38

M8 C

D0091305

Other Books in The Vintage Library
of Contemporary World Literature

Blood of Requited Love   BY MANUEL PUIG

The Guardian of the Word   BY CAMARA LAYE

History A Novel   BY ELSA MORANTE

The Ten Thousand Things   BY MARIA DERMOÛT

We Love Glenda So Much and
A Change of Light   BY JULIO CORTÁZAR

Aké: The Years of Childhood   BY WOLE SOYINKA

Correction   BY THOMAS BERNHARD

Maíra   BY DARCY RIBEIRO

Masks   BY FUMIKO ENCHI

One Day of Life   BY MANLIO ARGUETA

The Questionnaire   BY JIŘÍ GRUŠA

A MINOR APOCALYPSE

TADEUSZ KONWICKI

Translated from the Polish by Richard Lourie

AVENTURA

The Vintage Library of Contemporary World Literature

VINTAGE BOOKS   A DIVISION OF RANDOM HOUSE   NEW YORK

First Aventura Edition, April 1984

Translation copyright © 1983 by Farrar, Straus & Giroux, Inc.
All rights reserved under International and
Pan-American Copyright Conventions. Published in the
United States by Random House, Inc., New York, and
simultaneously in Canada by Random House of Canada
Limited, Toronto. This translation originally published
by Farrar, Straus & Giroux, Inc., in 1983. Originally
published in Polish as *Mała Apokalipsa* in 1979.
Copyright © 1979 by Tadeusz Konwicki.
Library of Congress Cataloging in Publication Data
Konwicki, Tadeusz.
A minor apocalypse.
Translation of: Mała apokalipsa.
"Aventura—the Vintage library of contemporary
world literature."—CIP t.p.
I. Title.
PG7158.K6513M313 1984   891.8′537   83-40384
ISBN 0-394-72442-9
Manufactured in the United States of America

TRANSLATOR'S
INTRODUCTION

A Minor Apocalypse is a hard book to pin down, for it keeps changing in the changing light of history. It was written in the late seventies. Gierek, ushered into power by the food riots of 1970, created an illusion of prosperity so convincing that Poles had begun to worry about "bourgeoisification": when the bubble burst, the country was in a state of ruin, a situation so grotesque and desperate that new, freewheeling energies were released. Independent publishing houses sprang up in Poland, one of which, Zapis, first published this book in 1979. It was also the time when the "Flying University" moved its lectures from apartment to apartment to avoid the gangs of police-sponsored roughnecks that often thwarted their meetings. The presses were always on the run, too, and sometimes whole editions fell victim to a raid. It was a time of courage and innovation, but it was not a time of hope. It would have taken a prophet to see what the year 1980 would bring to the history of Poland.

There is a touch of George Grosz in Konwicki's portrait of Warsaw, more than a little Orwellian surrealism, and a pinch of Dante in this comic inferno where the author disposes of his enemies with a satire as corrosive as battery acid. For Polish readers this was a *roman à clef* and there was little doubt that Andrzej Wajda was the model for the film director the narrator was settling his scores with. (Konwicki, by the way, has directed several films, including, most recently, one based on Czeslaw Milosz's novel *The Issa Valley*.) And the haughty ideologue at the Paradise restaurant seemed, to this reader at least, an attack on Jacek Kuroń, one of the founders of KOR (Committee for the Defense of the Workers, established in 1976 to aid the families of workers fired or imprisoned after the demonstrations at Radom and Ursus). But that is local gossip, incidental. More important is Konwicki's examination of the tensions, both tragic and comic, generated by a situation where conscience demands sacrifice and reality offers no hope that the sacrifice will be of any value or significance.

In the period of the great events, from the strikes of August 1980 to the imposition of martial law on December 13, 1981, reality seemed to be offering hope and *A Minor Apocalypse* seemed a different book. In those seventeen months it appeared as the bitter matrix from which the intellectual opposition had arisen, and at the same time, it could be faulted for its excessive bleakness, the nastiness of its convolutions, its narrow focus, which had not allowed for the workers' passion for justice.

But then came December 13, when Poland was cut off from the world by an internal blitzkrieg. And the period which one Polish writer called "the longest uprising in the nation's history" seemed to have taken its place with the other valiant, doomed insurrections of the past, described with such ironic lyricism by Konwicki in *The Polish Complex*. With the latest turn of the wheel, *A Minor Apocalypse* was revealed as prophetically sensitive to the necessity and the futility of the immolations required by Poland's history.

To shift from history to literature per se for a moment, as much as that is ever possible in a Polish context, it is worth noting that Konwicki has effected a certain mutation in the form of the novel. His first-person narratives, in which author and hero are closely or entirely identified, mix politics and confession, metaphysics and revenge, welding the bizarre and familiar together in a manner reminiscent of modern sculpture.

Jagged, eccentric, inventive, his work seems to be in the vanguard of new developments in the East European novel, as evidenced by Andrei Sinyavsky's new work *Good-Night*, with its author-narrator-hero, and by the conclusion of Vladimir Voinovich's *Chonkin* trilogy, which employs a similar device.

In the last three years Poland has been true to its tradition as a land of surprises. As this introduction is being written, Walesa has been released and is already on a collision course with the Jaruzelski regime, which has yet to suspend martial law. All that is certain is that by the time this book reaches the English-speaking public, Poland will have entered yet another phase of its cruel and exalted history, a phase which will color how *A Minor Apocalypse* is read and itself be revealed by this book.

December 15, 1982   Richard Lourie

A MINOR APOCALYPSE

Here comes the end of the world. It's coming, it's drawing closer, or rather, it's the end of my own world which has come creeping up on me. The end of my personal world. But before my universe collapses into rubble, disintegrates into atoms, explodes into the void, one last kilometer of my Golgotha awaits me, one last lap in this marathon, the last few rungs up or down a ladder that is without meaning.

I woke at the gloomy hour at which autumn's hopeless days begin. I lay in bed looking at a window full of rain clouds, but it was really one great cloud resembling a carpet darkened with age. This was the hour for doing life's books, the hour of the daily accounting. At one time people did their accounts at midnight before a good night's sleep, now they beat their breasts in the morning, woken by the thuds of their dying hearts.

There was blank paper close at hand, in the bureau. The nitroglycerine of the contemporary writer, the narcotic of the wounded individual. You can immerse yourself in the flat white abyss of the page, hide from yourself and your private universe, which will soon explode and vanish. You can soil that defenseless whiteness with bad blood, furious venom, stinking phlegm, but no one is going to like that, not even the author himself. You can pour the sweetness of artificial harmony, the ambrosia of false courage, the cloying syrup of flattery onto that vacant whiteness and everyone will like it, even the author himself.

Which way to turn in this last lap? To the bitter left or the sweet right? The same cloud was still outside the window, or a collective of clouds made uniform. On long, thin legs the rain flitted across the rusted windowsill. Once there had been something there. Forms, colors, scraps of emotion in violent movement. My life, or somebody else's. Most likely some made-up life. A collage of readings, incompletions, old films, unfinished fantasies, legends, dreams which did not come true. My life. A cutlet made of protein and cosmic dust.

Immersed in that cloud or in those few consolidated clouds was the Palace of Culture, which once, in its youth, had been the Joseph Stalin Palace of Culture and Science. That enormous, spired building has inspired fear, hatred, and magical horror. A monument to arrogance, a statue to slavery, a stone layer cake of abomination. But now it is only a large, upended barracks, corroded by fungus and mildew, an old chalet forgotten at some Central European crossroad.

A few windows wink at me like weak little flames. Flirting with unctuous familiarity. But who upended me? I've been set on my side. I've been set aside. I was lying on my left side and listening to my heart, which cannot be heard. I was thinking about the fragile chain of chemical reactions which causes my eyelid to rise, my stomach to rumble, the skin on my forehead to wrinkle, or makes the ordinary bladder creak with muffled pain. It causes that rush of words and images we call thoughts inside or outside of my head, it causes a cloud of waves—longing, a spasm of hatred—to appear; it causes a missile of fear of the eternal unknown to be shot out into space or fires a cartridge of the pleasure of knowing a morsel of truth. That little chain of chemical reactions suddenly broke one day for many of my friends, and I don't know where they are now, whether they are doing penance near a handful of phosphor aerating in the cemetery's earth or if they are receding in the convulsions and vibrations of their own individual waves, racing into the depths of infinity or ricocheting off the blank wall at the end of that infinity and will return here, where I will no longer be.

The first sounds of life could be heard in the building. This building, this great engine moved slowly into daily life. And so I reached for my first cigarette. The cigarette before breakfast tastes the best. It shortens your life. For many years now I have been laboring at shortening my life. Everybody shortens their existence on the sly. There must be something to all that. Some command from above, or perhaps a law of nature in this over-populated world.

I like the misty dizziness in my head after a deep drag of bitter smoke. I would like to say some suitable farewell to the world. For ever since I was a child I have been departing from this life, but I can't quite finish the job. I loiter at railway crossings, I walk by houses where roof tiles fall, I drink until I drop, I antagonize hooligans. I am approaching the finish line. I am in the final turn. I would like to say farewell to you somehow or other. I long to howl in an inhuman voice so that I am heard in the most distant corner of the planet and perhaps even in neighboring constellations or where the Lord God resides. Is that vanity? Or a duty? Or an instinct which commands us castaways, us cosmic castaways, to shout through the ages into starry space.

We've become intimate with the universe. Every money-hungry poet, foolish humorist, and treacherous journalist wipes his mouth on the cosmos and so why can't I too hold my head up high to where rusted Sputniks and astronaut excrement, frozen bone-hard, go gliding past.

And so I would like to say farewell somehow. I dreamed of teeth all night. I dreamed I was holding a pile of teeth like kernels of corn in my hand. There was even a filling in one, a cheap Warsaw filling from a dental co-op. To say something complete about myself. Not as a warning, not as knowledge, not even for amusement. Simply to say something which no one else could reveal. Because before falling asleep or perhaps in the first passing cloud of sleep, I begin to understand the meaning of existence, time, and the life beyond this one. I understand that mystery for a fraction of a second, through an instant of distant memories, a brief moment of consolation or fearful foreboding, and then plunge immediately into the depths of my bad dreams. In one way or another everyone strains his blood-fed brain to the breaking point trying to understand. But I'm getting close. I mean, at times I get close. And I would give everything I possess, down to the last scrap—but, after all, I don't own anything and so I would be giving a lot of nothing—to see that mystery in all its simplicity, to see it once and then to forget it forever.

I am a biped born not far from the Vistula River, of old stock and that means I inherited all their bipedal experience in my genes. I have seen war, that terrible frenzy of mammals murdering each other until they drop in exhaustion. I have observed the birth of life and its end in that act we call death. I have known all the brutality of my species and all its extraordinary angelicalness. I have traveled the thorny path of individual evolution known as fate. I am one of you. I am a perfect anonymous *Homo sapiens*. So why couldn't a caprice of chance have entrusted me with the secret if it is, in any case, destined to be revealed.

These words have a sort of gala quality, the luxury of an idler, the twists of a pervert. But, after all, all of you who from time to time put the convolutions of your own lazy brains into gear are subject to these same desires and ambitions. The same fears and self-destructive reflexes. The same rebellion and resignation.

Two drunken delivery women have knocked over a tall column of crates containing milk bottles. Now, standing stock-still, they are observing the results of the disaster, experiencing the complicated and yet at the same time simple process which transforms a mess into fun. The transparent rain has caught its wing on our building, which is rotting with age. A Warsaw building built late in the epoch of Stalinism, when Stalinism was decadent, the period when Stalinism had become Polonized and raggedy.

I have to get up. I have to rise from my bed and perform fifteen acts whose meaning is not to be pondered. An accretion of automatic habits. The blessed cancer of tradition's meaningless routine. But the last war not only took the lives of scores of millions of people. Without intending to, accidentally, the last war also shattered the great palace of culture of European morality, aesthetics, and custom. And humankind drove back to gloomy caverns and icy caves in their Rolls-Royces, Mercedes, and Moskviches.

Outside, my city, beneath a cloud the color of an old blackened carpet. A city to which I was driven by fate from my native city, which I no longer remember and dream of less all the time. Fate only drove me a few hundred kilometers, but it separated me from my old unfulfilled life by an entire eternity of reincarnation. This city is the capital of a people who are evaporating into nothingness. Something needs to be said about that, too. But to whom? To those who are no longer with us, who are sailing off into oblivion? Or perhaps to those who devour individuals and whole nations?

The city was beginning to hum like a drive belt. It was stirring from the lethargy of sleep. Moving toward its fate, which I know and which I wish to avoid.

A spider was lowering itself from the ceiling on an invisible thread. The poor thing, emaciated now because there are practically no flies left this time of year. He's been living with me like this since the spring. I have made his hunting easier. We have become friends out of necessity. For some reason he has no colleagues, and mine have expired. So first I will pray a little. For myself, for those who are close to me, and for my friends who are dead. This practical, compact prayer which sounds like a tearful ultimatum and which I composed myself.

The usual demands, a little politeness here and there. When I pray, skittish, blasphemous thoughts buzz about my head. I shoo them away, though they are only the measure of my modest knowledge seen against the enormous, old-fashioned structure of religious axioms encrusted in that dreary and melancholy edifice erected by people in epochs which were bright and dark, good and cruel. Then I spent a long time on my farewell, my endless despairing farewell, to drive away my evil, my evil desires, my evil spirits, with gestures of ritual.

I am free. I am one of the few free people in this country of utterly transparent slavery. A slavery covered by a sloppy coat of contemporary varnish. I have fought a long and bloodless battle for this pitiable personal freedom. I fought for my freedom against the temptations, ambitions, and appetites which drive everyone blindly on to the slaughterhouse. To the so-called modern slaughterhouse for human dignity, honor, and for something else, too, which we forgot about a long time ago.

I am free and alone. Being alone is a small enough price to pay for this none-too-great luxury of mine. I freed myself on the last lap, when the finish line could already be seen by the naked eye. I am a free, anonymous man. My flights and falls occurred while I was wearing a magical cap of invisibility, my successes and sins sailed on in invisible corvettes, and my films and books flew off into the abyss in invisible strongboxes. I am free, anonymous.

And so I'll light another cigarette. On an empty stomach. Here comes the end of my world. That I know for certain. The untimely end of my world. What will be its harbingers? A sudden, piercing pain in the chest beneath the sternum? The squeal of tires as a car slams on its brakes? An enemy, or perhaps a friend?

Outside, those women were still discussing the catastrophe with the milk. They sat down on the old, dark-gray, plastic cases, lit cigarettes, and watched the watery milk trickle down the catch basin, which was belching steam because, no doubt, hot water from the heat and power plant had again gotten into the water main by mistake. And then I suddenly became aware that no one had delivered milk for years, that I had forgotten the sight of those women workers of indeterminate age pushing carts of milk bottles long ago, and in my mind, that image was associated with those distant green years when I was young and the world was too.

They're probably making a period film, I told myself, and pressed my forehead against the damp windowpane. But all I saw was a normal everyday street. Small crowds of people hurrying by the buildings on the way to work. As usual when the temperature rises in the morning, a crumbling block of stone facing tore loose from the Palace of Culture and flew crashing down into the jagged gully of buildings. It was only then that I noticed the eagle on the wall of that great edifice, an eagle on a field of black, that is, on a field of red blackened by rain. Our white eagle is holding up pretty well because it is supported from below by a huge globe of the world, which is tightly entwined by a hammer and sickle. The gutter spoke with a voice deep as an ocarina's. Then the wind, perhaps still the summer wind or maybe now a winter wind, came tearing from Parade Square and turned the poplars' silver side to the sun, which was confined in wet clouds.

I was out of cigarettes. And when you run out of cigarettes you are suddenly seized by a desire to smoke. And so I opened the next drawer of my treasure chest, where I keep outrageous letters and old accounts, broken lighters and tax receipts, photographs from my youth and sleeping pills. And there, among tufts of cotton batting and rolls of bandages from the good old days when it was still worth my while to submit to operations, in those age-encrusted recesses I found a yellowed page from many years ago, a page like a cartouche on a monument or a gravestone, a page where I once began a piece of prose I have not finished yet. I began this work in that wonderful time around New Year's, right after New Year's Eve, with a nice hangover still throbbing in my healthy head. I began on New

Year's Day because I had indulged in superstition and wanted to celebrate the new biological and astronomical cycle with some work. Later I realized that my own New Year begins at the end of summer or the beginning of fall, and so that is why I stopped writing and have not written a word since.

And so there was that page, once white, now yellow, for long months, seasons, years, never finished, never completed, with its faded motto, which was to bless the wistful scenes, the exalted thoughts, the lovely descriptions of nature. I blew the dust from Warsaw's factories off that waxen corpse of my imagination and read the words, which were the credo of an old Polish magnate in the nineteenth century: "If Russia's interests permit, I would gladly turn my feelings to my original fatherland." What was it I had in mind then? Did I want to read that avowal every morning to my children before breakfast? Or did I intend to copy it out at Christmas to be sent to the magnates of science, literature, and film, my contemporaries? Or was I trying to win the favor of the censor for a piece that had come stillborn from an anemic inspiration?

The windowpanes rattled mournfully. Hysterical police sirens leaped from some side street. I glanced at the watch my friend Stanislaw D. had brought me from a trip to the Soviet Union. It was going on eight. I knew what that meant. Each day at that hour, an armored refrigerator truck carrying food supplies for the ministers and Party Secretaries raced through the city escorted by police vans. The cavalcade of vehicles flashed past my building splashing the puddles of milk on the street. The archaic milk deliverers, let out of some old-age home for the day, ground out their cigarette butts on the muddy sidewalk, exchanging furtive goodbyes.

Suddenly my doorbell rang. I froze by the window, not believing my ears, certain that it had not been working for years. But the elegant, xylophone-like sound was repeated, and more insistently this time. Pulling on an old robe, a present from my brother-in-law, Jan L., I moved guardedly toward the door. I opened the door. Hubert and Rysio, both wearing their Sunday best, suits which reminded me of the carefree middle seventies, were standing at the top of the stairs.

Hubert was holding a cane in his right hand and a sinister-looking black briefcase in his left. My heart began beating rapidly, and not without cause, for they came to see me only about twice a year and each of their visits had marked a radical change in my life.

"May we come in? It isn't too early?" asked Hubert jovially.

I was well acquainted with those artificial smiles of theirs, which concealed attacks on my comfort.

Now smiling freely myself, I opened the door hospitably, and as they entered, with much ceremony on their part, I instantly divined the purpose of this visit. Thanks to them, I had signed dozens of petitions, memorials, and protests sent over the years to our always taciturn regime. A few times it had cost me a contract, and many times I was secretly dispossessed of my civil rights; practically every day I was subjected to petty, invisible harassments which are even shameful to recall but which, adding up over the years, helped estrange me greatly from life. So we exchanged cordial hugs, smiling all the time like old cronies, but I was already quite tense and my throat had gone dry.

Finally we found ourselves in my living room, and we sat down in the wooden armchairs, all in a row, as if we were on an airplane flying off to some mysterious and exciting adventure.

"You look good," said Hubert, setting the sinister-looking briefcase down beside him.

"You seem to be holding up, too," I said in a friendly tone.

For a moment we looked at each other in embarrassment. Hubert was resting his sinewy hand on his cane. His one blind eye was motionless, the other kept blinking and regarding me with something between affection and irony. Once long ago he had been tortured, perhaps by the anti-Communist underground or perhaps by investigating officers of the security police, and because of that incident, now long forgotten by everyone, he walked with a cane and was in poor health. Rysio, whom I remembered as a blond angel, was now balding and had put on weight, the high priest of the plotless allegorical novel that uses neither punctuation nor dialogue.

We looked good, for old fogeys, that was true. But then the moment of silence grew a bit protracted and something had to be said.

"Would you like a drink?"

"A drink couldn't hurt," said Hubert. "What do you have?"

"Pure vodka. Made from potatoes. Imported potatoes."

"All the more reason not to refuse." Hubert's voice was thunderous as if tuned to some space larger than my cluttered room.

While I was getting the bottle and the glasses from the cupboard, they were both looking discreetly about the room. The liquid made from imported potatoes began to gurgle as I cowered at the edge of my chair. A cigarette on an empty stomach is bad for you, but a hundred grams of potato vodka is death itself. Or maybe it's better.

I raised my glass. "Good luck."

"Your health," said Rysio, finally breaking his silence and tossing off the contents of his glass.

Outside, the wind had died down for the moment and the poplars had turned their ripe and solid green toward us. My building was, as bad luck would have it, exceptionally quiet and our silence was becoming increasingly louder. But I made a firm decision not to speak and to force them to show their cards.

Hubert set his glass aside with a certain deliberation. "You're not going out much," he said.

"That's right. Autumn puts me out of sorts."

"A little depression?"

"Something like that."

"Are you writing?"

"I had just started."

He looked at me in apparent disbelief. Rysio poured himself another glass.

"What's it going to be?"

"No revelations. I just felt like writing a little nonsense about myself."

"You always wrote about yourself."

"You could be right. But I wanted to write about other people."

"It's high time you did."

"To drown myself out."

The whole thing seemed like an examination. And I felt like a Gymnasium senior taking his finals. But, after all, I had felt that way my whole life, a student at best.

"Well, Rysio," said Hubert all of a sudden. "Time to get down to business."

Rysio nodded.

"Something to sign?" I hazarded a guess, squinting accommodatingly over at the black briefcase.

"No, this time it's something else. Perhaps you might begin, Rysio."

"Go on, go on, since you started," said Rysio eagerly.

A sort of goofy warmth was rising in me. I reached for the bottle automatically, wanting to pour Hubert a glass while I was at it.

"Thanks, that's enough." He stopped me with a somewhat official tone. I took that as a bad sign.

Really I was indifferent. I am a free person suspended high above this city, who, from a distance and with serene amazement, observes the strange humans and their strange doings. Without thinking, I turned on the television on the table. I heard the sound of wind howling, the flutter of cloth, but after a moment, the image of a festively decorated airport emerged from the silvery dots. An honor guard was frozen across the screen, some civilians were shielding themselves against the wind with their overcoats while, above the honor guard and the civilians, red, sail-like flags swelled in the wind, and shyly interspersed among them were red-and-white Polish flags.

"Well, now," said Hubert, deciding to break the silence. "We haven't spoken with you for some time now."

I took a deep breath, which made me feel ashamed, and I sank deeper into my chair.

"Yes, we've been out of touch," I said in a worldly tone. "We're a vanishing breed."

"Everyone's out for himself," added Rysio.

"But I've been observing your activities."

"What activities," said Hubert with a dismissive wave of one hand. "We're the keepers of a dying flame."

"That's a fact. I really feel the country is dying," I said, without knowing what they were driving at.

"So many years of struggle. We've grown old, we've gone to pot putting out all those semilegal bulletins, periodicals, those appeals which are read by next to no one. Of course the young people read them. But young people get married, have babies, buy little Fiats, give up on action, and start growing tomatoes. We've been overrun by the bourgeoisie, a Soviet bourgeoisie."

"It's the end, the grave," added Rysio, pouring himself another glass.

Water was dripping onto the floor through the leaky balcony doors. I should have looked for a dishcloth to prevent any damage, but I didn't much feel like it, and I would have been a little embarrassed to do it in front of my colleagues. Our conversation was not going well. It was hard to chat about the things we reflected on all day and which we even dreamed about in our lousy sleep. Things had looked better at one time. We were children of the nineteenth century. Our fathers had been members of Pilsudski's Legions or his secret army, and during World War II we had been in the Home Army or the Union of Fighting Youth. That means, how to say it now, that means, how to explain it after all those years, that means, the hell with it, that doesn't mean anything now, at the end of our splendid twentieth century, a century of tyranny and unbridled democracy, foolish holiness and brilliant villainy, art without punch and graphomania run rampant.

I saw Hubert's good eye fixed on me. "Are you listening?" he asked.

"Yes, of course."

"We have a proposition for you. On behalf of our colleagues."

My spine went cold, and very slowly I put my unfinished glass aside.

"What is it you wish to propose?"

"That tonight at eight o'clock you set yourself on fire in front of the Party Central Committee building."

Nothing had changed on the screen—wind, the violent flapping of the flags, the waiting. Only now the reverent, solemn music broadcast from the studio could be heard.

I gulped saliva mixed with vodka.

"Are you joking, Hubert?"

"No, I'm not joking." He wiped some invisible sweat from his brow.

"But why me? Why are you coming to me with this?"

"Who else? Somebody has to do it."

"I understand, I understand everything, I just don't understand why me."

Hubert glanced over at Rysio. "I told you this would happen."

Rysio looked down at the floor. "Listen," he finally said in some anguish, "we've been discussing this for a long time. We've analyzed all the possible candidates. And it came out you."

My jade plant was on the windowsill. Only then did I notice how much it had shot up lately and how thick its young, strong leaves had grown. It had been sickly for many years and now suddenly, without any external cause, it had surged upward, sending out a large number of powerful, knotty branches.

"You see," said Hubert softly, "an act like this can make sense only if it shakes people here in Poland and everywhere abroad. You are known to Polish readers and you have a bit of a name in the West, too. Your life story, your personality are perfect for this situation. Obviously, we can't talk you into it and we won't even try, it's between you and your conscience. I only wish to pass on an opinion which is not only mine or Rysio's but that of the entire community which is attempting to put up some resistance. You'll pardon me for my lack of eloquence."

"I doubt whether my death would play the part you expect. I know people whose sacrifice would become a symbol the world over."

They looked at me with curiosity. Hubert rubbed his fingers, which were turning insistently bluish.

"No doubt you're thinking of Jan?" he asked.

"Naturally. The whole world knows his films, and his books are read in many countries in courses on world literature. Every year we're on tenterhooks waiting to see if he'll win an Oscar or the Nobel."

A barely perceptible smile appeared on Hubert's face. "That would be too high a price to pay. Too high a price for the country and our community. You're just right."

"All right. But what about our filmmakers, our composers? I can give you a few names better than mine right off."

"You're the one, old man," said Rysio, and reached for the bottle. He clearly felt I was weakening, which gave him heart.

"Life and blood have to be disposed of intelligently," said Hubert wearily. "Those others have a different role to play. Every nugget of genius possesses the highest value in this massacred nation. Their deaths would not enrich us very much and would impoverish us terribly."

"But why not you, or Rysio?"

They glanced at each other with distaste. My blubbering embarrassed them.

"Then why would we have come to you?" asked Hubert. "Let's be frank. Your death will be spectacular, another order up. Don't you see that?"

"You're the one, old man," added Rysio, who was soft-hearted and was now suffering along with me.

"Listen to me, Hubert. I never interfered in the functioning of our artistic life. I never butted into your affairs, the affairs of a careworn opposition in a country no one cares about. But now I must tell you what I think. You have bred blind, deaf demiurges, who in their marvelous artistic passions create beautiful, universal art but do not notice us crawling in the mud or the daily agonies of our society. They worked hard at guarding the flame of genius that burned in them and gladly exploited the regime's mass propaganda, which boasted of them every day and fed its own complexes with their world re-nown. You, the emaciated opposition, spared them no claques, either, anointing them with the charisma of moral approval. They grew fat on our exile, our humiliations, our anonymity. They hopped freely from one sacred grove of national art to another, for we had been driven out of them or had left of our own free will. When you went around pleading with them to sign even the most modest of humanitarian appeals which would displease our team of wanton rulers, they arrogantly sent you packing empty-handed, winking at their coteries to say that you were provocateurs, secret police agents. Their great-ness arose from our being voluntarily dwarfed. Their genius sprang from our graves as artists. Why shouldn't one of them pay for their decades of solemn, superhuman greatness with a cruel physical death?"

I turned off the television, where the civilians and soldiers were impatiently waiting for someone. A sudden hailstorm rat-tled past the balcony, knocking a condom withering on the iron balustrade off into the abyss. Those condoms were bouquets of violets bestowed on me by my neighbors from the upper floors on their days off.

"We're all racked by envy to one degree or another," said Hubert, somewhat taken aback. He was pale and strenuously rubbing his fingers, which were now turning even bluer. "But let's not talk about that today. Maybe some other time."

"But when are we going to talk if I carry out your command?"

"But, old man, you know," said Rysio, setting his glass aside, "these arguments are indecent."

"I never said anything even though my guts were turning. Hubert, do I need to tell you the names of the people who spent their whole lives walking hand in hand with the government while pretending to go their own way? And their works, which the more clever ones clothed in the garb of universal fashion, Weltschmerz, Western melancholy, and what is a sort of neuralgia of the left. And when we became Sovietized to such a degree that a cult of the illicit erupted here, an ambiguous desire for a lick of the forbidden, a pitiful delight in political pornography dressed in the lingerie of allusion, when there arose in Poland that aberration, that scheming contest of self-justification for all the sins of collaboration, they were the first, greedy for applause, anxious for success, they fastened on to the new state of affairs and littered art with the phony gestures of cunning Rejtans, they muddied our poor art, they stomped out the last of their own conscience in it. Why do you fall down before them when they climb up on your crosses to reach for the golden apples which feed their pride? Why do you pour admiration on them when their fate is opposed to yours?"

"You chose your own fate. This is not the time for that sort of discussion. Rysio, isn't it time for us to be going?" Hubert bent forward heavily and drew the black briefcase out from under the table, the briefcase which could contain an appeal for the abolition of the death penalty, a volume of uncensored poetry, or an ordinary homemade bomb.

"Wait a minute, Hubert." I stopped his hand. "Tell me here, in private, man to man, why have you designated me?"

He tore his hand from mine. "I don't designate. I have the same rights as you do. And the same duties."

"But there must be something about me that makes me suitable and others less so."

The rain had hazed the windows over. Nearby a child was

playing a melody with one finger, a melody which I remembered from years back, many years back.

"After all, you've always been obsessed with death," whispered Hubert hoarsely. "I never treated your complex as a literary mannerism. You're intimate with death, you shouldn't be afraid of it. You have prepared yourself, and us, for your death most carefully. What were you thinking about before we arrived?"

"Death."

"You see. It's at your side. All you have to do is reach out."

"Just reach out."

"Yes, that's all."

"Today?"

"Today at eight o'clock in the evening, when the Party congress is over and the delegates from the entire country are leaving the building."

"What about the others?"

"Who do you mean?"

"The people who are necessary to the nation."

"In sin and holiness, in conformity and rebellion, in betrayal and redemption, they will bear the soul of the nation into eternity."

"You're lying. You're choking on that garbage, your eyes are popping out of their sockets."

Rysio leaped from his chair, knocking over his glass. "Leave him alone!" he shouted, and began rummaging in Hubert's shirt. Hubert had gone stiff and extended his legs as if he wanted to look at his muddy boots. Rysio began pushing pealike pills through his lips, which had turned blue. He forced a few drops of water between Hubert's clenched teeth. Hubert moved his jaw, closed his eyes, then bit one pill in half and tried to swallow it.

Someone rang the bell. I opened the latch with trembling hands. A man, a bit on the drunk side, stood in the doorway holding on to the door frame.

"You should run yourself some water because we're going to turn it off," he said, belching a cloud of undigested alcohol.

"I don't need any water."

"I suggest you run your tub and your other faucets. We'll be cutting it off for the whole day."

"Thank you. So did a main burst, then?"

"Everything burst. May I sit down here for a minute, I'm dead on my feet."

"I'm sorry, but my friend isn't feeling well. I have to fetch an ambulance."

"No one's feeling good these days. I won't bother you, then. Stay well."

"The same to you."

He went off to knock on my neighbors' doors. I returned at a run down the hall. Now Hubert was sitting up straight in his chair. He smiled painfully, to hide his sudden panic.

"Should I call a doctor?"

"No need to. I'm all right now. Where were we?"

A swath of sunlight moved across the rooftops of the city like a great kite. My friend the sparrow hopped onto one bar of the balustrade and was surprised that I did not greet him.

"Hubert, is there any sense to all this? Do you really believe there is?"

"Now you're asking?"

"Why have you been so unrelenting all your life? In all ways. Is it hormones or some higher force compelling you?"

"Leave him alone, he has to go home." Rysio pushed me away.

"Isn't the Party building closer?"

"Not all deaths are the same, you see," said Hubert in a muffled voice. "We all need the elevated, the majestic, the holy. That is what you can offer us."

"For your sins, old man," added Rysio, and attempted a smile. "You have plenty of yours, and ours, on your conscience."

"But they have just as many," I said in despair, affected by the hysteria of that foul autumn day.

"They're not here. You're all alone with God or, if you prefer, with your conscience."

"And where are they?"

"Far away on a small, unhappy planet."

"Hubert, what a stupid joke. Someone put you up to it."

"No, it's not a joke. You know that perfectly well yourself. You've been waiting for us for years. Be honest for once and admit you were waiting."

He looked at me for a long moment with his one good eye and then began searching for his briefcase, which he had kicked under the table during his attack.

"Hubert, answer me—do you believe this is necessary?"

He walked heavily over to me, put his arms around me, and kissed both my cheeks with his cold lips. "Be at number 63 Vistula Street at eleven. Halina and Nadezhda will be waiting for you there. They're in engineering."

"The engineering of self-immolation?"

"Don't make things more difficult, old man," interjected Rysio.

A sudden fury seized me. "Don't talk to me like you're just one of the guys when you don't even use fucking commas and periods when you write."

At a loss, Rysio began retreating toward the door. "The lack of periods bothers you?" he said uncertainly.

"If you used punctuation, then maybe we wouldn't need show deaths in this country."

A lazy peal of thunder rolled from one end of the city to the other. The wind drove the balcony doors groaning open. I would have closed them but the handle had come off.

"Lend us five thousand for a taxi. It's too much for him to walk home in this weather." Rysio took Hubert's enchanted briefcase from him and then glanced out into the dark corridor.

I dug a five-thousand-zloty note out of my pocket. They took it without thanking me and started for the front hall. And then we were greeted by a sort of a droning, the high-pitched sound of telephone wires presaging bad weather. They had been making that glassy moan for years now, since the days when the world had still been a calm and normal place.

Hubert stopped before a heap of old slippers which had somehow or other accumulated over the course of a lifetime.

"When did you stop writing? I can't remember anymore," he said, looking askance and unseeing at the junk strewn about the floor.

"But I'm still writing."

"You've started writing again now. You're writing your testament. But I was asking about your fiction."

"I don't recall. Maybe five, maybe seven years ago. That's when I rid myself of two censors in one fell swoop, my own and the state's. I wrote a story for some little underground journal and that was my last piece. After that I was free and impotent."

"You were born to be a slave. Slavery emancipated you, it lent you wings, it made you a provincial classic. And then to punish you, it took everything away like some evil witch."

"Slavery has always perished at the hands of slaves," said Rysio. "You see what I mean, old man?"

That strange high-pitched sound, a sound that would be good for killing rats, made its first appearance in our building a few months ago. I spent weeks searching for its source, I probed the attics and cellars, but I didn't find anything. It would start up suddenly and then suddenly die down after forty minutes or so. During the day, at night, too. It kept the tenants in a state of constant, hysterical anticipation.

"But I'll finish writing this report. Not a report, a funeral dirge. I'll write it in my mind and then forget it at once. A literary work for one reader."

"Save your words, save the best of them for this evening. You'll have to shout with all your might there. Your most excellent thoughts. People will write them down and preserve them, like verses from the Bible. Your literary masterpiece."

He reached for my hand in the dark and shook it firmly. I thought that I caught a quick gleam of irony in that one good eye of his. Again I was seized by a fury.

"Who put you up to this? What son-of-a-bitch is after me?"

"Somebody has to do it. We're giving you the chance. You'll be number one. You'll surpass all your rivals. They'll belittle what you did under their breath. It will be your first absolute victory over them."

"But is it worth it? People should be setting themselves on fire every day over there. At the center, by the Kremlin wall, a fire would get raves from onlookers the world over. But our local fires, caused by negligence, just irritate the world and introduce unnecessary complications into the thrilling spectacle of the battle between good and evil. Listen, Hubert, could our solar system have gone off the course Providence assigned it and now be shooting off into the depths of the universe, where some mysterious cosmic fate will reconcile us all? Maybe some common win or common loss awaits us?" /

"What can be won or lost outside of what we have to win or lose?"

"All right, you better get going."

I opened the door. For some reason they loitered when leaving. Hubert began reading my neighbor's calling card tacked beside his bell. They were always a bit curious about my life, though good form required contempt for my existence. So he read that card, the shingle of a Secretary on the Central Committee, without knowing that behind that door an old pensioner had been dying for ten years, had been trying to die day after day but with no success. Drops of dirty water dripped down from the steps and the edges of the stairs. Our janitor, or as he is to be called these days, the building superintendent, an incorrigible lunatic, was washing the landing. He had already been on television and been written up in the papers, and still on he went washing our stairs, the only building superintendent in the country still doing it.

"Don't punk out, old man," said Rysio.

"I have to think it over."

"They're expecting you at eleven, Halina and Nadezhda," added Hubert.

"And if I don't do it?"

"Then you'll go on living the way you've lived till now."

They began down the stairs, supporting each other like two saints, like Cyril and Methodius. And naturally I remembered Rysio from those years long ago when we both were young. I remember one mad drunken night on some farm near Warsaw, the two of us sleeping side by side on a bed of straw. At that time Rysio was something between a critic and a filmologist. There was a drunken girl lying in between us, a girl I never saw again. We were both lying semiconscious on my green poncho, which I had obligingly spread out for us. The girl was moaning in her deep, drunken sleep. Rysio was fooling around with her, panting hoarsely with sudden desire, and so she turned her back to him. Then she was facing me and I could feel her damp, sleepy breath on my cheek. Rysio did not give up; unconscious but hard at work, he was fumbling at her, tearing at her clothes, slipping under her inert body, breathing wildly. And then, when I was already falling into a feverish sleep, Rysio clearly achieved his end, for he suddenly began moaning and pulling himself free on the frantic hay. Unaware of his ecstasies, she breathed her light calm breath on me. It was only in the morning when, hung over, we were all collecting ourselves on that rustic bed, that I struggled into my poncho, automatically put my hand in the pocket, and to my horror discovered that in the darkness of the night, it had been the victim of Rysio's passion, that he had made love to my pocket with a fierce and youthful fervor, perhaps even the first of his life.

Now Rysio wrote unpunctuated, amorphous prose, played adjutant to Hubert, and was a venerable figure in the literary world. I returned to my room to watch them through the window. Just then, by some miracle, an empty taxi happened by, but they missed it and walked off with dignity toward Nowy

Swiat. I was curious if they were being followed. But no car pulled away from the curb and no one came running out from the half shadows of any neighboring building.

At one point Hubert had hanged himself in his wardrobe; he had been hounded mercilessly during one campaign, for at that time, toward the end of the sixties, the regime still had strength enough for cruel spectacles and sinister campaigns. So Hubert hanged himself, but of course it was the first time he had ever done it and he didn't have the knack yet. The rod broke, the wardrobe turned over, and Hubert survived. Yes, he survived, so that years later he could deliver my death sentence to me.

There was another peal of thunder in the low, cramped sky. I went to the bathroom to wash up. The pipes began gurgling something awful, but what was left of the water came hiccuping out. I washed mechanically, wondering if it was right to wash and dress considering what was in store for me. But, after all, one should take death like communion, neatly dressed and with reverence. But did I have to die? Was someone going to force me off a bridge or douse me with gasoline? The decision was mine, wasn't it? I could die with honor or go on living dishonorably.

The bell rang again. I thought that Rysio and Hubert had forgotten something or were returning to call off the sentence. Dripping with the little water there was, I ran to the door. An old man with a large leather bag was sitting on the steps.

"Are you here to see me?" I asked.

"Yes, I am. I've been instructed to turn off the gas."

"But you've already turned it off three times this year."

"What do I know, first they tell me turn it off, then they tell me turn it on. They don't know what they're doing. Every day a house blows up, so to make it look like something's being done about it, they tell me to turn off the gas. It's a lucky thing your apartment's still here because I've got the numbers here of places which are gone." He showed me a dirty slip of paper.

"Well, then, why don't you turn off the electricity while you're at it. It doesn't matter to me."

"It doesn't matter to you," said the old man, with a sly smirk, and he sprang nimbly into the bathroom. "But it matters to me. I'm only authorized to turn off the gas."

And indeed, in a fraction of a second, he had turned the valve, had taken apart the grate on the heater, and was already sitting on the edge of the bathtub lighting a cigarette that was falling apart.

"It's nice to take a warm bath, if only to wash your butt, you'll pardon the expression," discoursed the old man, glancing about the bathroom. "But what can you do, orders are orders. Maybe you should have a little talk with the manager, you know what I mean. Speak to his hand."

"I don't feel like talking with the manager. I'm going to die today."

The old plumber began chuckling merrily. "Why'd you think that one up for today, isn't there enough going on? That Russian Secretary's coming today. They've got the whole town decked out. There's been bands playing everywhere since this morning. They say there's some sort of festival going on, some big holiday of theirs, maybe it's one of ours, too. They've filled up the stands with goods, everywhere, by the Palace of Culture, down by the Vistula; people have been standing in line since early this morning and you're getting ready to die."

"I'll be dying to spite them."

The gray-haired plumber wiped away tears of laughter. "You're a funny one. If we started dying to spite them, there'd be no Poles left. You know what, I'll reconnect your gas, but I'll seal up the valve handle. I'll leave it open wide enough so you can use the gas, just you be careful."

"I don't have any need for gas. Why don't you take the little heater as a souvenir."

"You're pretty touchy. I can take no for an answer. Sign here, please."

I accompanied him back to the hall. He took the opportunity to feel my coat, which was hanging by the door.

"Nice wool. Foreign."

"Take it. Wear it in good health."

"What are you talking about? I can pay you. I'll give you fifty thousand."

"I'll give it to you for nothing. The only thing is, when you put it on, give a sigh for my soul, would you."

"You must be an artist, right? You like a good laugh, right?"

But he rolled the coat up skillfully, packed it in his bag, and then was already at my neighbor's door, pressing the doorbell, a severe look on his face.

I returned to my room and sat down in the armchair which was still warm from Hubert. The wind bore scraps of music across the city. It was good to give the coat away, it would make getting dressed easier and make it easier to jump into the next world. I would return my life to them the way I had been given it: angrily. A symbol. Yet another symbol. In relation to eternity or to the idiots of the present day? A complicated and indecipherable gesture. A gesture to stigmatize our puppet regime consumed by servility or to indict the eternal Russian hidden behind the moldering façade of the Soviet Union? A protest against the slavery of a society, or of a nation. What sort of freedom are we talking about, for which, of all the many freedoms, will I leap into the fire, the sacred fire of death? What is this anyway, nonsense or Ascension?

I could always disappear down some mouse hole at the last minute, I told myself in consolation, but I knew I would not go anywhere but where I had been ordered to, where I had to go. I dressed modestly but neatly. They had ordered me to shout, and for me, that was the worst of it. I might be able to stand the fire, but not the embarrassment. A warrior must be bold and reckless. And I had botched many erotic possibilities because I was too embarrassed to unbutton my pants.

I turned on the television. I had to do something, my hands were shaking, I couldn't collect my thoughts. An airplane appeared on the screen, and beside it two fat men were kissing each other on the mouth. It was our Secretary and theirs, the Russian one, the tsar of tsars, master of half the world. Ours had the kindhearted face of a cardinal or a janitor, or, as they say these days, a building superintendent. History and heredity had endowed the Russian with the face of a Kalmuck. They hugged each other and then listened to the national anthem. But the "Internationale" is our national anthem now. A hand-me-down from our big brother, like some vest.

I put my ID in my pocket. You don't go anywhere without it. Last name, first name, date of birth, father's name, mother's name, height, eye color, none of it important. What is important is the code on it, a few letters, a row of numbers. That's how I am known to the police, the municipal government, the health service. That's how the computers know me and make sure I don't escape, that I don't hide from my oppressors, and do not give my insolent protectors the slip.

I left the house. I had to leave those four walls. Leaving an apartment is not the same thing as making a decision. I had the whole day ahead of me. Fortunes are made and dynasties destroyed in the course of twelve hours, empires rise and fall in the course of twelve hours.

Walking down the stairs, I glanced at my mailbox and even opened it on the off chance. It scraped open, scattering bits of rust. All it contained was a tattered cobweb. Just as well. The post office hasn't been bringing me any good letters for years now.

Outside, I was struck by the great clamor of music. Public-address systems were booming, bands were thundering, somewhere a military drum was banging away with dismal persistence. By the Palace of Culture, which at one time had so fascinated me as a sacred place, as a terrible grave mound where evil spirits linger in penance, anyway on a platform by the Palace, a large number of fresh-faced couples wearing embroidered Cracovian coats and bodices decorated with sequins, wearing peacock feathers and Zywiec lace, were skipping about and dancing. The leader of the dance was tapping his foot and singing in a low voice with a Russian accent: "I'm from Krakow, yes, I am!"

Out of habit I got in line at a newspaper kiosk and bought a pack of cigarettes, but the newspapers were already gone. That was a bad omen, too. To succeed in buying a newspaper in the morning has always been our first success of the day. A man with a newspaper under his arm is an attention-getter. One time I even began an intimate relationship with a girl who had been gazing greedily at my newspaper. No one reads the newspaper, even though it's a lot of work getting hold of one. But you have to have a newspaper. Such is the custom.

A man with a thin face and somewhat unhappy eyes came out of the apartment building on the other side of the street. I knew him by sight. The whole street knew him. He was a character, an eccentric, a dignitary who, for reasons unknown, had not built himself a castle-like villa in the government district and had gone on living with us, the common cattle of the People's Republic. He looked at me and I looked at him; we did not bow to each other because it would not have been becoming for him and honor would not permit me to. He got into a black Mercedes and drove off down the street, a security car pulling out quickly behind him.

I have always had some strange premonition that my fate would be interwoven with his. I suspect that he, too, entertained similar misgivings. And so I have been stealthily observing the dignitary's meager life, his comings and goings, his boring, interminable speeches on television; I followed his official travels in the newspapers and always had a friendly greeting for the government refrigerated truck which brought him German sausages, chuck roasts, giblets, and low-fat cottage cheese. I supposed that he, too, struck by some evil thought, had also taken a discreet interest in my equally boring life.

I came out onto Nowy Swiat, which was overgrown with a shrubbery of flags, red flags and red-and-white flags. But in those red-and-white flags of ours the red has slowly increased over the years, while the white has diminished. And now our flags are red, too, with just a little white band at the top. And so those old small buildings, like brick larvae permanently shedding their plaster cocoons, discharged the bad blood of festive flags and dozed by the narrow canyon of the street down which schoolchildren and office and factory workers were marching. Above the festive crowd there was a gigantic fluttering banner with the words: LONG LIVE THE FORTIETH ANNIVERSARY OF THE POLISH PEOPLE'S REPUBLIC.

I fell into thought, contemplating that slogan, which attracted the attention of a pensioner with a newspaper under his arm.

He smiled knowingly at me. "You noticed, too?"

"Excuse me, noticed what?"

"Come on, don't pretend."

"You mean the fortieth anniversary."

"They've added on a good couple of years there," he said, chuckling. "My memory is good."

"You think that's what they did?"

"I don't think so, I know so."

"Let me see your newspaper. We'll have a look at the date."

"You're not very perceptive. For quite a while the dates in the newspapers have been all squashed together, as if somebody had stepped on the type with his boot. See for yourself."

He thrust the newspaper at me and I grabbed it from his hand. "Hey, what are you doing!" protested the pensioner. "My wife hasn't read it yet."

"I beg of you. I must have a newspaper."

He began tearing the thin twist of *Trybuna Ludu* from my hand.

"Let go, let go, or I'll call the police."

"I'm very ill. I may go to the hospital. I may be dying."

"That's what they all say."

At that moment the newspaper tore in two, and what remained in my hand was the precious half with the movie, theater, and television schedules, the list of emergency wards and pharmacies, the notices of lectures and public transportation routes not in service. He had ended up with the half nobody ever reads—the political dispatches, the speeches, including the speech of the dignitary I knew, essays on the collapse of capitalism, and appeals for increased ideological awareness.

"Thief! Thief!" shrieked the victimized old man in Russian, but no one paid any attention to him because, on that festive day, everyone else was shouting too.

I slipped quickly into the crowd, bearing my loot away with me. I found it somehow pleasant to have been called a thief in Russian, a word I remembered from my childhood. I also had today's guide to Warsaw in my hand. Just then I was courteously saluted by two young policemen. "Please come over to the gateway with us, sir."

We entered a short passageway whose walls were damp with urine. Just in time, too, for it had started to rain again.

"ID," said the taller of the two.

I handed him the dilapidated little book which, in the first fifteen minutes of my journey, had already proven necessary. My journey to where? A chill went through me.

"What's the date today?" I asked.

"Why do you want to know?" said the shorter of the two mistrustfully.

"It's worth knowing."

They exchanged glances, and then the taller one said emphatically, "The twenty-second of July."

"What do you mean July? It's late autumn. It's hailing out."

Without answering me, the taller one began to jot down my personal data. The shorter one was looking at me with un-friendly eyes. His colleague showed him something in my ID, and he nodded his head.

"Aren't you surprised that we're writing this down?" he asked.

"It's happened quite often to me."

"That's not good. And where are you going?"

"To the Family."

"What does that mean?"

"It's a dairy bar, my favorite one."

I still wanted to ask what year it was, but I sensed that would be overdoing it. Somebody was walking over to me from the darkness of the gateway.

"Hey, how are you," he said in Russian, giving me a friendly whack. I saw that it was Kolka Nachalow. "I know him. What's going on?"

"Keep moving, please," said the taller policeman, stressing his words.

"Hey, young man, easy does it. Where's your number?" he said, still speaking in Russian.

"Excuse me?"

"There should be a number here," he said, pulling on the sleeve of the uniform.

"We're from the Goledzinow Police Academy."

"There still should be a number there!"

A bit crestfallen but trying to maintain their dignity, they returned my ID and walked away.

"You need some bricks? Some good Stalin bricks."

"Are you crazy? What do I need bricks for?"

"For your dacha, your house. They're tearing down the Warsaw Steel Mill. You can buy them cheap."

"No, thanks."

"I've got good contraceptives from a government store. I'll let you have them at the state price, fifty zlotys."

"I don't use them."

"Then maybe we can split half a liter."

"Thanks, but I'm not feeling well."

"I can sell you some Szostakowski salve. Straight from the Baltic."

I don't remember how I knew Kolka Nachalow. He'd been around Warsaw for years, always involved in odd schemes. Apparently his father, a KGB general, had been a counselor in the Security Forces in Szczecin. When he retired, he took off his Polish uniform, put his Soviet one back on, packed up, and went home to Moscow with his family. But Kolka stayed on. He liked it in Poland, even though sometimes he'd get smacked in the face when he was drunk.

"I've got to get going," I said, to say something.

"I've got to run, too. Which way are you going, left or right?"

"Straight ahead. To the other side of the street."

"All right then, stay well. If you have any trouble, you can always find me at the Paradise."

He walked off, almost at a run, while I stood at the end of the gateway watching a young man in provincial clothes who was either bowing respectfully to me or to someone behind me. But there was nobody standing behind me, and so I returned the bow with a certain surprise. The young man smiled timidly. A blond with earnest eyes, there had been plenty of boys like that in the Home Army underground during the war.

"And then suddenly death came. Cruel death came on that cold, starlit night," recited the young boy from the provinces in a subdued voice.

You run into more madmen all the time; no one is treating them anymore because the psychiatric hospitals are packed with government officials of every sort. At one time it was the oppositionists who were hospitalized as a warning, but soon there were no places left for them because it had become fashionable for high officials to protect themselves against a fall, being deposed, or sentenced, by signing themselves into the madhouse.

Feigning indifference, I walked past the boy and crossed the street. I plunged into the warm, rancid-smelling interior of the Family dairy bar. There was an enormous line in front of the cashier. This new bit of bad luck disconcerted me. I circled uncertainly around the small, cracked, glazed tables and had decided to leave when someone called out in a friendly voice from the line, "Hello, there!"

I wanted to run away, because I had recognized Rysio's brother, but it was too late.

"Is that you?" I said, annoyed.

"What'll you have?"

"Maybe some hot milk and a roll."

"They've run out of milk, but there's buttermilk."

"All right, buttermilk, then."

Waiting for Rysio's brother and my breakfast, I racked my brains trying to remember his name. I ran feverishly through Slavic names, Western names, and all names of ancient origin, but somehow none of them matched the severe profile of the Marxist and philosopher so heartily hated by Rysio. The two brothers held each other in contempt.

Twenty minutes later we were sitting together at a table which had been cleared.

"How are things going, Docent?" I asked to be polite.

The philosopher choked on a sip of buttermilk. "I can't abide such titles."

"Forgive me, I didn't mean any harm."

He took a bite of his dry roll and, out of habit, began a lecture. "At the present time the word 'docent' has an offensive ring to it."

"I didn't know."

"Please don't interrupt. That form of reward, the granting of the title 'docent,' has not worked out in practice. Now we have a great army of docents and they're causing great problems. You see, some of them are barely out of high school, and the exams they took were a crime. And what ambitions! We have to train them, to complete their education. We've formed a special department to educate docents. I'm the director. Do you know what that means? An enormous program, a gigantic assignment, there's supposed to be classes twelve hours a day, but they're always playing hookey. Medical excuses, phone calls from their wives, or, worse, from the Central Committee. I'm losing patience now. There, you see," he said, glancing at his watch, "my lecture starts in five minutes. I have to run. Too bad."

"To the docents?"

"No, to the Censorship. I'm giving a lecture at the Censorship."

"Are there docents there, too?"

"There are, but that's not the point. The Censorship has formed an independent department for allusions. I'm giving the instructional lectures. Allusions in works of art, allusions in the mass media. You're grimacing? You always were ill-tempered."

"The buttermilk's gone sour, that's the only reason."

"I, my good man, am a devotee of allusions. I have created a theory of how allusions function in a socialist society. Are you listening?"

"I'm listening, I'm listening . . . I was just thinking about something."

The same provincial youth was sitting at the other end of the restaurant and smiling again.

"So, in our situation," continued the philosopher, "allusions play a vital role. Not calling a thing by its name reveals what it is; allusions have suggestive power, they reach into the listener's subconscious. Therefore, an undisclosed truth becomes a public truth. The tension caused by the hunger for truth or, rather, I would say, by people's complex about truth, those dangerous tensions are artificially eliminated by a skillfully employed allusion. For that reason, allusions should not be repressed; quite the contrary, they must be encouraged, people must be taught to make more intelligent, more meaningful allusions. After a certain amount of time, people will prefer an allusion to the truth itself. Because an allusion is, in its own way, a sort of an art form. An allusion is truth clad in metaphor."

"I was always an admirer of the Censorship."

"Let's be frank, not everything functions correctly here. We're constantly suffering from all sorts of aggravating shortages. But really, one has to admit, the Censorship has certain ambitions, and one should be fair about it, it has been leading the way in the dynamics of social change. And that's no accident, either. Our system is an intellectual system, born of intellectuals. Who could think up a better censorship than an intellectual?"

"Rysio was at my house today."

"Which Rysio?"

"Your brother."

"That idiot. I say that because, in the end, he's my brother. And so I didn't use a harsher word—'provocateur.' An idiot with unbridled ambition. I'm surprised that he wasn't appointed a docent. He has dreams of a career on a world scale. That's why he writes that unpunctuated, dissident prose. But he doesn't understand my theory of allusions in prose. And so his novels seem truthful, but they are completely untruthful; they seem modern, but they are absolutely old-fashioned. He's an ass, if you'll excuse the expression."

The provincial youth was keeping his eyes on me, his lips moving soundlessly. Someone was arrogantly complaining about a rotten egg at the kitchen window. Offended, the woman cook had broken into tears and had begun removing her apron and cap, ready to quit. The cashier pulled out the cash drawer and, carrying it in her arms, ran over to comfort the cook. A passing band blared down the street. We all glanced out the window, dull with dust. But it was only a band of kindergarteners.

"You shouldn't even say hello to them," said the docent.

"To who?"

"Those dissidents of yours. They're the same sort of apparatchiks you find working for the state. They're dissidents with lifetime appointments. The regime has grown accustomed to them and they've grown accustomed to the regime. The opposition, the regime, they're the same thing, part and parcel of each other. You should write for the Censorship. They'd appreciate you. You had a flair for allusions. And allusions represent a higher initiation into art. You remember what Joyce used to say? That thirty years wouldn't be enough for the literary nitpickers to decipher all his allusions. He didn't have a state censorship and so he created one of his own and imposed it on himself."

There was a heavily fly-specked calendar on the wall. The date it showed was April 1980. And I didn't know whether that was an old, forgotten calendar or next year's. The cashier returned to her booth. The cook was back at her stove in the kitchen. Defeated, the customer was eating his rotten egg in despair.

"I remember you as a brilliant young philosopher," I said after a moment, and he froze watchfully, with a hunk of stale roll by his lips. "You were in the young Catholic intellectual circles. What drove you to Marxism? Was it laziness?"

He threw the roll furiously onto the table. It ricocheted off the empty salt shaker and fell to the ground. It was immediately seized by a clochard I knew who made his little nest on our street. The clochard leaned on a six-foot-long, freshly stripped stick like an apostle.

"I'm listening, go on, please," said the philosopher, trying to control his agitation. We both glanced up at the television set suspended from the ceiling over the bar. From the static and snow an image emerged—a gigantic automobile bearing both Secretaries, ours and the Soviet one. They had just been stopped by steelworkers dressed in white like cooks, who began kissing our leaders on the mouth with listless enthusiasm.

"You dreaded taking responsibility for your own life," I said, finishing up the buttermilk. "You were afraid of a blank sheet of paper, afraid of the Censorship, afraid of competition from other dynamic philosophers. And so you hid behind the iconostasis of the Party, you served on commissions, committees, you threw your weight around, a big-shot official. Now you govern while others work. Now you're a slothful, lazy, evil god lording it over your talented contemporaries."

I could see fine drops of sweat on his forehead. He leaned toward me with an indulgent smirk. But though his hands were resting on the table, they were trembling hysterically.

"You're a fool, too. Don't you realize that we're experiencing the next great flood? An ocean of shit from the east has inundated us from the Bug River to the Elbe. And one must survive this cataclysm. Survive physically. And save one's soul. We were lucky that the Russians collapsed, eaten away by the leprosy of Communism. You should pray every day and thank your gods that the Russians have been rendered inert by that idiotic doctrine, depraved by that ghastly life, exhausted by that moronic economic system. Every night you should thank heaven that they can't stop writing those huge books, that those scraps of ideas from the nineteenth-century idealists are still flitting through their brains, that they're standing in lines, that they're hungry for fashionable clothes, that they're reading bourgeois Polish weeklies, that, in a word, they're splashing about in the mud in the cellar of humanity. Imagine a free, democratic Russia with a capitalist economy. In a few years a Russia of that sort would be producing art of such genius they'd have the world on its knees. A Russia like that would truly overtake America in industry. And a Russia like that would suck us up like a vacuum cleaner sucks up cobwebs. Without tanks, without deportations to Siberia, it would swallow us up by virtue of its cultural supremacy, by the height its civilization had reached. Everyone would be making tracks to Russia, the way they do to America now. You too would be searching for Russian grandmothers and grandfathers among your ancestors, you too would be wanting to travel to Kamchatka as part of some humanitarian campaign to reunite families. You see, they're kissing them, without any feeling, under duress," he said, pointing at the television screen, where young people were now kissing both the Secretaries. "But they ought to kiss that Kalmuck's feet with genuine, intelligent, proud gratitude."

I sat there, a bit battered by the philosopher's lecture. I wanted to counter him and regretted that Hubert wasn't with me. He was looking at me the way a snake looks at a laboratory mouse, yellowish froth or the remains of the buttermilk drying at the corners of his mouth.

"Tell all that to Rysio sometime," he said sadistically, seeing me weaken. "That ass, with his band of cunning, stupid colleagues is hard at work sawing off the branch he's sitting on. The branch will break and they'll fall together into an enormous Russian vat. And while they're falling into that abyss, they'll knock all of us off like pears off a tree."

"You're a Cassandra. The raging prophet of Polish nationalism," I said in a weary voice. "But our chauvinism is a zero, a nothing, a gob of spit on the highway of the world. It won't give us any breakthroughs, Mr. Ex-Philosopher, Mr. Former Student of Pascal and Sartre. I won't tell anyone about this conversation. Let it be forgotten."

"You've bet everything on their card and you're afraid of losing," said the philosopher, and began to laugh mockingly. "Me, I couldn't care less. I have demonstrated another point of view to you. I'm a drop of protein in the ocean of chaos we call the universe. It doesn't matter to me."

He rose violently from the table, took his cup, his plate, and carried them to the window along with the dirty utensils. He was precise even when excited. Then he left without saying goodbye.

The boy from the provinces was sitting closer to me now, at the next table. Again, seemingly in my honor, he was reciting a verse that sounded familiar.

"And the door slammed dully behind him like a closed book or the heavy lid of a coffin."

I left the dairy bar. The boy sprang from his table, too, in fear of letting me out of his sight. He didn't look like a stoolie. Our watchdogs dress fashionably, they're Europeans with doctorates in sociology or law. But this one had a good-natured face, and he probably hadn't even started shaving yet.

I entered the dense crowd, but he stole up behind me, awkwardly colliding with people like a bumpkin. In the middle of the street a police car was dispersing schoolchildren carrying flags. A police officer leaning out the open window was making signals to the cadets from Goledzinow.

A young man clothed in fashionable baize and wearing mirrored sunglasses (although, I must say, no one had seen the sun for a week) walked over to me.

"May I ask you for a light?" he asked, crumpling a Gauloise between his fingers.

"I'm sorry, I don't smoke."

"That's no problem. Would you come with me over to the gateway."

"To the gateway, for what?"

"For this." He showed me the small metal plainclothesman's badge.

"I've already been checked once today. By that gate, on the other side of the street."

"No problem. We'll just do it again. Your ID, please."

I handed him my well-worn document, which had once gotten soaked in tea or juice of some sort. He took it in his hand and pretended to be reading it. On the other side of the apartment building on Nowy Swiat which had two pet stores in it, on the other side of it, the Gorski Street side, an enormous silent crowd was standing on the small asphalt square. They were all holding jars and plastic sacks full of water, little aquariums in which little fish were moving dreamily about. Red ones, gold ones, gray ones, black ones, white ones. The fish were silent, and their dealers, perhaps connoisseurs, were not speaking, either. So they stood there with their limpid, illuminated handfuls of water and examined each other's fish.

"It's curious that I'm the only one whose papers are always being checked," I said to the plainclothesman, who would have looked right in an American film.

"Sometimes that happens," he said impassively. His tone could even have been termed friendly. Of everything that could have been modernized in this underdeveloped country, the police were the first. And so that modernity of his seemed to possess an element of superiority over my inferiority. I felt a little ill at ease.

Meanwhile, behind me, police cars were howling on the street; there was a deafening roar from the motorcycles in the honorary escort. Light, scattered applause broke out. The plainclothesman glanced over my head with neither excitement nor curiosity, the way a mechanic looks at a well-functioning machine.

"Do I look like an assassin?"

"Ask your wife," said the elegant plainclothesman, closing my ID. "Thank you. You may go."

I returned to the street, passing the boy from the provinces, who began reciting in a stage whisper, obviously for my benefit: "The earth of sorcerers and soothsayers is dying away, the earth of prophets and messiahs who still have not succeeded in saving the world."

I would have bet anything I knew where that was from. It sounded like a fragment of one of Hubert's poems or of Rysio's amorphous prose, more likely Rysio's, because he liked to step on the pathos throttle when there was no need to.

A great cloud of virulent exhaust fumes from poorly tuned motors floated down the shallow ditch that was Nowy Swiat Street. Accompanied by a band of kindergarteners, the schoolchildren walked off toward Swietokrzyska Street. Linked in a hug, both Secretaries flashed past a ways down on Krakowskie Przedmiescie Street.

I had left the house on impulse. I had felt something clearly and had wanted to make a decision. But now everything had fogged over. I remembered Hubert and Rysio's visit with a sort of oppressive disbelief. Maybe it had all been just a dream.

Such things had already happened to me. A couple of years ago I called up my publishing house in the morning to request them to change the title of my new book. The editor was polite but surprised. She maintained that she did not know anything about the book and did not see it on her list, but would go check on it right away and call me back. But when she had finished her courteous speech with its undertone of nervous surprise, I suddenly realized that I was acting out a dream I had had a couple of hours before. A dream in which I had been writhing in shame over the title of a book I had never written and would never write. I unplugged the phone at once so that she would not be able to call me back.

I spotted a calendar between a trombone and some cymbals in a store that sold musical instruments. The date was clear: October 1979.

"What's the date today, and the year?" I asked a man operating a portable soft-drink cart.

"I've got no time for nonsense," he answered impolitely. "You can see what the traffic's like. And they haven't brought me any gas yet, either."

"Yes, we're running out of gas."

Hold on a minute. I left the house with a definite decision. To set myself on fire tonight. Why set myself on fire? The sun had just broken through again. At once the city became more cheerful. Why did I listen to them, anyway? My usual lack of character? But what is character? But, after all, I know the answer perfectly well, I understood all that a long time ago. Character is a lack of doubt, character is stubbornly persevering in an intention no matter how senseless it is, character is a lack of imagination, character is inborn dullness, character is the misfortune of humanity.

I lacked character. I'll walk around like this until evening comes. Still, I could sidestep the whole business. And at some point I will. I was standing at a bus stop. The ticket taker sauntered past, wider than she was tall, an appalling elephant from the municipal transportation system. She was eyeing the prospective passengers suspiciously.

"Excuse me, ma'am," I asked timidly. "Is number 155 still in service? I heard it was canceled."

"How should I know. I saw it at the traffic circle the day before yesterday. Wait and you'll see."

Character has outlived its day. In ancient, primitive times, when biologically weak man struggled against omnipotent nature, character was useful, beneficial; with hideous labor it shoved the heavy stone of human impotence forward. We learned to praise ourselves, to admire character, to prostrate ourselves before it, make a fetish of it. But today no one has the courage to discredit character, although, psychologically speaking, it is now a throwback, simply reactionary. In today's ambiguous world, character means despotism, tyranny, absolute intolerance. At last it is time to admire a lack of character, inner weakness. Our epoch is that of noble doubts, blessed uncertainty, sacred hypersensitivity, divine wishy-washiness.

I squeezed into the packed bus. Asphyxiated by the reek of the exhausted passengers, I finally remembered what was exacerbating my mood and general frame of mind. It was my hangover, of course. An enormous hangover, a number-one hangover. But what was the good time that had caused it, what were the circumstances?

There is no poverty in my country. Few people beg on the street corners, and if somebody does, it's without the conviction, inner strength, and moral right peculiar to true beggars. Nobody divides matches into four parts, nobody counts grains of salt. Besides, there'd be no sense in dividing up a match nowadays. Scarcely every third one lights as it is.

Our contemporary poverty is as transparent as glass and as invisible as the air. Our poverty is kilometer-long lines, the constant elbowing, spiteful officials, trains late without reason, the water cut off by some disaster, or a water shortage, a store unexpectedly closed, an infuriated neighbor, lying newspapers, and hour after hour of speeches on television instead of sports events, the compulsion to belong to the Party, a broken washing machine sold in a state store where you can buy anything for dollars, the monotony of living without any hope whatsoever, the decaying historic cities, the provinces emptying, the rivers poisoned. Our poverty is the grace of the totalitarian state by whose grace we live.

Yes, that hangover had debilitated me. And they had blackmailed me because what else could Hubert's fainting spell be called? They had carefully stage-managed an irrevocable death sentence. Probably some expert in psychology had anticipated all my reactions and instructed them how to disarm me. Perhaps I had even been purposely driven to that hangover. That giant hangover, that total hangover.

But for a while now I've been having dry hangovers, uncaused hangovers *an sich*. After a day of perfect behavior, after a dull evening watching television, after a peaceful night's sleep, I wake up in the morning with a terrific hangover. And if that weren't enough, my life's work of stimulating my imagination causes me splitting hangovers of a purely intellectual variety, even when I'm lying quietly in bed. The hangover is my most faithful companion, my doppelgänger.

We had barely managed to reach the Tamka district on the bank of the Vistula when for no reason the bus broke down. The driver simply pulled over to the curb and announced with vindictive satisfaction that we wouldn't be going any farther because there'd been a breakdown. Quietly, without a murmur, like busy little field mice, the crowd vacated the interior of the bus, which was covered with inspiring slogans.

I set off toward the Vistula, figuring that Vistula Street ought to be located near the river. I'd welch on them at the last minute, I'd give them the slip and vanish. But I'd have to feign loyalty until the evening. I would doggedly walk the Stations of the Cross, which the mysterious hierophants of the rebellious had assigned me. The invisible politburo of the last people who suffer insomnia in this sleeping country.

But still I could not collect my thoughts and still did not know what I was going to do. When I recalled Hubert and Rysio's visit, it seemed to me a sinister morning dream. But then it would become hard to breathe, there wasn't enough air, and in a spasm of hysteria I wanted to flee. But flee where?

The Vistula's water was dun-colored, slimy, close to flood level. A few sailboats regaled in flags were struggling with an unfavorable wind in the middle of the current. On the other side of the river, above the fading jungle of the zoo, there was an enormous neon sign blinking on and off: WE HAVE BUILT SOCIALISM!

I had spent many difficult moments by that river. Those bushes trampled by punks had once been my hermitage. I would stare for hours into the clear space of the water, still pure back then, and would digest the sweet bitterness of some defeat in love or the acidic bitterness of a literary disaster. My sins, my pains, my shame flowed away to the distant sea like the wreaths on St. John's Day.

To leap into the water forever, that would be good. But my miserable brothers want me to leap into the fire.

I wanted to spend a long time, as long as I possibly could, looking for that building on Vistula Street. But, as bad luck would have it, I found it right away. A tenement from the Stalinist period. Coming to the end of its days. Destined to be demolished. Wearied by all the years. Never caressed by repairs, never cleaned of mildew, left to its own fate, like all the buildings in our city. Now only one floor was in use. On all the others the windows had been broken, the doors broken in, the walls pissed on. But that was no problem because on the horizon could be seen the precipitously positioned piles of stone which had been doomed to the short, hard life of the butterfly.

"Poland, Poland, Polska, Polsha!" chanted a smallish crowd in Polish and Russian, having gathered on the boulevard by the river carrying an enormous portrait of our guest, the angry Kalmuck. Above their heads the wind tore at our nation's flag, all red, with just a white band at the top. There were similar little crowds on the other side of the river. They caught sight of each other and began waving their portraits and flags in a mutual greeting that violated all protocol, just for the hell of it.

The boy from the provinces was standing at the corner of Vistula Street with an uncertain smile. He was following me like a dog. In one hand he held a red-and-yellow maple leaf.

I had already crossed the street and was about to enter the dilapidated stairwell when a police whistle pierced the air. A traffic sergeant wearing a white, slightly soiled cap was approaching me with a dejected air.

"You jaywalked," he said impassively. "Your ID, please."

"I've already been stopped today. Twice."

He looked at me with a touch of mockery.

"Do you think I'm going to run you in? No, I'm a human being, too."

But he looked at my poor document with no curiosity at all. "So how much will we pay?"

"Whatever you say."

"What's the big hurry? You got too much cash?"

"That's right. Too much. I won't be able to spend it all now."

He didn't want to open his bag and hunt for his tickets. It was obvious that he had had a lousy night, too. Water from the last downpour was still dripping off the peak of his cap. He didn't feel like talking, either. So he just wagged a threatening finger at me and returned my ID.

But when I was already on the stairs he said laboriously, "Be careful. Just in general, be careful."

Bands were booming tumultuously away in the heart of the city. A great rumble arose from the Praga side of the river. Close by, windowpanes shattered. Probably an artillery salute.

On the landing I was passed by a gaunt old man in crumpled clothes who was carrying an old-fashioned, strap-bound briefcase. For a moment my eyes met his, dark and glittering with the embers of fanaticism. It was Comrade Sacher, who had been a member of the Politburo many years ago. I stopped in amazement by the cracked banister and stared at the back of that wretched old man who had once been driven around in bulletproof limousines and protected like the royal jewels. A nod from him could change the names of cities and cause heads to roll. Now he was a defenseless old man living in retirement and no doubt on his way to stand in line for noodles made practically without any eggs.

Suddenly he turned around and looked at me from the

depths of those eyes which had once hypnotized women comrades devoted to the revolution.

"Good day," I said mechanically.

"Good day," he answered in a hoarse voice, and went outside.

I pressed the doorbell beside a door painted gray-blue. No one opened it for quite some time, though I did hear an authoritative voice behind the door drawling out its words ponderously, followed by short bursts of enthusiasm. Finally, the door opened as far as the chain would allow and I saw an anemic, lackluster girl.

"Hubert sent me. I'm here to see Halina and Nadezhda."

She undid the chain and let me into a front hall full of old junk and baskets of useless clothes, with cheap prints on the walls and cobwebs everywhere.

"Are you here about the technical end?"

"Yes, you could say that."

"Then come in, please."

She was not the least interested in me. Just as if I had come from the cleaner's for her dirty laundry. I felt a certain irritation, blessed irritation. I would offer resistance. Passive resistance.

The room was strangely reminiscent of the makeshift furnished rooms from the years of the German occupation. There were some folk rugs on the wall, some wooden furniture from a Cepelia store and some flowers, a bit dried out, in a clay jug. In one corner a television was glowing, and a man with a white beard was lying on a couch in the other.

"I have a few pamphlets for you," said the girl. She was small, slender, haggard, like all young people today who had been born into a socialism all ready for them, built by us.

"What kind of pamphlets?" I asked in surprise.

"Pamphlets concerning the technical side of things. About your predecessors, from various countries. They're worth reading."

I took the several pamphlets from her, not knowing what to

do with them. I only knew that I would never look at them.

The peeling spines of the classic works by Russian dissidents grinned at me from the shelves.

"Watch this! He's going to take off his clothes!" shouted the man with the white beard, pointing at the television.

We moved closer to the set. The girl turned up the volume. The Presidium appeared on the old-fashioned television set's large screen. Our Secretary was in the center, seated alongside the Soviet Secretary, with his Asiatic features. They were holding hands. There was an enormous Roman numeral XL above them and beneath it a banner in both Polish and Russian which read: WE HAVE BUILT SOCIALISM!

From behind the platform the next speaker was advancing toward the mike. I recognized him as the official who lived across the street from me. He was moving without hurrying toward the rostrum decorated with a star, not quite a Soviet star but somewhat similar to one.

"Comrade Kobialka," said the man on the couch excitedly. "I've been observing him for months. Watch, today he's going to take off his clothes.

The Congress Hall grew quiet and we held our breath. This was the terrible fate, the inconceivable plague, the uncontrollable epidemic seizing the entire Party. So far, no one had been able to avert it. It deprived everyone of sleep, made hearts beat faster, and at the same time rendered everyone listless. Participants and observers alike. Security men and reactionaries.

Comrade Kobialka walked up to the rostrum, holding a stack of cards with his speech on them in front of him like an alibi. With large suffering eyes he glanced up at the ceiling and then brought his gaze down to the audience. Then, slowly, almost imperceptibly, he began to part his lips in a hideous, indecent, appalling smile.

"No! No!" cried someone wildly in the Congress Hall.

But, as if manipulated by some unearthly power, Comrade Kobialka began to sway behind the mike and, prolonging the motion, tore his cards into four parts and let them fall, with no show of concern. They fluttered down with aggressive haste onto the delegates in the front rows, from which there rose at once a strange, hysterical sob.

Comrade Kobialka opened his lips. For a moment he tormented his audience, ominous, frozen in silence; then he spoke, his voice sonorous and strong: "Comrade traitors! Comrade swine!"

A second later there was violent interference on the screen, which was crisscrossed with white streaks, followed by a screeching sound; the image kept appearing and disappearing as if someone was trying to switch off a set but couldn't quite manage it. And so Comrade Kobialka would appear for a brief moment and then vanish again. When he was on screen, his lips would be moving violently, but nothing could be heard, because they had managed to disconnect the audio. Comrade Kobialka was delivering his mute speech, his accusation for which he had been preparing himself for a quarter of a century, his credo formed over many sleepless nights, his confession rising in a throat parched with all the depths of humiliation. Comrade Kobialka was shouting all that soundlessly, while, for a few seconds, the audience in the hall sank into a preternatural trance.

Finally, as in a dream, someone rose slowly from his folding chair, someone else tore himself away from the wall, then hands, a bit imploring, a bit rapacious, reached through the motionless wall of the Presidium's members, and the image returned to normal speed. Still shouting soundlessly, Comrade Kobialka took off his jacket and threw it on the red-carpeted steps, undid his tie and hung it on the microphone. Then he tore off his white dress shirt without unbuttoning it and, finally, began pulling off his pants. But by that time the agents were almost to him. He had become entangled in his falling clothes and was now staggering dangerously. Then they reached him, grabbed him by the arms and legs, and dragged him off behind the Presidium into the wings. But he kept struggling; he wriggled out of their grasp, spitting froth in all directions, kicking out his legs, his head tossing like an epileptic's, and then he disappeared behind a crimson curtain with one last flash of his snow-white shorts, imports from the U.S.S.R.

Suddenly there was a card on the screen showing two doves kissing each other. One dove was red, and the other was red with a white tail. The magical Roman numeral XL was there beneath them. The sound of Tchaikovsky's Fifth Symphony rose majestically.

We were silent for a moment, as if at the graveside of someone who had just been buried.

Finally, I said, "He's my neighbor."

"I used to like him," said the man with the white beard. "He must have been quite a drunkard."

"Everybody drinks," said Halina.

"But he was serious about it. And that's why he ended up like that." The man with the white beard was trying to turn over onto his other side, but after a brief effort, he gave up.

Halina walked over to the door which led into the interior of the apartment. "Excuse me for a moment, please."

I was left alone with the man on the couch. He looked at me for a very long time, then he finally moved his lips and said, "It's you."

"Yes. Me."

"Come closer. Please, sit by me. I'm paralyzed." And when I had squeezed onto the edge of the couch, he added, "Partially. Do you remember the war?"

"Which war?"

"Ours, of course. Our great war."

"I took part in it. I thought I would never forget it until the day I died. But I forgot it a long time ago."

"I remember it. It lasted a long time for me. For ten years after the war, I was in Soviet camps."

He looked me over closely. "No, it's not what you think. They didn't put me in prison for Communism. I was in the Home Army camps. Not only for Home Army people, they had everybody there in those camps, they were like the Tower of Babel. But there were a lot of Home Army people there, that's why I called them that."

Tchaikovsky rose slowly and grandiloquently behind those two red doves, one of which had a white tail. The fingers on the old Home Army soldier's right hand were fidgeting nervously on a fold in the blanket. I guessed that a stroke had affected the right hemisphere of his brain, and now his hand lived a life of its own.

"Would you like to be turned on your other side?"

"Yes. You noticed?"

I helped roll the thin and tremendously heavy body onto its other side. Now he was facing the wall, which had no hangings on it. And that was better.

"You're afraid, of course?" he asked softly.

"I still don't know whether I'll do it or not."

"Fear is human. I used to be afraid. Up until the moment I was told that my wife and daughter had died in prison. From then on I ceased being afraid. Torture is more horrible than death."

"I haven't been able to collect my thoughts since this morning. I want to concentrate and see my situation clearly. I want to make up my mind, but I can't."

"But my wife and daughter weren't dead. They were alive and free. They had wanted to break me, but they only stiffened my resistance."

"Do I have to do it?"

"I don't know. Back then we knew everything, now we don't know anything. The world was simple back then. Now it's out of joint. It either went out of joint itself or it was thrown out of joint by ideology, like a hurricane. Maybe it's weakness, but maybe it's strength."

"What's weakness or strength?"

"Your death."

"My not untimely death. Death right on time."

"We're dying anyway, minute by minute. And the world's dying along with us, true or not?"

"The world can't die. Many generations have thought the world was dying. But it was only their world which was dying."

"Well said. But if the world isn't dying, then you have to live somehow."

"What does that mean?"

"That means you need to have a human death."

The doves disappeared. The Congress Hall appeared on the screen again. Someone was speaking, the audience was thunderous in its applause, and one person had begun cheering exuberantly. Everything was back to normal. Back to abnormal normality for a while.

"You lie there and you watch this handful of young people, a little group haunted by something—pangs of conscience for the sins of their parents, anger at the nastiness of existence, a spasm of the species' collective morality. But they're swimming against the current, aren't they, and they're not making any headway," I said.

"We're living through a terrible night, a nightmare. We have to scream to wake people up."

"Oh, my brothers, from the forests and the camps, in exile, despair, in this fucked-up life of ours, what should I do?"

"You'll know when the hour comes."

The door opened and I saw Halina blocking the view of the other room. "Please come in."

I went in, she closed the door. By the window, against the light, stood a girl with an enormous head of matted, felt-like hair which seemed to give off a glow.

"This is Nadezhda," said Halina.

I bowed, but the girl with the reddish hair remained motionless. An ashen shadow crossed her face.

"Do you know where it's supposed to happen?" asked Halina.

"By the Party building."

"No, that decision has been changed. It will be in front of the Congress Hall, where the congress is taking place."

Who changed the decision, I thought. These children? A Masonic lodge? Or some strange demiurge chained in a Warsaw dungeon?

"It doesn't matter to me," I said and immediately realized that those were the words of Rysio's brother, the philosopher.

The walls shook. There was a roar from the Vistula. A last belated salute. Somebody had either forgotten one or the gun had gotten jammed.

"You'll need gasoline and reliable matches. You don't happen to have any with you, do you?"

"I thought I'd buy some at a gas station."

"You need coupons for that. And besides, they'll gyp you and sell you watered-down gas."

"So what can we do, then?" I asked with a certain sense of hope.

"You stay here. With Nadezhda. She'll fill you in on the details. I'll go to a drugstore I know and buy some thinner."

"But today's a national holiday."

"No problem. They're taking inventory right now and I have some money to bribe them."

"I've got a little, too. May I pick up this cost?"

"It's a long way till evening. You'll have enough time to spend it," she said, smiling, and added, "Nadezhda's grandmother was Lenin's lover, did you know that?"

"No, that's the first I've heard of it." I bowed again to the motionless girl by the window.

Halina put on a short jacket because the wind had started attacking the windows again, and she left quietly, closing the door behind her. The gale was rattling the poorly puttied panes and carrying the sounds of music and the cheering crowds blurred by distance. We were facing each other, she could see me but I could not make out her features. For quite a while neither of us said anything and I, wonder of wonders, did not feel ill at ease. I could have stood like that until nightfall. Finally, she began moving toward me, slowly at first, almost dreamily, then quicker and quicker until finally she fell to her knees, seized my hand, pressed her lips to it, and said in a strangely low voice, "You're a genius."

Realizing that this was a compliment I did not deserve, I tried to lift her back up, but only got myself entangled in her hair, dry, matted, and reddish, like Lenin's in his youth.

She sighed precipitously and tore herself from the floor and ran off to the room where the gray-bearded man was lying.

All right then, I said to myself, but no other thought came into my head. I looked stealthily around. It must have been Nadezhda's room, because the stern and bearded faces of the Russian dissidents were looking down at me from every wall.

She returned a moment later, smiling merrily, yet rubbing the corner of one eye with the back of her hand.

"You're not angry with me?" she asked in a low and throaty voice.

"Of course not, what for?"

"I'm always acting like a fool and then afterward I feel ashamed of myself. I can't get used to Polish ways. With us things are simple. If you love, you love. And if you hate, you hate."

"Different countries, different ways," I said diplomatically.

She took a bottle of some black liquid and two small glasses from a cupboard.

"Shall we drink to us making up?" she asked, still crying a little but already laughing infectiously. She had green eyes, dimpled cheeks, and was a little on the plump side.

"But we're not angry with each other."

She filled both of the glasses nearly to the brim. "It's a Siberian fruit brandy. I brought it here from Moscow and I told myself that I would only drink it on the most important occasions. I was in love with you, you know."

"And I'm still in love with you."

"Irony, always that irony. But I'm telling the truth. One time you were pointed out to me from a distance and I fell in love with you just like a crazy woman."

"Could you be confusing me with someone else, perhaps?"

"No, I've even read your books. You have a Russian soul. Only sometimes it feels a little Polish, a little false."

By a strange coincidence some brass band on some platform close by, over near the banks of the Vistula, began playing an old waltz, "On the Hills of Manchuria," which for me was a lovely, fateful song.

She handed me the glass with the mysterious herbal brandy but did not withdraw her hand. And so we were both holding my glass, which brimmed with Siberian aquavit. My heart missed a beat hearing that old-fashioned waltz.

"To your health," she said.

"To your health."

"To our health."

For a moment that rankled me. That toast was out of place. What's the difference, I tossed off my hemlock in one gulp.

"You might sit down," she said, indicating an iron bed covered by a fur of some sort. No doubt Siberian, too. "It's not healthy, all that standing and standing."

"To tell you the truth, health doesn't matter to me anymore."

I looked down at the bottom of the glass, at the dregs of the herbs. God only knew what they did to you.

"You have a hangover. I could see that right away. I haven't offended you, have I?"

"Nadezhda, or as we say in Polish, Nadzieja—it means Hope in both languages."

"Oh, how nicely you said that. I should give you a kiss."

Which she did. For a moment I felt her hot, wide lips near mine. The band was still playing "On the Hills of Manchuria," a melody by which I seem to have first glimpsed the light of day or night, whenever it was I came into this world.

"What do you think of me?" said Nadezhda, closing her slightly slanted green eyes. I took the opportunity to observe that beneath her strange, transparent blouse, which looked like an enormous kerchief or a theatrical poncho, or rather more like a risqué habit than anything, she was wearing no brassiere. She had already been a bit corrupted by our half-Western Poland.

"I am thinking the best of thoughts, O daughter of the steppes and fallows."

"You Poles can't be trusted."

"Could I have a little more of that Russian folk ambrosia?"

We clinked glasses. The melody of the old waltz soared over the building like a white Caucasian swan, though I wasn't so sure there were any swans in the Caucasus.

"Oh, how I loved you."

"You're always using the past tense, my beautiful Nadezhda. I mean, Hope."

"I was even going to commit suicide."

A slight chill ran down my spine again. She was either a little on the crude side or on too familiar terms with death.

"Your prose had a direct physical effect on me."

"I'm not writing anymore."

"My God, why not?"

"Too boring."

"How can you be bored by literature! You can't say such things. You're an artist, a genius, the whole world is watching you."

The Siberian brandy was doing its job. The room was swaying from side to side, inviting me to dance Cossack style. The band finished playing "On the Hills of Manchuria" and then struck it up for a second time. But now it seemed slower, as if it was trying to inscribe every note on my dissolving brain.

"And so how do you like it here, my child, in this demi-Europe of ours, this ex-demi-Europe of ours?"

"Not very much."

"You imagined Poland differently?"

"How did you know?"

"I know you people."

"You mean Russians?"

"I mean you Russian women. Though I knew some Russian men, too."

"And how do you know Russian women? From Turgenev, Tolstoy, Leskov?"

"But you said I had a Russian soul."

"I said that?"

"When we started."

"Still, you're different."

"And Poland is different, too?"

"Yes."

"Better or worse?"

"Both."

"What does that mean?"

"I miss Moscow."

"That city is missable?"

"I'd walk barefoot through the snow to get there."

"To Moscow?"

"Yes, to Moscow."

I was tempted to ask why she didn't fly back on Aeroflot with her shoes on, but I resisted that temptation.

"You're patriotic, Nadezhda?"

"You're the Polish nationalist."

"You see, my slant-eyed child, that is our fate—whatever we say to you, you always respond by calling us chauvinists."

Suddenly she pressed herself against me. The wistful notes of that waltz from my childhood drifted like cigarette smoke into that girlish, Russianized room.

"Oh, why are there always quarrels between Russians and Poles! Aren't we all Slavs? Wouldn't it be better if you just joined us of your own free will? We'd both forget all these useless grievances, these grudges, and all the bad blood which has kept us divided for so many centuries. We can love you, just give us a little love, too."

"But, you know, there are no Russians left. Your granddaddy, Lenin, murdered the last of the Slavs, the upper classes. Now it's strictly Asia from the Bug to Khabarovsk."

She pushed me away so hard that I fell onto the pillow.

"I knew that I'd be disappointed. Oh, God, I'm so unhappy!"

Again she went running out of the room. I got up with some effort and sat at the bony edge of the bed. That Siberian lovage weed had gotten the better of me. It had fallen on fertile soil; I mean, it had come splashing down on my poor defenseless hangover, my senile illness. Yes, I remember, yesterday I was drinking alone. I had put a tablecloth on the table and set out a plate, silverware, and a piece of cheese. Without haste, with an air of dignity as if at a respectable party, I poured myself half a liter of pure vodka made from domestic potatoes. At first I talked to myself politely and with some humor, later on I think I grew abusive. They were testing the public-address system outside my window. They switched to wild music and an anonymous voice asked to be excused for making so much noise at such a late hour.

Again she returned, laughing and wiping her slanted green eyes. "I take everything seriously and naturally you were just joking."

"I probably was, my Hope."

"I should strangle you this very second and then I'll have some peace."

"You can't strangle me before my time is up."

But she paid no attention to my allusion. She walked over to me, rested her delicate knees, yes, truly delicate knees, against mine and placed both her hands on my throbbing neck.

"Are you afraid?"

"Like anyone would be. I'm afraid that I'll become more and more afraid."

"A colleague of mine from the university did the same thing you're going to. By the Kremlin."

"Many people have done it."

"Do you mean that it's not worth doing, then?"

"I don't know if it's worth it. Maybe one time it will turn out to have been worth it."

"Didn't you ever feel that I was thinking about you?"

"I never knew you existed, Hope."

"Oh, that's not a very nice thing to say. You're so common, and I thought . . ."

"All my strength is in the commonplace."

"You've reconciled yourself to that?"

"A long time ago."

"You mustn't. Man is a strange, uncommon, splendid creature."

"Especially Russian man. He's a God-bearer."

"You're starting again."

I grabbed her wrists, her hands still squeezing my neck lightly. And the band was still playing my undoing, "On the Hills of Manchuria."

"In this country you have to get used to the commonplace. To you it seems banal, bourgeois, insipid, but it has certain virtues which turn out to be necessary fairly often. Do you write poetry, Hope?"

"I do."

"Once a week?"

"Sometimes even more often. I can't live a normal life like you people do here."

"We don't live a normal life. We live the way we're told to live."

"Do you believe in God?"

"I do. I mean, I try to."

"You see, you only try. Like all the rest of you."

I'm ashamed to say it but warmth was emanating from her ample Russian body. I thought that I could see the almond-shaped, wide-open eyes of her nipples among the colored spots dappling her dress. I imagined the hot, massive, womanly breasts beneath that transparent fabric. Breasts which would not be fashionable west of the Vistula. Then I felt indecent humors stirring in my old, hangover-battered body.

"I'd like to take you away to my country, to old Russia. Where the horizon is distant like nowhere else on earth and the sky is so big, the biggest sky. You try to protect yourself from greatness because you have no courage. You should spit on everything and go searching for God."

"It's too late now, my too-late Hope."

She felt my pulse but I could catch the beating of her blood too, at her strangely thin and fragile wrists. Somewhat taken aback, I noticed that my thoughts were growing confused. That I was staring through the silk or cambric of that strange habit of hers. Dissidents looked down admonishingly from every wall.

"You know what, let's run away," said Nadezhda all of a sudden.

"What are you talking about?"

"Come on, no one will see us. We'll run away from everyone."

"But where to, my little granddaughter of Genghis Khan?"

"We'll see. There'll always be a place for the two of us."

"You'd leave them alone? But then who would save the world?"

"You're a cynic. God, why do I have to love you. Had I known . . ."

Suddenly the clouds dispersed, revealing a bright-blue sky. A pure, enormous sun came flaring through, making the day as warm as August. A large rectangle of light blazed on the floor. And the band was still playing "On the Hills of Manchuria."

"I'm a positive cynic. And that's why I suit you. We're the same."

"You don't know how to bring off something really mad, do you? You never could."

"My dear Nadezhda, it's not nice of you to reproach me when Halina has gone out to buy thinner."

She was about to say something, but she fell silent. She was looking at me with those slanted eyes, which weren't green at all, though they should have been. Her eyes had intense violet depths and even seemed a little phosphorescent to me. She knelt down in front of me.

"It's a pity I didn't dare to get to know you sooner."

"You're confusing me with someone else."

"No, I swear to you. Ask Halina."

"You felt lost here in Poland and so you were looking for a soul mate. A wild, crazy, Russian soul mate."

"Why do you dislike us so much?"

"I dislike everybody. Or, if you prefer, I like everybody. Even those two poor Secretaries, yours and ours, who may be kissing each other reluctantly on the mouth at this very moment. But you, you I just love, Nadezhda. I fell in love with you at first sight."

"But you're still a Pole. A White Pole."

"Come here, sit beside me."

"For what? The feeling's passed."

"That'll make it easier."

"I'm indifferent to you."

"Fine. All the more reason for you to sit down on this virginal bed of yours."

"And how do you know I'm a virgin? I may have had three husbands already."

"The first one was an artist, the second was a section head in the Central Committee, and the third was a Pole who took you out of Russia."

"Keep going. It's revolting. At least I'm recovering from my giddiness."

She smelled of henna or some Siberian herb. And that hair could have been underwater vegetation in some mysterious Siberian river. She sat down beside me with an angry look on her face.

"My dear Nadezhda, you're mocking me. You are all mocking this old man who's no good for anything now but burning."

"I don't feel like talking."

"You have to talk to me, it's your duty. You have to stifle me, stun me, numb me."

To my surprise I noticed that her enormous head of hair, a

cap of pure gold, was trembling slightly and she was hiding her face with her hair.

"No, come on, Nadezhda, you can't do that. Why are you crying?"

I put my arms around her and pulled her over to me.

"I don't know myself," she sobbed. "I'm just so upset."

I kissed her on the cheek, where a line of tears was flowing.

"I love you. I've come to love you in the course of an hour, in the space of an entire epoch, the final era of my finite stay on earth. Do you believe me?"

She nodded her head docilely. I became aware of her warm weight in my arms. There had been many times like this. Many nights, dawns, late afternoons. But now it seemed I was holding a body blessed by Providence, the magical body of the woman you dream of your entire life. A body both girlish and womanly, a body that was both an adventure and a refuge. For the first time I was seized by a sort of keen longing for this young woman who was joined with me in a sisterly, or perhaps only human, embrace.

In a word, I had been overcome by a feeling of melancholy and anxiety, of blissful ease and dark premonition. The music from the brass band outside grew stronger and an incoherent desire arose in me. She was pressing herself harder and harder to me, as if trying to press through the transparent wall of the inevitable.

So my hand went searching for her in that habit of hers, and to my surprise I found a frayed hole and could confirm that she was indeed naked beneath that shawl, that poncho. A thought on that subject had almost reached me, but it never quite arrived, for I had glimpsed the gentle hills of her breasts and it felt as if it was the first time in my life that I was seeing the beautiful breasts of a woman. In a state of great amazement, balmy with delight, I laid my head in the shadowy pass between those breasts.

Somewhere in the back of my mind was a throbbing, vague

awareness that I was taking part in a rite of magic. And that panic, that eclipse, that fever which is always with me in those moments of sin, all that ambiguous animalism vanished in the melody of our confused whispers and kisses.

Then I wanted to enter her and I could not. Abashed, I struggled against her resistance, but it wasn't her resistance, for she wanted me, it was her innocence resisting. Finally, I penetrated the warm and thrilling darkness.

"Oh, God," she whispered.

And at that moment the telephone near our heads began to ring shrilly. To me it sounded like the shriek of a pneumatic hammer. It had been waiting, treacherously concealed on the windowsill, and now was alarming us with all the mechanical power it had.

I faded. She grew still. The bell was urgently clamoring complaint and disapproval.

"Answer the phone!" shouted the sick man from the other room.

I rose, covered her with that habit while she hid her face with a shoulder so strikingly beautiful I had never seen its equal. At that moment the arm of a young woman bent at the elbow seemed painfully perfect to me. Without taking my eyes from those amazing ovals held in lucid gold skin, I picked up the receiver, heavy as an oar. Her hair, reddish, full of life, greedy, was spread out against the coarse gray blanket on that hospital or prison bed.

"Hello," I said, my voice hoarse.

"This is Halina. Everything went fine. The only thing is, what color gas can do you want? There's a choice. Red, yellow, or blue?"

"Gas can?"

"You know what it's for. So, what color?"

"Does it have any meaning?"

"I don't know. It could. So I thought I'd ask."

"All right, I'll take blue."

"So long, then. I'll be right back."

Again clouds saturated with the black of a storm were being driven across the sky. The band had fallen still, I don't know when. A little crowd was forming by the building and chanting ecstatically, "Poland, Poland," first in Polish, then in Russian: "Polska, Polsha!"

They were carrying a crumpled banner whose peeling letters formed the slogan: LONG LIVE JULY 22, 1999! I replaced the receiver.

Suddenly Nadezhda stood up and without looking in my direction left the room as if she were walking in her sleep. A bit dumbfounded, I stared at a silvery crack in the window. Then I noticed the rest of that Siberian brandy in a glass, either mine or Nadezhda's. I brought it mechanically to my lips and took a sip of the bittersweet, gritty dregs. I was trying to control my chaotic thoughts and make some sense of a bizarre situation.

Down below, the youth from the provinces was standing by a broken streetlight and toying with a red-and-yellow maple leaf. He was waiting for me.

The best thing would be to slip out of there and wait for Halina on the stairs. But how? The room had only one door, on the other side of which were my unsatisfied Nadezhda and that paralyzed old man, who made me very uneasy. I found myself in a snare, as writers used to say. Ensnared by the sorcery of a slant-eyed Russian girl. My hangover was throbbing, the little hangover I'd picked up the night before.

The door banged open. Nadezhda entered holding two glasses of tea in her hands. She was smiling as if nothing had happened, but there were still traces of tears in those slanted eyes.

"Will you have some tea?" she asked in her normal, that is, astonishingly low, voice.

I took my glass without saying anything. The rectangle of sunlight had already begun to climb the opposite wall. The street bands had struck up again but none of them were playing "On the Hills of Manchuria."

"Halina's on her way," said Nadezhda.

"Are you angry with me?" I asked uncertainly.

"Maybe I am," she said, but then was quick to add, "I'm angry because I met you in the first place."

I looked at her with grief in my heart. She shook her heavy veil of red hair onto her back and drank her strong hot tea, staring deliberately into her steamy glass.

"Nadezhda, have you lost your mind?" I said finally.

"Why? What do you mean?"

Now confused myself, I too began staring into my own glass. "You know what I mean. I'm just passing through. Tomorrow I'll be far away. Why did you do it? Why did you agree to?"

"Maybe that's the reason."

"How are you going to survive in today's world?"

"But I'm a Russian lady," she said, and broke into laughter. She stirred her tea with a teaspoon though there was no sugar left in it to stir.

"Before this, I would have said that it was a pity we hadn't met earlier."

"But now you know that we met at the proper time."

"I don't know anything, Hope. My ears are ringing and none of this seems real to me. I sometimes have very real dreams."

"No one believes in dreams anymore. Dreams are debris from a bad day. Dreams are poems by bad poets that never got written."

"Your Polish is improving all the time."

"I can speak very good Polish when I want to."

"There's so much I want to tell you. If only I weren't ashamed, if only there were time."

"I know everything you want to say."

"You know me that well?"

"I don't know you at all. Today is the first time I ever saw you in my whole life."

"You said that you've read my books."

"I said that? All Poles and all Russians are writers. I might have said it, but I had no idea you were a writer."

"What does that mean, Hope?"

"It means that I fell in love with you in the course of fifteen minutes, just like you did with me."

"You're joking; I thought Russians didn't joke."

"There's still a few seconds left to think it through. Do you have the courage to run away?"

"Without liberating the world from slavery first?"

"We'll be free."

"I'm free already."

"So, I'll be free, too. Two people, that's the beginning of a society."

A door slammed inside the apartment. Nadezhda put her empty glass aside and walked over to me. She looked into my eyes with her enormous irises, which were green, after all, like old-fashioned wine decanters.

Suddenly she put her arms around me. "Well, my dear, what will it be?"

"You think we were destined for each other even though we missed each other by a few decades?"

"Yes, we were destined for each other."

"For what?"

"We still have seven hours ahead of us. A seven-hour eternity. That's a good bad title," I said.

She kissed me tenderly on the lips. "It's good there."

"Where?"

"There. You know. I've been there."

"What are you talking about now?"

"I was once freezing to death in the taiga but I was rescued. Ten or twenty minutes, but it seemed a lifetime to me."

"Hope?"

"What, my dear?"

"Nothing's definite yet. Everything's in my hands, and in yours."

"We can't run away now. We let our last chance slip by."

We kissed, our lips salty.

"If you want, I'll go to the stake with you."

Just then someone knocked at the door. We stepped back from each other. Halina came in carrying a blue plastic gas can in one hand. She took off her beret and began whacking it against the arm of the chair.

"Raining again?" I asked, to have something to say.

"They've even screwed up the seasons," she said. "It's all happening at the same time—snow, sun, wind, rain. The best thinner is imported from New Zealand. We'll buy matches in a hard-currency store and then we'll bring them to you later. Did Nadezhda fill you in on the details?"

"Yes, she did."

"Do you have any questions, any doubts?"

"I don't know what to do with myself."

"But I gave you the pamphlets."

"Yes, but I don't know what to do with myself until eight o'clock."

"I don't know, either. Maybe you'd like to say farewell to your friends, to the city."

"This isn't my city."

"The best thing to do would be to take a sleeping pill and go to sleep. We'll wake you up."

"Thanks, but I'll be all right."

"Nadezhda, why are you standing there looking out the window?"

"I'm thinking."

I picked up the blue gas can. Heavy hand luggage for a long voyage.

"Well, I'll be going, then," I said, none too decisively.

"You'll be under our protection. Don't be afraid of anything. And eight on the dot by the Congress Hall. We'll be there, too."

I bowed and the gas gurgled listlessly in the plastic container. Nadezhda was still facing the window. The soft red glow around her hair was like that of an ash-covered coal in a cold stove. I went out into the other room.

"You're leaving?" asked the sick man.

"Yes, it's time to be going."

"But I am staying. God's forgotten about me. I outlived my time and my legend. That is the greatest agony and I know what agony is. I envy you."

"Now I remember. I've heard of you."

"You might have. My memoirs were translated into thirteen languages. In Poland they were sold on the black market. Then a few generations passed and stamped out my memory. No one remembers anymore."

I shook the can, and the liquid gurgled merrily. "They'll forget about me, too."

"God forbid. Do you think we are witnessing the extermination of our people?"

"Nobody knows. It's wonderful and it's terrible that nobody knows what his own gestures, actions, and follies actually mean. We're worried about the death of our nation, but at the same time the entire galaxy is hurtling off into an abyss, nothingness. It's hailing again. What an autumn."

"I'd say it was still summer. I don't like thinking about solar systems. While we're on earth we should hang on by our fingernails. But I shouldn't say that because I'm holding on by one broken fingernail."

"So, do I have your blessing for the road?" I rapped on the rough side of the gas can.

"It isn't worth it to live so long," he said, and closed his eyes. He looked oddly young in spite of his white beard and gray hair.

"You know what, I have the feeling that all over the world people are buying gasoline and hunting around for gas cans just as I am. Because I have an unusual instinct for mimicry. Once I did something, it would always turn out that everybody else was doing it, too. I'm right there in the middle. Right in the statistical mediocre middle. That's been my bad luck in this life."

"If you can't be first, then be last. That's a good position, too."

I looked at him closely and without sympathy. I knew that he was also observing me through the slits of his eyelids. Could he have been placed there to nudge me on my way to my destiny? Could he be lying under that crumpled coverlet in a morning coat and striped pants, ready to jump up and dash off to a holiday banquet after I left?

The congress was still being televised. With a solemn expression the Soviet Secretary had just handed some sort of standard or banner to our Secretary, who knelt down and obsequiously kissed the edge of the embroidered material. The camera shifted to the audience, where there was an immediate outburst of enthusiasm. Everyone leaped from his seat, applauding fervently; some people even raised their hands and cried out in ecstasy, but I didn't know what they were shouting because here, as in most places, these inspirational programs were watched with the sound off.

Then the gray-haired man, a living relic or an ordinary agitator, then that gray-haired holy figure raised his right hand in a gesture of farewell, or blessing.

"All right then," I said, and left.

On the stairs I examined the vessel full of fiery balsam. It held a good five liters. I tried opening the cap. It worked well. Light blue, the color of innocence. Innocence is inconspicuous. I could go, I had to go, but where? I'd figure it out on the way.

On the landing I stepped on a piece of broken glass. The glass was smoky, though I couldn't tell why. I looked out at the sky through it. Again the sky was gleaming with reflected light from the sun. Nowadays no one watched eclipses of the sun or moon. People in all the social systems and military blocs had gotten their dates screwed up. I didn't see anything interesting in the weary sky, a sky debilitated by anomalies in the climate, and so I glanced over at the wall, where I found only some antigovernment graffiti, the usual stuff which the government no longer had the strength to erase and paint over.

I walked downstairs, and there in the vestibule I bumped into Sacher, the venerable old revolutionary with the fanatical eyes. He was on his way back from the line and was carrying some booty, his briefcase bulging like a python which had just eaten its fill.

"Don't I know you from somewhere?" said Sacher, stopping and blocking the way out.

"Yes, you know me. We met only once but in dramatic circumstances."

"Was I awarding you a medal or appointing you to something?"

"No, you were throwing me out of the Party."

He smiled, which dimmed the cold gleam of fanaticism in his eyes. A fanaticism unrelated to the present, like a forgotten scar.

"I never threw anyone out of the Party. You are mistaken."

"You did once. A professor of Marxism's little group of followers."

"Oh yes. Who was that?"

"It's not important. What's important is that I have no grudge against you."

"We had to act like that. It was the right thing at that stage. Afterward things grew confused. But back then I was able to help save the country."

"How are things going?"

"Fine, thanks. I've gone back to philosophy. Actually, the history of philosophical doctrines. I've gone back to where I belong. I'm free. Free at last."

"So you're free, too?"

"What, you too?"

"Of course. I'm meeting more and more free people all the time."

"Because you can really be free only under slavery. Forgive the cliché, young man. Do you like walking?"

"Of course."

"You should take walks, then. Long ones. At least ten kilometers. You'll do your best thinking. You'll observe nature, human behavior, even the sky. There's movement in the sky, too. Both literally and figuratively. And, young man, movement, if we go back to the classical philosophers . . . But am I boring you?"

"But are you happy? Don't you miss the power, the impunity that comes with ruling people, the exaltations of a power equal to God's?"

Sacher broke into hearty laughter and took out a not particularly clean handkerchief to wipe his eyes. "I'm a philosopher. And a philosopher knows how to forgive himself and those who are close to him."

"What's there to forgive?"

"That they failed the test. That's our original sin."

"You know, I remember that evening quite clearly. After being frisked by dozens of agents, X-rayed and checked out by supervisors, we arrived at the Party sanctuary, where the Politburo was meeting. I remember the round table surrounded by all those faces I was used to seeing on posters hanging on office walls. The faces of our judges."

"But you don't have any regrets, do you?"

"Of course I don't. I remember the gesture you made and the words you said to me: 'Rights as a Party member suspended.' That gave me my freedom back."

"I went through the same thing about fifteen years later. Wasn't there a supper break ordered in the middle of the hearings?"

"Yes, you rose and said in an unofficial, even human voice, 'Comrades, it's time for a little something to eat.' "

"Somebody said those exact same words during my hearing, too. And what was the menu for you that night?"

"It wasn't for me, it was only for you. We went off into another room where there were steaks, sturgeon, hams, maybe even caviar on tables decorated with flowers in Japanese vases. We both smacked our lips, victims and executioners, we wiped the mayonnaise stealthily from our beards, we tore juicy oranges in quarters, even though things were pretty bad in the city and there weren't even enough lemons for people with the flu."

"You see, it was the same story at my hearing. Though I don't remember any caviar. Maybe that's the socialist humanism which neither you, a young man, nor I was able to perceive. Well then, are we quits?"

"It's all the same now," I said, and glanced at my gas can, along which a spider was crawling meaninglessly.

"Take long walks, that's my advice. I've got to run home and watch TV. My favorite program, *The Zoo Show*, is on tonight after dinner and my favorite animals will be on."

"You won't be seeing your innocent little *Zoo Show*. There's a Party congress today. From morning till night. It's on television, in the papers, in the movie theaters. In every home."

"Mother of Jesus, now you've upset me. What a lousy break. Well, I'll go for a walk. Good luck, young man."

He made his pitch-black eyes light up like a cat stepping into the dark, and muttering complaints, he began climbing the rickety stairs.

I went outside. A rather tipsy woman was pushing a baby carriage with a child in it. To break the monotony, she would let go of the handle and then catch up with the carriage, pretending that she was about to kick it. It careened toward the street, which was littered with remnants of colored tissue and letters which had torn loose from the banners.

Suddenly I saw a great cloud of dust coming from the Poniatowski Bridge, and the center span, like a mighty elevator, slid majestically into the water, which bubbled for a time. Only then did I hear the echo of the hollow boom. Small human figures were running in all directions from the remains of the bridge.

"Son-of-a-bitch," said the tipsy woman, with admiration in her voice. "Sleep, little one, sleep." She rocked the child in the carriage. "First time I ever saw anything like that."

"Me, too. Houses have collapsed right in front of my eyes,

but bridges—never," I said politely. "The demonstrators were probably walking in lockstep."

"No big deal. There's a couple of other bridges. What are you carrying in that jug there?"

"Gasoline."

"Aw, too bad, I'm dry as a bone. The soda carts aren't working, they haven't brought them their gas yet. Sleep, little one, sleep, or I'll give you a kick."

And zigzagging slightly she set off toward the Vistula, where a slogan made of wreaths and lit candles—reading WE HAVE BUILT SOCIALISM!—was floating down the center of the current. But the end of the slogan had already been mangled; it had been in range of the bridge disaster. The last two letters were badly mauled and were floating off toward the other bank. Seized by an eddy, the exclamation point was sinking.

"And perhaps your dreams, agonies, sadnesses, adversities, created me like a cloud of cosmic dust."

I turned around abruptly and saw the young man from the provinces with a maple leaf in his hand, smiling timidly.

"Where's that from?" I asked.

"It's from you. I know it by heart."

"And why are you here?"

"I came here from Stargard."

"You came to see me?"

"Yes, to see you. It's just that I didn't dare go to your house. Please, help yourself," he said, offering me an open soldier's haversack filled with heavenly apples. "From our orchard."

I bit into the sweet, juicy fruit, unknown or, rather, forgotten in this country.

"You must write poetry."

"No, prose."

"But I can't help you now. I'm out of things now."

"I don't need help. I only wanted to make your acquaintance. We read you at home in the evenings. The whole family. Dad says you knew each other when you were children."

"And what is your name?"

"Skorko. Tadzio Skorko."

"Doesn't ring a bell. It's possible, though. And so what do you want from me?"

"Nothing. If you would allow it, I'd like to walk with you."

"You picked a bad day."

"I know. Will you let me? I'm leaving tonight."

I took a hard, critical look at that Tadzio from Stargard, and no vanity began chirping in my exhausted soul, no pride began grumbling. But I was an old-timer. I was familiar with all these talented, delicate, sensitive youngsters who quickly grow up into venal, brutal louts.

"I'll carry your can for you."

"All right, if you want to. But you picked a bad day, Tadzio. I can give you the address of more important artists who can do more for you."

"Let me walk with you, I beg you. It's very important to me."

He turned and stealthily wiped a tear away. But I was unbribable. That only put me more on my guard. He could walk with me if he wanted to, but he wouldn't soften me up. These days no one reads books the way they did a hundred years ago. Government pamphlets and Proust, sensationalistic American crap and Joyce make the same impression when consumed. That tripe stuffed with black letters is swallowed and then excreted at once. No one has shot himself in the head because of a novel's sad ending. As a rule no one even remembers a novel the next day. And now this boy was laying quotations on me which could be mine but could also just as well belong to some other pen-pusher.

A window opened, the glass rattling. "Hello, hello there!" Someone was calling me.

I turned around and saw Halina leaning out over a rotted windowsill.

"Wait, please! I'll be right down!"

Perhaps they'd given up on it, I thought. And suddenly that

seemed a shame, a waste of thinner, a waste of my nerves, a wasted opportunity. I had already grown a little used to it all.

The winter days were coming, those terrible, black, short days followed by even blacker, endlessly long nights. And my subscription to life had expired a long time ago. I was living past my limit. I was getting on everyone's nerves, God's included.

"Give me the can," said Tadzio softly.

"Here, but be careful you don't spill any," I said without conviction.

"We'll bring it back to the store. Maybe they'll give us a refund." A moment before, it had been a terrible, death-dealing liquid. And now it seemed no more than fermented lemonade to me.

Halina came running out of the building, hastily pulling on a green sweater that dated from the Second World War. She had been joined by some little dog that had come running up behind her as if it wanted to grab her calf between its teeth. The little dog was barking shrilly.

"Hubert has fallen ill."

"Where?"

"In the Volga movie theater."

"He already had an attack this morning."

"He's dying. We were called. We've got to get over there."

She set off at a run toward the escarpment of the Vistula. The sun had appeared again as if spring were, after some reflection, now approaching. Bands were groaning off and on in the city and echoing strangely; the bass stammerings of the loudspeakers roared like God's voice thundering on Judgment Day. The little dog had joined us and had at once selected Tadzio as its pal.

A police whistle stopped us. Two young functionaries were beckoning me with crooked fingers.

"I'll kick them in the belly," I said. "Whatever happens, happens."

"You can't provoke them," said Halina. "I forbid you to. I'm in charge of this operation."

"So, I'll crack them in the face. Doesn't matter to me."

"I forbid you to," gasped Halina.

The policemen didn't move from where they stood. They were waiting for me. I walked over to them with a provocative amble, glancing up at the Florentine sky above Warsaw. I purposely fastened the top button of my jacket so they could see that I had no intention of going for my ID.

But they saluted me politely, and then one of them asked with a stammer, "Excuse me, s-s-s-sir, how do we find Parade Square?"

"It's straight ahead. Follow the escarpment and then straight all the way to the square. What's the matter, don't you know the city?" I asked impertinently. "What do they teach you in those schools?"

Suddenly it flashed through my mind that if I were arrested my problem would be solved. That was one way out. Even an honorable one, in a certain sense.

But instead of unfastening their three-foot-long nightsticks, issued to them on some special anniversary or another, the policemen grew even more embarrassed and the stammerer removed his cap and bowed humbly to me, peasant style. "We're not from around here. We're s-s-s-sorry to bother you and we thank you."

"Well, watch it in the future," I said, returning to Halina, whose hands were clenched in nervous anxiety.

We ran up along the old paved lane which for years had been overgrown with the kind of grass we call chickory where I come from. Halina was running up ahead. I could see her bare legs, unattractive, too thin, with short, rough stubble on them. She was of the new, physically weak generation. They were all small, thin, shaggy. But it was in them alone that any resistance to the authorities had smoldered. Over the years, the authorities had grown ugly, too, but in a different way—they had turned into fat, growing sideways; they had become womanish.

And so to my surprise, running behind Halina, I realized that she was also a female, but, as if she were a female of another species, she had no effect on me. She looked back at us a few times and I saw her face, really not all that bad-looking, perhaps someone of her species would have discerned Gothic or perhaps even Byzantine features on it. But she was alien to me, just as her whole tribe was, which might be that of the first Christians in the falling Rome of Communism. Then I suddenly felt old, but the feeling did not make me sad in the least. My own world had been more colorful, a hierarchical world, the world of social injustice, the world of the brutal struggle for existence. Mine was a different struggle and mine a different passivity. My falls seemed deeper, my flights higher. I know this is what a generation feels when it departs for nonexistence. I know that the present age compels them both to a pettiness and to a greatness much like ours, though theirs is adapted to the future. But I swear to God, I feel sorry for them and not for myself.

Well, we reached the Volga movie theater, which in my day had still been called The Escarpment. Out front a jagged neon sign advertised a Soviet musical comedy, *The Radiant Future*, but I knew that a Polish film, *Transfusion*, directed by Wladyslaw Bulat, was actually playing in that theater, behind that façade. A new practice had evolved in recent years— Polish films which, for some reason, made the regime ashamed in front of the Russians, were released on the q.t., with Soviet films advertised on the marquee. Thus they played in many cinemas to good houses and the directors, venerated by the regime and by dissidents both at home and abroad, competed for that form of distribution. There had even been bribery scandals.

My testament. My last will. A troublesome document because there is no inheritance, no legacy. I made no fortune. I acquired nothing. I didn't even collect any memorabilia-type junk. No interesting letters from eminent people. No souvenirs from my travels, no traces of my literary inertia. The only material goods, if they can be called that, are my remains, which I am willing to the Academy of Medicine's anatomical laboratory, for young surgeons to practice on.

But it is shameful to go without leaving anything. I ought to make a few notes to the living so that some good comes from my life, my brief presence on earth, where I took other people's places, where I snatched tasty morsels from the mouths of those I loved, and where at times I provided some irritation for my contemporaries.

Mentally I rummaged through the couple of desk drawers which conceal my spiritual and material possessions. A few old photographs, a few out-of-date documents, some dried-out ballpoint pens, a damaged fountain pen which once brought me luck but then ran out of luck. Cuff links I'd been given for a birthday, little light bulbs, I don't remember what they were for, somebody's master's dissertation written about me when I was briefly in vogue, letters that hadn't been thrown out due to absentmindedness and containing compliments from a cripple, pills for hyperacidity too old to be of any use, bits of tobacco, burned traces of forgotten cigarettes.

And yet I do see something I could offer to posterity, though I find the idea a bit intimidating. I am referring to two old prescriptions, refilled many times, two pink sheets of paper with an unfashionable, even antediluvian letterhead. A doctor friend wrote them for me, I don't even remember when. He left the country a long time ago, vanished without a trace, simply expired from our life here. Those two prescriptions are for a shameful ailment, and it is with a certain embarrassment that I speak of them. And yet I know that those nasty, unappetizing, even dishonorable flakes can be the most grievous thing in the world. Delicate people struggle for years with this unpleasant condition, not daring to seek advice. So, unable to do anything else and taking my masters as my model, I would like to be useful in some small way.

To come to the point, I bequeath my poor descendants who suffer from dandruff a proven remedy which will liberate them from their complexes and make them happy, even if only for a short while.

Here is the prescription for the ointment:

> Ac. salicyl. 2.0
> Liq. carb. deterg.
> Sulfuri ppt. aa. 4.0
> Ol. Ricine 6.0
> Aoleps suille ad 40.0

And here is the prescription for the compound:

> Ac. salicyl. 2.0
> Ac. biborici 2.0
> T-rae chinae 5.0
> Ol. Ricine 1.5
> Spir. vini 70° ad 100

First, the ointment. Generous amounts of this unguent should be rubbed into the scalp, preferably before going to sleep. In order not to soil the pillow, I recommend that the entire head be wrapped in an old towel or that a plastic shower cap be worn, or something of the sort. The ointment must remain on the scalp for the entire night. In the morning, when bathing, I urge you to wash your scalp carefully, perhaps even several times. Watch out for your eyes. Keep them free of ointment.

Even if applied only once, this treatment will definitely produce positive results. In order to keep the scalp clean, I recommend that the other mixture be used once a week. If, after a while, the dandruff returns, the ointment treatment should be repeated. But I recommend that the compound be used every week midway between your first and second washings.

I would also like discreetly to bring up another hideous affliction. Constipation happens to even the most splendid, lovely, and spiritual of persons; sometimes it is brief, sporadic, sometimes horrible, lasting for months. And such persistent constipation is able, shameful to say, to make the most exalted existence miserable. For that reason I hasten with discreet aid for this problem. Obviously my advice will not be of help to everyone, but it may bring relief to many worthy people.

And thus I encourage those who trust me to drink a glass of cold boiled water in the morning upon waking. Dried prunes taken in the evening before retiring can also be a source of considerable benefit. At critical moments, when life is becoming truly disgusting, you should down a glass of booze in good company, but I point out that it should be no less than two hundred grams and preferably around three hundred.

If my prescriptions do not produce the desired results in any specific case, which, of course, can happen, I can only beg your forgiveness, and as a consolation I will give the injured parties an effective rule for winning in the card game called Twenty-one. I learned this trick in my youth and was later to shine in many games of Twenty-one. I was taught the trick by a folk doctor, a mysterious wanderer, or by an old gypsy before his death. In any case, whoever it was was a magical figure and did not seem to be a part of this world.

There are two methods, because where I come from there are two ways of playing Twenty-one—using the whole deck or leaving the tens and picture cards out. So, when you're the dealer and using the latter method, make a separate pile for the nines. Then shuffle them back in casually, nonchalantly. Naturally, one of the players will notice what you're doing and accuse you of stacking the deck. Propose that he shuffle. He'll shuffle the cards for quite some time with a vengeful grin on his face, sometimes even for several minutes, in order to wipe out anything you may have done to them. Watch this closely, seem afraid, but remain calm. The more he shuffles, the more he brings defeat upon himself. Because in practically every hand, or at least in the statistical majority of them, your opponent will go bust.

When playing with a full deck, you must separate the picture cards, tens, and nines, into one pile, and everything from eight down in the other one. Shuffle as you did before.

I am sincere when I say I don't know how this trick works. And I never looked into it, either. I even think it's better not to succumb to the temptation of being too inquisitive. It's enough that it works.

On the other hand, one may well doubt whether a last will is the proper place for revealing secrets on how to cheat people at cards. But I humbly submit that people who have been successful at playing cards their whole lives will burst into laughter at such naïve sorcery. On the other hand, people who have had no luck at cards will try my method once or twice and will occasionally even clean out the lucky players, thereby bringing Nemesis' scales into momentary balance.

There was a large crowd in front of the movie theater, but it wasn't clear what they were waiting for, since the show had already begun. On the other side of the street a meat store's enormous window was filled with a large "50" made of kielbasa. The meat industry was celebrating the fiftieth anniversary of the Polish People's Republic. But the kielbasas were dummies and sawdust was sifting out of a few of the more obviously damaged ones. A line of old women stood sleepily by the gilded plate-glass door. The store was closed today on account of the holiday, and so this was the first shift of tomorrow's customers who were lining up.

On Foksal Street a group of people who had been drinking were swaying and reeling while waiting in line for taxis. This was a special taxi stand which served only drunks. Taxi drivers who worked in the alcoholic sector would pull in there.

And so those three little groups sluggishly ambled along, plunged in the grayness of their clothes and the hopelessness of a holiday to which everyone was indifferent. An airplane flew low over the rooftops, carrying tourists who were circling above the city for the holiday. But today something had gone wrong, some defect, and the silvery, rust-eaten machine began plunging toward the beach on the other side of the Vistula with the obvious intention of nose-diving onto the golden sand of that broad shore.

We went into the movie theater along with the stray dog and Tadzio, who was carrying my gas can. There was a large party going on in the lobby; it was the opening of an exhibit of paintings by a former minister of culture and member of the Central Committee. He had spent his entire professional life making artists rot in jail and hounding poor art, and now that he was retired, he had suddenly begun to envy his victims and had taken up painting himself. The movie had already started, but little groups admiring the ex-minister's muse were still crowding around his trashy art. On every canvas there was a naked young woman with her pussy prudishly painted out; in one, her hands were behind her head, in another her hands were above her head, and in a third they were holding up a preciously rendered breast. And their titles—*The Dream, The Premonition, Call of the Senses*—had all been conceived during his sleepless nights as a minister.

The creator himself was bustling about, glass in hand, among his guests and peering lewdly at some haggard young women who had not made it in to that showing of the movie. His guests were also men of distinction—generals from the security police, governors, high officials from the Censorship, vice ministers. They too had become part of the artistic elite. They were writing memoirs and sensationalistic novels, carving tree roots, composing hit tunes, and sculpting busts of their colleagues who had passed away. Any of their children who did not wish a career in politics were placed in art schools. And so now the regime had its own art. The regime is self-sufficient. It creates reality and mirrors it in art.

"Excuse me." I walked up to the creator of the paintings. "Did someone fall ill here?"

He took me cordially by the arm. "Not at all. We're all

feeling excellent here. You should go to the bar. I recommend the Soviet wine from the Caucasus. Don't we know each other from somewhere?"

"That's ancient history. I was once a client of yours when you were a minister."

"That's what I thought. Many people come up to me on the street. They remember me, and with gratitude, too. Could be worse, isn't that so? Fortunately, a lot of nonsense has been avoided. For I was always, first and foremost, a human being."

"I've stopped being an artist."

"And I'm just starting," said the former minister with a laugh. "I'll make my name yet. You don't have any grudge against me, do you?"

"God forbid."

"Let's have a drink and get things on a first-name basis. Call me Lutek."

"You'll excuse me, but I'm in a hurry. A colleague of mine passed out here."

"Not here. Maybe in the theater. The atmosphere's pretty heated in there. That Bulat is awfully clever. He knows how to deal with them," he said, pointing a finger upward to where the Lord God and the Politburo reside.

I slipped away between two palm trees which had at one time been placed there for the opening of a series of Soviet films and then were forgotten. The dog was sticking obediently close to my leg.

"Excuse me." I stopped the ticket taker. "I'm looking for a friend who was taken ill here."

"Don't try that one on me. We're sold out. Leave the theater or I'll call the police."

"We received a telephone call. I swear it. We're family. Every minute counts."

He hesitated, inspecting us with a suspicious eye. But clearly the dog made a good impression, for he reluctantly drew the deep-red curtain aside and said severely, "Over there, on the left. Ask the manager. But nobody better go into the theater."

The film's dialogue came rumbling out of the dark theater. We tiptoed along the corridor to the left. There was a partially open door and a bright, wing-shaped patch of light on the floor.

"Oh, God," whispered Halina.

Inside the office Hubert was lying on a few chairs which had been pushed together, his head resting on his own dark brief-case, which had carried so many noble appeals to the world. Pale and solemn, Rysio was squatting by the sick man as if trying to catch his faint words. The theater manager kept monotonously dialing 999, the number for ambulance service.

"I know a special secret number for the shift boss at the ambulance service," I whispered, walking into the middle of that clerical cell.

"We all know it," grunted the manager, "but that jerk has his answering machine on: 'This line is not in service. Please dial 999. Thank you.'"

"What is it, Rysio?" I knelt at Hubert's feet.

"They've killed him," he said solemnly.

"Who's killed him?"

"The things they're saying out there on the screen, it makes me sick and I'm a healthy man," said the manager, continuing to dial. "How could they allow it."

Halina knelt on the other side of him. A burst of laughter came from beyond the curtain, but it died out quickly.

"They've killed him," Rysio repeated stubbornly.

The dog was sniffing Hubert's feet, his old, ruined, low boots.

"I won't allow it. I'll appeal to the Central Committee," roared a voice from the invisible screen.

I looked at Hubert's dark, grizzled head. It looked as if he was dying. From time to time his eyeballs would tremble beneath their lids. In the course of the day black stubble had grown out of his skin. His cheeks were thin, he had become thinner, a dark shadow of his former self. Why was there always so much strength in that skinny body of his?

"The hell with them, the sons-of-bitches!" shouted the manager, but not very loudly.

Very slowly Hubert opened his eyes and then saw me. "What time is it?" he asked barely audibly.

"Doesn't matter. How do you feel?" I said.

"Here." He pointed to his chest. "There's a hole here. I'm cold."

He was slowly regaining consciousness. All of a sudden the dog began yelping, but no one quieted him. A garden spider floated down on an invisible thread past the sick man's head.

"Maybe you'd like to say something important," moaned Rysio.

Hubert looked up at me with painful effort. "Are you going there?"

"Yes."

"You won't back out?"

"I already have everything I need," I said, my eyes indicating Tadzio, who was holding the blue gas can in both hands. As if he had understood our conversation, the boy jiggled the container. Hubert closed his eyes.

"You see, I'm giving you the slip," he said.

"No. The ambulance will be here any minute. You'll write a lament on my death yet."

He tried to smile. "And where's Bulat?"

"He's keeping an eye on the projector," said Rysio eagerly. "Do you want him to come in?"

Hubert blinked his eyes to indicate yes. Rysio rose from his knees.

"We're all responsible," an actor's baritone boomed on the soundtrack.

"Do you love Bulat?" I said softly.

Again he tried to smile. Halina wiped the fine beads of sweat from his forehead with her kerchief.

"You spared him. You're sending me instead of him."

"I'm happy to have lived during his lifetime," he whispered.

Again I felt a certain annoyance. It's not bad enough that he's better than I; on top of that, I have to die. Nobody knows who I am anymore. I gave up on my fate as a total loss a long time ago. But still people remember, they always remember me at bad moments.

"The ambulance is on its way!" cried the manager triumphantly. "I scared them, I said the Soviet attaché was at the premiere."

Halina came back in with a glass of water. Hail as fine as salt was falling again. In spite of ourselves we looked at the window lashed by the freezing wind.

"Not only new buildings need to be built, but a new morality as well," said the voice from the screen we could not see. His words were met by thunderous applause in the darkened theater.

"People go to the cinema as if it was confession. To purge themselves of their sins by communing together through allusions. In the safe darkness of the theater they wink at the author and he winks at them. They embroider their own condemnation of force and violence on the cloth offered them by the director. It is a one-time magnetic performance which vanishes the moment they leave the theater, freed of their pangs of conscience, their moral pain, the specter of responsibility. They go home to sin again in pursuit of their private interests through their obsequiousness and their betrayals."

He was looking at me but he wasn't listening. That is, he was listening but he wasn't taking it in.

"Terror grows strong and then it grows senile," he said, barely audibly. "How many freezes and thaws have we lived through already, how much of the regime's fury, how much of its surprising apathy. The most important thing is that the people have been waiting."

"Who's waiting? A small percentage of the stricken, misfits, cripples with deviationist leanings. In any society they lived in they would be searching for a place where their deformities would fit in. They would sign up for the Salvation Army, they would join religious cults or anarchist groups. The silent majority sleeps in torpor. It gets along somehow, it finds warm little corners, spins a cocoon of relative prosperity. It was the great epidemic of bribes which saved this system. Bribes and baksheesh have humanized an inhuman society. From the highest Secretary to the lowliest night watchman, everyone is on the take and everyone is stealing. We sail on a boundless sea of sanctioned theft. Our ship will never break up on the rocks by the shore because we'll never see the shore again. This system began its career with Lenin's slogan: 'Steal what's been stolen.'"

"You hear that, they're applauding again," whispered Hubert. "They can still see, still hear. Your death will bring them back to life or redeem them."

The ticket taker glanced into the room, checking to see that he hadn't been tricked. The dog was lying beside me and had begun picking fleas from his genitals with his teeth. Halina had bowed her head, lost in prayer or in remorse for all our sins.

"Is that man from the opposition?" asked the manager, bringing his mouth confidentially close to my ear.

"Yes, but everyone knows it. Don't worry."

"It's no good. Jesus, they've got plenty on me already. If he's so weak what's he going to the movies for? Let him sit home and watch television, goddamnit," he said, and turned on the television angrily.

The machinery groaned, black and white bands flickered across the screen, followed by an image of the Party congress. Both Secretaries, ours and the Soviet one, presented one another with medals and then kissed each other on the mouth.

"The time is coming when we will ask everyone who he was and which master he served," said the voice from the screen. There was another burst of applause. Someone close to us, hidden by the dark-red curtain, was applauding the loudest. It might have been the ticket taker or the ex-minister, now a painter.

Rysio tiptoed back into the room, bringing Bulat with him. I hadn't seen the artist for a long time. He had aged, but he had grown more dignified as well. His head, with its mane of long gray hair, was held high. Bitter lines enclosed his tightly drawn lips on either side. He approached the catafalque made of chairs and lifted Hubert's lifeless hand.

"I'm here, my friend, I'm here. Help is on the way. I'm sorry that I had to leave."

"I know, I understand. It's getting a great response, isn't it?"

"Yes, not bad at all. I'm glad to have been of use."

"No, don't talk like that. That's the most important film of recent years, maybe even of our lifetime. For the first time there is a work of art wiser than I am, than all of us."

I should have hid in some tree hollow and waited out the time until evening fell. They were immobilizing me, they were taking away my faith in the meaning of what I would do that evening. What could my suicide mean set against the immortal greatness of a work of art that would rouse humanity for centuries to come. I suddenly lost interest in heroism and infamy, sacrifice and cowardice. I had simply lost interest in everything. I looked with disgust at the blue plastic container which that nitwit from the provinces was still holding.

"Move away," hissed Rysio. "Can't you see they want to talk privately."

I took a step back and my foot came down on the dog's tail. He jumped away with a yelp and then, furious, showed me his teeth. Yes, pride was overcoming me, immobilizing me, making me shiver as though with some illness. Somehow everyone is satisfied with the places fate and the chain of genes has assigned them. And they modestly go about doing the bidding of the Great Entropy. But I feel offended by fate, my limitations, God. I desire something which I cannot do, I dream of what cannot be. I am drowning in the sixty liters of my own poisonous fluids, me, a flawed, two-legged mammal.

But wasn't this a good moment for humility? To sprinkle my balding skull with a handful of ashes and go off to the stake?

Suddenly two attendants carrying a stretcher and a young twerp of a doctor came into the office. The doctor ceremoniously unbuttoned Hubert's shirt, listened to his heart, then took his pulse, while we all looked piously on.

He made a sign to the attendants, who placed Hubert ably on the stretcher.

"To the government clinic or a regular hospital?" asked the doctor.

We looked at each other helplessly. Bulat was the first to break the silence. "Maybe the government clinic is better. I'll call the Central Committee right away."

"Aha," said the doctor conclusively. "That means we'll be going to the emergency ward for the time being. The patient does not have authorization to use the clinic."

Bulat had been holding Hubert's hand all this time. They were looking into each other's eyes.

"Thank you, Wladek, thank you," said Hubert softly.

"And I thank you. You've given me a lot of yourself, Hubert."

"I'm happy if that's true."

They began carrying him out. But they couldn't fit through the door. They had to tilt the stretcher. I ran over to help. Then the patient became aware of me as well.

"We'll be meeting soon," he whispered.

"If we do."

"And if we don't, it will still be as if we had."

They forced their way through the door and were out in the darkness of the corridor.

"Hubert, I'm not promising anything. I still don't know myself for sure!" I shouted after him into the cinema's red-tinged darkness.

"Quiet, don't shout. If you don't, someone else will," I heard Hubert whisper scornfully. "We gave you the chance. One of many chances for a little immortality."

I ran after him. "Hubert, that's all you have to say to me?"

"Listen, you were always a hysteric."

"But hysteria's the fuel I run on, it's my energy source."

"I feel weak. Goodbye. Hang on. There has to be some sense to it all. I'm not leaving you. I'll be with you. Oh, God, I'm going under already."

They carried him through the lobby, past the ex-minister's paintings of young nudes. Before the curtain came back down, I caught a glimpse of the guests circulating, holding glasses of Soviet wine. They looked without special interest at the grimy stretcher and the motionless, powerless body of the old battler who had galled their consciences for years, causing them to lose sleep, killing their appetite. But perhaps he did nothing of the sort. He was only an item, an entry in recurrent police reports like a drunkards' hangout, an auto accident, a stolen barrel of herring, like daily life in a small, luckless country that just keeps on dying.

Someone was standing by the curtain that blocked the entrance to the theater. He was holding the edge of the plush curtain in one hand. The screen was visible through the opening and I could see the enormous back of a man looking out the window.

"Is that you?" someone whispered, and I recognized Bulat's voice.

"It's me."

"I haven't seen you for a long time. I thought you'd left the country. One time over vodka someone swore that you had died abroad."

"I'm still alive. Is that the end of the film?"

"The last scene. I don't like it, but that's how it has to be."

Seen from outside, the window on screen opened. A man of indeterminate age, unshaven, covered with mortal sweat, climbed up on the windowsill. A clock was ticking behind him, or a faucet dripping. Somewhere beneath him, in the abyss of the courtyard, children were shouting as they played. He was looking at the sky. We could see clouds gliding quickly over the city; he looked down and we saw the stone courtyard and a child riding a bicycle. The man tried to swallow; he choked on his own saliva, looked back into the room, and then finally whispered to himself, "Lying has killed me."

With a sleepy gesture he moved toward the camera as if tearing himself away from someone's hands and then came flying at us. Then, from above, we saw him falling, spinning, buffeted by the wind, falling slowly, terribly slowly, as in a dream, and then, just as he was about to hit the hard ground, he stopped, halted forever in a freeze frame.

There was a moment of piercing silence as the sound faded out. The chandeliers and footlights came up slowly. Then the audience exploded with enthusiasm, rising from their seats, shouting, yelling for something; someone was running in front of the screen, where the curtain was still falling.

"They're calling for you, Wladek," I said, nudging him past the curtain. "Go on out there, they want to thank you."

"There's no need to. It's better like this."

He withdrew into the dark corridor, dragging me along. We were standing beside a display with stills from the Soviet film *The Radiant Future*.

The crowd was pouring out the exits, cramming their way through, pushing up against the glass poster display cases, but they didn't see us. Our hearts in our throats, we listened to scraps of conversations, sighs, sobs.

"This is a triumph for you," I said softly.

He ran his fingers absentmindedly through his white hair, an old man still young.

"I'm the only one who knows the truth. But I don't know if it's a good truth or an evil one."

We were colleagues at one time. I wrote a few screenplays for him, I flirted with one of his wives. Who knows, perhaps I, too, had played some part in his triumph.

"Do you remember your first premiere?"

"Oh, don't remind me. When I replay my films in memory, a sudden suffocating panic overwhelms me. If you think about it, that crowd should knock the cases over and lynch me right there in the middle of our ex-minister's opening. Look, I started with a film that slandered the Home Army, that is, the very milieu I came from, then I made a film glorifying the ill-fated Home Army. When the country was wasting away in a stupor, oppressed by the hopelessness of a situation that was half occupation, half freedom, I was making psychological films. I took a little of this and a little of that. I was trying to keep up with certain world trends. And then I made a film lampooning the intellectual elite and then I did one that smelled of anti-Semitism, though there really wasn't any in it. Do you see the iron logic in the path I've taken?"

"You did what the others did."

"Oh no, you're wrong. My artistic biography is the curriculum vitae of a fellow traveler. I always thought I was doing what could be done at a given moment. But look closer at the consistent thrust of my ideas and statements. I was carrying out the Party line in Technicolor. I rolled along with it from one error to the next."

"Stop it, Wladek, you're having a bad day, though you should be having a good one. It's not true. The public always loved you, and the audience is always right."

The corridor was slowly emptying. Somewhere the bands had struck up again, their music cutting through the drone of the public-address systems. I could also hear that stray dog barking. Halina and Tadzio from the provinces were looking for me in the deep recesses of the theater.

"The public loves me because I'm one of them. You know what, you know I'm going to say something sacrilegious—Poland has been raped. She defended herself for a long time, she scratched and bit, but in the end she submitted. And she took a certain delight in that passive, unwilling submission. She felt an ambiguous, strange, and somewhat filthy pleasure in being raped. Poland lies at the crossroads of Europe, screwed by lowlife. I was raped too. They screw me, the brutes, but I submit and resist at the same time. I moan a little, softly, I bite when I can. I've been raped and I don't hide the fact that they rape me. Maybe that's why I've been forgiven for my films, maybe that's why I am loved. I was forced to discover new aberrations, God willed me on to new perversions. And you, why don't I hear anything about you? What are you doing these days?"

The sun was shining like a flashlight outside the large dirty windows.

"I'm writing. Actually I just started writing again. This morning."

Bulat was trembling. Noticing that his hands were shaking, he put them in the pockets of his old tuxedo, which I remembered from his first premiere, the first timid, partial, unpromising success of a great career.

"Only Hubert," he said, looking out the window, "only Hubert was able to entice me onto a new, slippery, dangerous path."

"You're thinking about *Transfusion*?"

"I'm thinking about *Transfusion*, which is his film, though he didn't write a single word for me, didn't give me even one silly gag for it. Now I'll kick and bite as much as I can. Which means as much as the censor will allow me to. And he'll allow me more than he allows the others because the country looks forward to my films. You see the hookup here? I can kick the Party in the teeth because I have the right to do it, but I have the right to because I have served the Party. What are you hiding from me?"

"I'm not hiding anything, Wladek. What do you have in mind?"

"Hubert made me promise to come with my crew tonight to the Congress Hall. He never asked me to sign anything, he never forced me to make any risky gestures. But today he demanded my presence by the Palace of Culture."

"Maybe he expects that life will imitate your art."

"Don't be so vague. I'm upset today. I left my medicine home. And then there was Hubert's attack. He'll come out of it, won't he?"

"He may."

"Today when I was standing by the curtain and clinging to it, it occurred to me for the first time that those people probably do need me. I have to get to work. Work elevates me, and I work better when I'm elevated. Another hookup. It's taken hold and won't let go. When I'm on edge I start to understand more. God will judge it all. There probably is a God. That's what I always thought to myself. In my bad moments. And in my good ones, too."

"And I feel offended, Wladek."

"By whom?"

"By everything. I haven't been writing for years. I lost faith. It's not for me. Too many levels."

"What levels?"

"All those levels of existence. Us down here, and up there, high above us, the ceiling of the universe. I've chosen nothingness."

"But you're writing."

"I'm writing. I'm writing my testament. But I don't know if I'll finish it or not. I took a different path. Maybe mine's worse than yours, maybe it's better. That we'll never know."

"Do you have any grudge against me?"

"Sometimes I think I do, sometimes I think I don't."

"I showed you my path. Try it. It's very simple. All you have to do is look people in the eye and check to see if they're accepting what you're doing. Do what people want."

"It's too late. I'll do what I want to."

"You'll do that because you think that's what they want, but it isn't. Listen to me and stop pouting. Come see me, I'll be glad to help. If, of course, you accept me."

"I just don't know if I do accept you."

He shuddered, withdrew his hands from his pockets, and rubbed them feverishly. "It's cold. God, I'm cold."

Then suddenly the lights went out. The broad corridor now looked gray and dismal. The newsreel beginning the next scheduled show broke off in the middle of a word.

"The light's off!" roared the projectionist from his little booth near the ceiling.

"Sons-of-bitches!" shouted the theater manager somewhere in the dark.

"Hello!" cried Halina, losing her way in the labyrinth of curtains.

"Maestro!" chimed in provincial Tadzio.

Suddenly I recalled a four-line poem by my late friend Wilhelm M., who once lifted his head above a half-full glass at daybreak and, looking up at an unseen sky, said:

> Day after day passes slowly.
> Life's neck is ever longer.
> Everything's fucked as fucked can be.
> We're not free, we're not free.

"You know what, Wladek?"

"What?" he answered in the half darkness, still rubbing his numbed hands.

"It isn't true. I haven't been offended. It's just that I don't know how to or can't play with a stacked deck. I'm an old-fashioned guy."

"I don't really see what you mean."

"Everything goes against me. My world, I don't know if it's good or bad, but it's my own, it got me started, gave birth to me, taught me the rules, and that world crumbled into ruins after the war. That fucking war completed some sort of cycle, some lap on the track of infinity. And now we're at the finish line on our hands and knees. Decadence. The end that comes before an unknown beginning."

"Oh, people have always complained about the immorality of the world."

"That's no consolation to me. I'm still a little boy from the provinces. What I miss is—men, real men with honor and dignity. Self-controlled, brave, ascetic, chivalrous. And now everywhere there's only little women in pants. Mannish women with long hair, frills, and décolletage. Greedy, avaricious, shameless women with penises concealed in their lace panties. Wladek, I miss men. My generation of men died off. I've been left alone with nothing but pussies, women, cunts; I'm going under because everything is against me. Everything is a slap in the face to me, an offense, I'm being kicked out of life."

They were whistling in the theater. Outside, the wind was driving clouds of golden leaves toward the two lines by the meat store and the one at the taxi stand. The theater's employees were running desperately up and down the corridor.

"You're just weak," said Bulat softly. "You don't know how to live in a world devoid of hierarchy. You don't have the courage to construct your own system of values, you cling to the ruins which the mill of time is grinding into the atoms which will be the beginning of the next civilization, if there is one. But I'm fighting. You see, that's how I got through these two terrible hours, which were like being born again."

"Wladek, do you know where I'm going now?"

"Home. Or to dinner."

"Come on, Hubert told you. Why pretend."

He combed his gray mane with his fingers and put his hands back in his tuxedo.

"I'm going to South America tonight. I'm afraid I'll be taking a flu with me," said Wladek.

"Do you want to change places with me?"

"But you can't take my place and go to America."

"But you can take mine by the Congress Hall."

"You think so?" he said, drawing out his words.

"I'm just asking."

"Forgive me, but that's your business. Yours and theirs. From me they want films. And I'll make them for them. Then I'll see, maybe I'll follow in your footsteps. Or maybe by then no one will be demanding any more sacrifices."

"But why me?"

"I don't know. Ask the people in line or in the theater, ask Hubert or the Central Committee. Best of all, ask yourself. I've been speaking out against the death penalty all my life. Against death by execution or by a person's own hand."

"Well, it's farewell, then."

He pulled me to him and hugged me with his trembling arms. We spent a moment locked in a brotherly embrace. No doubt he was thinking about his next film, he may even just have gotten an idea for a good scene, but I still could not collect my thoughts enough to extract any point, any meaning clear and simple as a proverb from this magma.

The dog started barking, our little mongrel with the short, fringy legs. All the colors known to dogs were present in his coat. And then I knew I would name him Pikush, in memory of a dog I had known once which had disappeared without ever having been named, a true unknown dog.

"Where did you disappear to?" said Halina angrily. "We were even looking for you in the basement."

"Excuse me, it was my fault," said Bulat, and she cooled off at once. Good-looking men can calm women down, and vice versa. "We hadn't seen each other in a long time. And we're both off on long journeys. He's my friend. A friend from my youth."

He put his arm around me one more time. In the theater people were stamping their feet furiously. The lights flashed on for a moment and then immediately died out again.

"Can I ask for your autograph?" Tadzio thrust a crumpled notebook at Bulat, who sighed with despair but then spent a good while writing something in it.

"So, goodbye, then," I said.

"Goodbye."

But somehow I couldn't walk away. Jumping up in the air on his short legs, Pikush was ardently licking the tips of my fingers.

"So I'll be seeing you," I said.

"Farewell, old friend."

"Best of luck."

"Same to you."

We raised our hands in salutation, captains of two sinking ships. Mine was sinking, it was true, but his was sailing over the seas. We parted warily like two gunslingers in an old Western.

Again I found myself in the lobby, where the exhibition was being held. Their coats on, the last of the guests were bantering by the door. The retired minister, the creator, caught sight of me. Fresh as a daisy he ran over to me. The wine had gone to his head, his reddish-blond and balding head. He took me by the elbow with friendly condescension.

"Well, how about a few of us popping over and seeing the girls?"

"What girls?"

"They're outside Warsaw. You know, old colleague, out in the provinces you can still find girls who'll put out for good old Polish zlotys."

"Are they expensive?"

"Not too bad. Around a hundred thousand, but you can find some for around fifty thousand, too."

"That's expensive, Mr. Minister."

"Today it's on me. We're leaving for the cars now. And what sort of impression did the show make? A positive one?"

"It did."

"I think so. People like that sort of thing nowadays. A little artiness, a little spice, but the main thing is—no politics. We're already pretty close friends, I guess."

"Of course, Mr. Minister."

"So, come with us, brother, you can ride with Comrade Makolagwa. If you ever need a passport, he can arrange it for you in a minute."

"No, thanks, maybe some other time."

"By then those girls'll only be accepting foreign currency. But as you prefer. You have my number?"

"Lutek! Lutek! We're freezing here by the door. Come on, hurry up!" his comrades called.

"You'll regret it. Too bad. Goodbye! Take care!" He ran off

with his sexy little strut to his group of comrades, who were undertaking an expedition to the wilds outside Warsaw.

I regarded him without anger. Those emotions had died out a long time ago like some childhood fever. He did not remember those times, and we didn't think about him, either. In the new context he was an amusing older man with mild erotic tastes.

"Somehow you keep slipping off," said Halina unpleasantly.

"What do you mean? And what are you, sister, my keeper?"

"Well, we're doing a lot of walking, but we're not getting where we're going."

"And where is that, may I ask?"

"To the hard-currency store, to buy matches."

"I'm sorry. I forgot."

We walked out onto the broken steps in front of the movie theater. The group from inside was in a car, warming up its two-stroke engine. Two-stroke engines have come back into style here because they're cheaper and easier to service. It was even hoped that grain alcohol would be successfully adapted as a fuel for them. A mob of teenagers was following the demonstration down Kopernik Street, which, for some reason, had been dug up. They were carrying an old banner, or maybe it was a new one, for they all had been torn by the wind; in any case, they were carrying a banner which read: LONG LIVE THE THIRTY-FIFTH ANNIVERSARY OF THE POLISH PEOPLE'S REPUBLIC, and shouting in thin, hoarse voices in Polish and Russian: "Polska! Polsha! Chemodan! Polska! Polsha! Baraban!"

We started after that mini-parade toward Ordynacka Street. There were piles of fresh snow or hail rapidly melting along the walls. Tadzio was swinging my gas can casually as he went.

"And Nadezhda," I asked, "how did Nadezhda end up here?"

Halina looked at me for a long moment. "How do you mean? Like everyone else. She married a Polish diplomat and came to Poland with him when his tour of duty was over. She divorced him in Warsaw and married again. A journalist. Now she's engaged to an engineer who's studying forestry, but I don't know if anything will come of it because Rysio Szmidt's fallen in love with her."

"That I don't believe."

"Why don't you believe me?"

"Because she was never married. Maybe her grandmother brought her here, the one who was Lenin's lover."

For a long time Halina walked lost in thought.

"Maybe that's how it happened," she said finally. "It interests you? There are more and more Russians in Poland all the time."

"And more Poles in Russia all the time."

I realized that these young people, plain as they were, no doubt pursued love among themselves. I had only just noticed that Halina was mindful of her obligations as a woman. Her eyes had been discreetly made up and there was a thin layer of lip gloss on her narrow lips. The longer I looked at her, the more I was convinced that there was something attractive about her. There was even something a bit indecent about her, as there sometimes is about young nuns. She was regarding me more fondly now too. In a word, we had been joined by an invisible thread, some ambiguous understanding which would not amount to anything but which helped us bear each other's presence.

"You're a bit of a nationalist," she said.

"A bit. I'm old-fashioned. And you?"

"We're not nationalists anymore. We'd be ashamed to have any of your provincial complexes, grudges, or fantasies."

"So you people are universalists?"

"You're being ironical, aren't you?"

"No, I'm just the conscientious sort. I'd like to understand."

"We're interested in man. Wherever he is, whatever time he lives in. Man above all. Man, singular, helpless, lonely."

"That's a portrait of me—singular, helpless, lonely."

"You're a bit of a scoundrel. I've read your stuff."

"I'm known as a moderate moralist."

"All right, all right. My parents used to tear your books out of my hands and rap my knuckles for reading them."

Holiday bands were blaring away somewhere around the corner. Flocks of strange, colored clouds were sailing across the sky.

"Maybe we could go for a coffee, Halina," I asked. "I'm not feeling well. I had some sort of accident yesterday but I can't remember anything about it."

"But now you've come back to life?"

"No. I liked you right from the start. I was looking at your legs when we were walking up the escarpment."

"You know, I'd prefer a more business-like tone from you."

"You must have a boyfriend?"

"I've had lots of them. Does that shock you?"

"More of a disappointment, I'd say."

Past the clouds there was a long banner made of colored balloons which read in Polish and Russian: WE HAVE BUILT SOCIALISM.

Birds were circling in dismay over that garish caravan.

"Halinka, don't you feel the least bit sorry for me?"

She quickened her step. We were already near Nowy Swiat, where market stalls had been set up for the holidays and made to look like country inns, ancient pagan Slavic temples, and Russian bathhouses. Peasant choirs were belting out popular folk songs.

"Old fart," Halinka muttered, looking at me without anger.

I'd been out of the game for years, but now I stick my hung-over head out into the world and I find temptation everywhere. All right, let her buy the matches. We'll use them to make a bonfire by the Vistula.

We stopped in front of the hard-currency store, which was located on the site of a famous massacre. Halina looked in her purse.

"You're shelling out for me again."

"You know this routine is becoming distasteful."

She went into the store and we were left by the plate-glass door, which had a crack running across its width. Pikush sat down by my foot and began to look closely at me as if he'd known me for years.

Holiday crowds were surging up and down the street. But they were not walking with dignity, their heads held high, looking about with a benevolent eye, as I remember people doing in my youth. These crowds rushed about as if nervously gathering mushrooms. They nosed around the booths, peeked in back of them, formed sudden lines, and then, for reasons unknown, dissolved those lines a second later. These were crowds looking for prey, the chance to buy some indispensable something, a lucky find among the usual state junk.

Oh, God, where are the faces of my countrymen of yester-year? Where is all that diversity now? Faces lovely and rough, handsome and misshapen, pleasant and slightly askew. And those rough, ugly, crooked faces were interesting, attractive. And where is that variety of features, types, and complexions? Where is the charm and beauty of those alluring people who grew up on the shores of the romantic rivers of Central Europe?

Here, on every side, a stream of disagreeable faces, if they can be called faces. Mean, sloppy, branded with a hereditary and irreversible ugliness. Occasionally, the oval, melon-like head of a state or Party apparatchik would flash past among them. They can be distinguished by a certain alcoholic puffiness, their thin, ugly hair forming nasty locks on their sweaty skulls. They can be recognized by their small, quick, suspicious eyes, their plump, spongy cheeks, and the absence of a mouth, replaced by an aperture for issuing reports. Jesus God, when did some evil witch punish this society by turning it into a great herd of Neanderthals?

I remember when it happened, I remember that terrible period of transformation, pupation. It was at the end of the sixties or the beginning of the seventies. New strains came into being, begotten by Party Secretaries, managers, policemen, censors, docents appointed to their posts, prison wardens, and treacherous artists. Merciless, the genes passed the nastiness of the parents' occupations, the herpes of their moral abominations, the carbuncles of their venality on to the faces of their offspring. The disastrous lives of the fathers and mothers had prematurely disfigured their children's outward appearance. No one sings the praises of the beauty of Polish women anymore, no one admires the knightly nobility of Polish men.

"And I realized that the land of my childhood no longer existed. That it lives only in me and will crumble into dust along with me in one of the hours that approach out of nothingness," said provincial Tadzio all of a sudden.

"Did I write that?" I asked.

"Yes, that's from you."

"They must be putting up the pickled cabbage in your house now. Your father's probably already spread out the apples on the hay for the winter."

"It's too early for that. After all, we're only halfway through the summer."

"What do you mean summer, sonny boy? Didn't you see the snow in the gutter?"

"A freak event. Up our way people say there's a glacier coming."

"Maybe a glacier will solve all our problems. A glacier'll be fair, don't you think?"

"You're not feeling well. Maybe you'd better go home. It's not far."

"I need something to eat. To fortify me. Will you join me, Mr. Young Poet?"

Halina came out of the store with a good-sized box of matches. Pikush greeted her like an old friend.

"Swedish. The best they had," she said.

"The Swedes are making shoddy stuff now, too."

"I was in there so long because they didn't have any change. Finally, they gave me some Indonesian currency. Test out those matches beforehand."

"I'll test them out on myself, Halinka."

"I'll leave you now. But you'll be under our protection. I'll be seeing you."

"We'll see each other again?" I asked with a strange feeling of hope.

For the first time she smiled good-naturedly at me.

"Don't be afraid. Of course, we'll see each other."

"Halinka," I said, taking her by the hand to keep her from going, "there's something I meant to say but I don't know what it is. Do you have to go?"

"I do."

"And Hubert?"

"I called from the store. He's in intensive care. In critical condition," she said, and turned her head away abruptly.

"Did you, did you," I hesitated, "did you love him?"

"You ask too many questions."

"There's a great deal that binds me to him. More than binds him to me. I feel horrible today, but my hand should be as steady as a watchmaker's. Halinka, what does all this mean?"

"You should be going now. It's hard for everyone. Very hard."

She turned around and walked straight into the heart of the crowd, which knew nothing of her and would never know of her. Her gray jacket vanished quickly into the faded colors of the crowd.

"Did I invite you to dinner?" I asked Tadzio.

"You did, and thank you very much."

"And I'm inviting you, too, Pikush. Let's go to the Paradyz, where, once upon a time when it was still called the Paradise, I started out on this shitty life of mine. Does bad language offend you?"

"It's not too nice," replied Tadzio. "My family has a lot of respect for you."

"Well, you see, I don't like bad language, either. But sometimes a vulgar word is like a breath of fresh air or an abrupt change of mood, a sudden feeling of refreshment. But since

I've gotten to like you both, I'll avoid certain expressions, though God knows they come to my lips."

"Maybe it would be better if we sat down for a little while so you can rest."

"There's no need. I know myself. You see, son, I drank some buttermilk this morning and then later I was treated to a Siberian brandy. Ordinarily that would mean trouble, but as you can see, I'm still on my feet, even though I am feeling a little strange. So let's go have some dinner. And keep an eye on my gas can."

"I am. I am."

We set off toward the Square of the Three Crosses, led by Pikush, who kept checking to make sure we were following his meandering trail.

A bunch of guys, not young but dressed as newspaper boys, were fast approaching us from Aleje Jerozolimskie. It was a group of some sort of activists, probably from a youth organization. They were scattering a special edition of *Trybuna Ludu* and calling out shamefacedly:

"Poland awarded honorary title of First Candidate for membership in the Union of Soviet Socialist Republics!"

"Extra! Poland a candidate for membership in Soviet Union!"

"Great events in Polish history at the threshold of a new millennium. Extra!"

No one was picking up those newspapers from the ground, but no one was trampling them angrily, either. People with an eye for the long run twisted their heads around and tried stealthily to read the front page, which had been printed in red. Nowy Swiat Street looked merry, wainscoted in flags. The peeling plaster and the shattered waterspouts were nowhere to be seen. Only one tenement, beside which grew a birch tree that had witnessed the German occupation, only that musty tenement had caved in on itself, felled by the pressure of that innocent tree, but a kiosk had been set up in that dark breach. The kiosk contained folkware and a potter from the provinces, a bewildered old man who was frantically spinning the slippery potter's wheel with his bare foot.

We walked up to the rotary at the intersection of Nowy Swiat and Aleje. There I suddenly caught sight of my friends Andrzej M. and Jozef H., who were out taking their traditional walk toward Okolnik. Jozef H. was gesturing, pressing one arm against Andrzej M. and blocking his path, carried away by some modest, commonplace revelation. Andrzej M., bent slightly forward as if his stomach had been removed, was listening to his colleague's arguments with a pained expression and was clearly absorbed in his own thoughts. They walked right past me like that, about twenty feet from us, and did not notice us walking in the opposite direction. We always used to go out on those walks together. But today they had gone without me. And nothing had happened. Maybe they even felt less constrained.

There was a festive, peaceful air by the aging Party building, which was showing cracks at various spots. Security agents disguised as traffic policemen were loitering apathetically by the corners of the building. An enormous banner reading WE HAVE BUILT SOCIALISM was fluttering on the building's long wall. No doubt, the slogan had to be repeated many times to dispel the doubts of the Party members.

Then suddenly, and for no special reason, I felt like looking at the world around me, to see nature as it is in fall or summer, to see that something which, it seems, is dying out and which had been mourned for years before indifference was finally victorious. So I was standing beside the building which housed the Censorship, a tidy building whose exterior had recently received a coat of paint. I was looking in the direction of the Poniatowski Bridge, which had unfortunately collapsed a few hours back. It was no great catastrophe, there were other bridges. Anyway, I was looking toward the Vistula and I could see the blackened tops of the houses on the shore, I could see the poisonous mouth of the river, the beaches of Praga, and the tangled, yellow vegetation of Grochow and Goclawek, a large, raggedy meadow which had not surrendered. But it was slowly shrinking as the jam-packed city encroached on it more and more with every year. A crippled landscape, ugly yet at the same time beautiful, because it was all we had left, and so that dolorous sight, gale-tossed and lashed by hail every quarter of an hour, still gave me some heart. Pikush was squirming at my feet, whining and begging for dinner.

Yes, after dinner, I'll read that scrap of newspaper which I tore out of the old man's hands this morning. I'll take a peek at the obituaries, you can learn more about Polish life from the obituaries, even though they are censored, than from our annual information almanacs. Then we'll see.

My friends had already vanished into the half darkness of Smolna Street behind a small monument apparently erected to the Mother of the Partisan, a monument reminiscent of the brass paperweights found on Party officials' desks. In our city it is rare for a monument to signify anything, to be dedicated to someone famous or to some event which touched us all. Our monuments are erected to ideas, abstractions, metaphors. And that is why no one ever even thinks of those poor monuments; even the regime, its absentminded donor has forgotten about all those pitiful tons of cast iron.

"Give me the gas can," I said.

Tadzio handed me the container. Containing what? I shook it. The gas made an indecent gurgle. We were approaching the glass door, currently broken, of the Paradyz.

Yes, my last two friends had walked past me without saying hello. I really do have one foot in the grave. Little by little, without even noticing it, I had been left alone on earth. I don't have anybody to call up when I've got the blues. I pick up the phone, I play with the cord, I dial a few numbers at random, and then I replace that white vulcanite bone. But, after all, at the end everyone, or nearly everyone, is left alone in the world. They get through it somehow or other. For there is no one to complain to. Those who would have understood are long gone now and those who are still around still don't know what it's all about.

The cloakroom attendant bowed politely, though he did not have to return my greeting. For in our country cloakroom attendants are millionaires. Mysterious masters of our nocturnal vices.

"Major," I said to him, "I would like to leave my gas can and my dog with you."

"Sure, I'll take your little flask." The cloakroom attendant laughed, hiding my gas can under the counter.

"Do you think there might be a bone for the dog? Go on, Pikush, go to the man. The major loves animals."

"You guessed it. I have a basset hound at home. A friend of mine, a minister, brought it back for me from one of his official trips. I'll be good to your Pikush."

I looked at myself in the mirror. I had respectable parents but, despite that, my face is not all that respectable-looking. I have adapted to my environment. At least no one can complain that I'm too old or too young. Too handsome or too ugly. I am simply just right for these times. Oh, God, it'll be evening soon. What have I gotten myself into! My head felt heavy, my thoughts were out of joint. I woke up, after all, in a certain mental condition which may have been awful but was at least familiar, part of my routine, and, ultimately, harmless. Now I was in this terrible provisional state, a chaos of doubts and insubstantial consolations. It's illogical, not credible, and not to be taken seriously. Not to be taken seriously? There are Swedish matches in my pocket and five liters of gasoline in the cloakroom. All the worse then if it's not serious.

Tadzio returned from the men's room, straightening his short, double-breasted provincial overcoat.

"Someone's asking for you," he said, with a timid smile.

"Where?" I asked.

"Out there, in the corridor."

"Wait for me. And you, Pikush, whom I'm glad to say

turned up today, you wait here, too, Pikush, who turned up to accompany me in my final hours. Am I talking too much, Major?"

"Oh, you like to talk." The fat-faced cloakroom attendant laughed. "In Poland we always find time to shoot the breeze."

This he said somewhat strangely. In a prophetic tone of voice. And all I wanted to do was outtalk the barbed lump growing in me, that mouthful that I had not eaten.

"I'll be right back, boys," I said, and plunged into the blue cellar-like darkness of the corridor. A man with a puffy face, wearing an ordinary suit, was standing next to a flirtatious young woman, the restroom attendant.

"This way, please," he said, showing me a red door as if he thought me fully aware of what was going on.

I pushed the half-open door. We entered a white corridor of the sort you see in the basements of Warsaw's better apartment buildings. He walked ahead of me and turned an iron valve on a metal door. One of us or one of them? A guard or an agent checking papers of illegal currency traders? He shoved me into a spacious room where a few men seated at a large table were watching the Congress Hall proceedings on a large, foreign-made color TV.

"Oh, so it's you, then?" said a tall man in surprise. He was good-looking but he had rotten teeth. Dressed in Harris tweeds, which had come back into fashion, he looked like a depressed artist. There was a look of melancholy and negligence about his face.

"What's the good word?" he said, without lowering his eyes from the television.

"Nothing new. I just came by for some dinner."

"Came by for dinner?" asked the sour-looking but elegantly dressed man with an ominous familiarity in his voice.

For a moment we all looked at the speaker on the screen, who was laboriously reading from a large stack of cards. He was pronouncing his words badly, using a strange folk accent that nobody ever actually used. But he was involved in what he was doing and his quick eyes welled with a certain eagerness.

The elegantly dressed man turned his icy gaze onto me. He looked at me for a long time, but it was difficult to guess what he made of me.

"Search our guest, Zenek."

Zenek, who had brought me there, was a master of the frisk. In a fraction of a second I found myself against the rough white wall with my hands in the air. His hands were on my back, under my arms, even at my crotch.

"Some loose cash, apartment keys, part of a newspaper, imported matches, Swedish," stated Zenek, as if it were for the record.

"And no cigarettes?" asked the elegantly dressed man.

"No."

"Then what are the matches for?"

"I ran out of cigarettes. I was about to buy some at the cloakroom . . ." I said in an indifferent tone of voice so as not to prolong the point.

"Show me the newspaper," said the elegant man, and began perfunctorily glancing at the pages from *Trybuna Ludu*. He tried to piece them together, as if they were some note smuggled out of prison.

"So what's to be done with you, then," he sighed, ceasing to read.

I kept a careful silence. The basement-like room had no windows, even though it looked like some sort of makeshift dwelling. There was even a sofa covered with a blanket in the corner. I realized it must be a contact point.

"What do you think, men, should we release the citizen?" he asked his colleagues.

They smiled expressionlessly, clearly used to their chief's style.

"What is that fucking asshole saying now. Zenek, turn down the sound."

Zenek walked obediently over to the television and turned the dial.

"Goddamnit, he can't even speak correctly. Doesn't it get on your nerves?" he said to me.

"I really wasn't listening."

"Aha. Are you writing anything interesting these days?"

"Only in my mind."

"You write in your mind?" The elegant man laughed. "What a smart guy this is. And what's it about?"

"Same as always, life."

"You took yourself a pretty long break there. We know, we've visited you a few times. Do you remember, you reported the break-ins to the police? One time we drank your cognac, another time we took your porno magazines. Well?"

"Well, what?"

"You weren't surprised by the burglars' sense of humor?"

"Nothing surprises me anymore. Not even you not calling me sir, when you're young enough to be my son."

He looked over at his colleagues, who smiled, but without any great conviction.

"That's how I talk to everybody. It's a habit."

"There was a time when I would have smacked your face for that habit. But now it's all the same to me."

Zenek and the others at the table froze in horror. The toilet flushed loudly next door in the men's room. Then the bathroom attendant shouted indignantly after someone: "You take a crap and leave me twenty zlotys, you miser!"

The elegantly dressed chief rose lazily, the way they like to the whole world over. He rose unhurriedly, with all the ominous ceremoniousness of the enraged policeman and walked over to me. For a moment he looked me over with a hard eye.

"Why are you trying to charm me?" I said sleepily. "I've had the pleasure of meeting with the Gestapo, the NKVD, and with the good old prewar Polish police, who hated so-called intellectuals. You bore me."

"So, you're comparing us to the Gestapo?"

"You said it yourself."

Suddenly he struck my face, and I immediately felt the warm, salty taste of blood on my lips. My gums used to be much better. Now even a toothbrush makes them bleed.

"Zenek, put the cuffs on him. You're behaving like a hooligan, sir."

My only victory was that he was calling me sir. His subordinate put the handcuffs on me with a sort of official efficiency.

"So where were we, then?" said the elegantly dressed man, addressing his colleagues at the table.

He was drawing out his words as he had before, but I could see that he had been put off a little. He didn't know that I had left my own murder weapon in the cloakroom. I was seized by a perverse, vengeful sense of satisfaction at seeing this poor fool playing his old-fashioned game for his own sake, for his colleagues, and for my colleagues, who had thrust me out on the road to saintliness.

His retinue was keeping a respectful silence. But in a certain sense that silence worked against him. "One uhlan's saddlebags, hold the potatoes!" cried someone on the other side of the wall. The chief flipped through the blank cards on the table, pretending to be thinking.

He might kill me right here, I thought, with a bizarre sense of hope. Kill me skillfully, painlessly, instantly. For him it would be just a trifle and for me it would be a great relief. It wouldn't be that much of a loss for our side, either. They could always make a little hay out of the death of a writer while under arrest. And poor hung-over me, I wouldn't have to wander around until evening and die a thousand times in the meantime.

"What have you been doing today? Please tell us everything, and in the order it happened," he said, finally sitting down at his desk.

"I woke up in a lousy mood. I lay in bed thinking about myself, my failures. I thought that life really wasn't worth it. I imagined how nice it would be if some accident or some skillful person, something, deprived me of my boring, rotten life."

"And then?"

"And then I got washed and dressed, still floundering around in pessimism."

"Did anyone visit you?"

"Yes. First the superintendent. He advised me to run some water because they were turning it off."

"And then?"

"Then the plumber came to turn off the gas."

"Why were they all out to get you?"

Then one of the assistants moved, making his chair squeak, and said, "They turned off the water in the whole district. My house, too. I had to wash at the office. Those bums should drop dead."

"Foksal Street's all dug up," added a second.

"And last spring they dug up Nowy Swiat," interjected Zenek. "They cut the telephone lines while they were doing it. For months I had to go running out to use phone booths. And you think the phones in the booths work all the time, either? Shit, every couple of days some punks would rip off the receiver and pull the insides out of the phone."

"Over by us on Kolo Street," began another of the assistants, "a wall gave in. Roof to basement."

"All right, all right," interrupted the chief reluctantly, but the flood of gripes had taken the dignity out of the interrogation. "Let's get back to the point. No one else visited you?"

"No one. I left the house at once."

"For what?"

"To have some breakfast. I go to the Family dairy bar, you gentlemen may know it. It's by the hard-currency pastry shop where the Blikly Company used to be."

"And after breakfast?"

"After breakfast I went for a walk and had a look at the film *Transfusion*. An interesting film, plenty of strong dialogue. I'm surprised it was released. I recommend it to you, gentlemen. It's worth seeing."

A few bars of Prokofiev echoed in the cellar pipes.

"You're not feeling well?" asked the chief abruptly.

"Nothing unusual. I'm suffering from a hangover and I don't know how I got it."

"Zenek, give the gentleman an injection."

In an instant I was nailed to the chair. This time both of the chief's assistants lent a hand. In a fraction of a second they had pulled back the sleeves of my jacket and shirt. Someone tied a length of rubber tubing around my arm, and Zenek was already rubbing one of my delicate veins with pleasure.

"I protest!" I wanted to shout in a piercing tenor, but it came out as a sort of unfortunate cough. I knew that a strong cry that carried was an effective means against injustice. But everyone was shouting nonstop in the bar and, outside, the demonstrators were shouting and on the television the Party delegates were shouting the names of both the Secretaries, ours and the Soviet one. And so I couldn't really count on my shout being heard.

Zenek stuck the needle energetically into my vein. Out of the corner of my eye I noticed that it was the type that can be used only once. At least there was something humanitarian about that. For I knew that even in respectable hospitals, bandages barely washed out in lukewarm water were used and reused.

He injected the entire large dose. I didn't feel anything. It wasn't out of the question that the ampule was a dummy. They used injections like that which contained no drugs, only a salt solution. Our domestic pharmaceutical industry had also been on the skids for some time now.

Zenek could read the disbelief on my face. He patted the vein with a piece of dirty cotton and said tenderly, "The injection's good. It's a real one. American."

"You meant to say Soviet," corrected the chief.

"Yes, Soviet."

They stepped back from me. I rolled down the sleeve on my now sore arm.

"All right, let's start all over again," said the chief. "Who visited you?"

"The superintendent, the plumber."

The elegantly dressed man rose, walked over to me at a normal speed, and flicked my cheek with the tips of two fingers as if trying to brush off a little spider. I began howling and leaped to my feet. It felt as if a pair of invisible tongs were trying to tear my poor head off the top of my spine.

"So you see, the injection does work," said Zenek in a confidential tone. "You better tell the truth."

"Now you are like one enormous testicle. Even a little breeze will cause you pain." The chief went back to his desk. "So who paid you a visit this morning?"

"Hubert. And Ryszard Szmidt."

"Very good," praised the chief. "And who else?"

"Only those two."

The chief rose from his desk and started toward me.

"Hubert and Ryszard!" I shrieked. "Only them."

"Is he telling the truth?" the chief asked his sidekicks. They shrugged their shoulders noncommittally, but he returned to his place.

"I'll accept that. And who did you meet during your walk?"

He was crumpling a sheet of paper and looking at me matter-of-factly, dispassionately.

"I met a dog. Pikush. He disappeared many years ago. He lived among strangers, and so of course he was unhappy and missed me. And now he's turned up by the Vistula."

He snapped the ball of paper at me, striking my forehead. I howled and fell out of my chair. And that was even worse. It took me a long time to pull myself up off the concrete floor.

"I met a girl I knew when I was out walking."

"What's her name?"

"I didn't say what I meant. I meant that I picked her up while I was out walking. I don't know her last name."

"And her first name?"

"Halina."

"Halina," repeated the chief, and glanced over at his associates. There were violent thuds on the other side of the wall as if someone were boring his way through to us via the sewers. "Help, they've poisoned me. God, where's the toilet!" The usual stuff you hear in Polish restaurants.

"You're not feeling well," said the elegantly dressed man. He could have even been good-looking if it wasn't for those teeth. He was clearly afraid of dentists or didn't have the time for them.

"Not too well," I admitted. "I feel bad today."

"What do you think—why have we invited you in for a little chat?"

"I don't know," I said apathetically. "Everyone gets called in."

"You don't like it here, do you?"

"It's not really much of a place."

"No, I mean in general."

"I don't like it in general, either."

"That's just it. There's a lot of things I don't like myself. You too, boys, right?" They agreed, without putting much feeling into it. "For example, I don't like my work. That torturing another person can give you pleasure—that's just something hack writers have dreamed up. My work makes me nauseous. You don't believe me?"

"I have a few doubts. I must have read too many of those hacks."

He rose again and made a point of lighting his cigarette with one of my Swedish matches. He looked closely at the crisp imported little flame and then blew it out. He walked over to me like a concerned physician and jabbed my chest with his index finger. I yelped and leaped to my feet again.

"I don't know her last name, but I know where she lives."

He broke into laughter, normal laughter, and no longer seemed the least bit demonic. He was about to strike me again but then thought better of it.

"You think we don't know? I touched you because I wanted to make sure that the injection was still working. So where were we? Aha, I know. So, my work is repulsive and deserves to be condemned. But there's more than one way to do the job and I'm just doing it one of those ways, isn't that right, boys?" he said, fixing his eyes on them. They were quick to agree. "The point is that every level of society has people like us in it, people like you and me. Because you and I are oppositionists. Though you are a negative oppositionist and I am a positive one. You deal with ceremony, the superstructure, aesthetic form, and I deal with pragmatism, daily life, the functioning of the infrastructure. You represent noble passivity while I am trivial action."

He stroked my hair and I began to groan.

"Please don't feel inhibited here. Your shouts, groans, and tears prove that we're doing a good job. We get checked up on too, and we have to watch out that no one who isn't serious wangles his way into our ranks, no one from outside the circle of ideological oppositionists."

"But what about our Soviet advisers?" I asked, and immediately lost consciousness.

I came to on the rough surface of the floor. Zenek was pouring a pail of water over me. There was an alpine waterfall roaring in my left ear, a tornado from the Indian Ocean. The conch of my ear had swollen, separating from the skin on my head. Grumbling, Zenek lifted me from the floor and seated me back on the chair.

"We won't speak about such things," said the chief severely. "I hope you will keep that in mind."

"Yes, I'll try," I breathed out of the corner of my mouth at my swollen ear. On the television screen the dean of Polish artists, a man nearly a hundred years old who resembled a dead tortoise, was paying homage to the leaders of both parties. On one side he was, to my surprise, supported by Bulat and, on the other, by a talented young woman pianist. They were actually carrying him, holding him by his elbows dry as blown eggs, and he was nodding his bald, bent head monotonously. The Presidium was clapping in unison and the worthy old man's long-dead skull twitched to their rhythm.

"I'll tell you something else," said the elegantly dressed man. "The First Secretary is also one of us. He belongs to the great army of positive oppositionists, though he is not our leader," he said, laughing again and raising the finger with which he had struck me before. "And here we come to the specific dialectics of what I would call our time system. You're looking at my assistants with some anxiety. Don't be afraid, they're loyal and true. Besides, they wouldn't dare inform on me, they'd be afraid of saying the words, the words would stick in their throats. They're part of it, too, out of complicity. Just like you."

"May I ask one question?"

"Go right ahead."

"Then why aren't we free?"

He returned to his desk and sat down, leaning over the desktop. He rummaged about as if searching for the right paper. "Because that is how the system is. A tectonic system of global politics."

"So we've taken ourselves prisoner and we're keeping ourselves behind bars, is that it?" I asked shrewdly.

His eyes flashed with approval. "That's it. We've given the oppressor the slip. We've outwitted him. We are free because we have imposed our own slavery."

"Is History our oppressor?"

"What would you prefer?"

"I'd prefer History. There's more honor in that."

"History, History." He smiled, putting out his cigarette on the sole of his shoe, for there were no ashtrays in the room. "Strange and mysterious. Mass movements, economic collapse, epidemics of psychological vices, the aspirations of individuals damaged by rebellious genes and, as well, the metaphysics of time, without which there would be no History. Here we are blabbing away and you must be dreaming of your dinner. Well then, maybe we'll see each other this evening?"

Without saying anything I tried to rise from my chair.

"Zenek, give the gentleman a hand. And so, till tonight."

"What is it you have in mind?"

"Time will tell, that's it, History will tell. So you see, things went rather smoothly. I am not even requiring any discretion on your part. Back in the primitive old days, they used to shove a piece of paper at you to sign, to enforce your silence. I just need a handshake on it. We're from the same tribe or, if you prefer, the same soil."

And he really did extend his hand to me but withdrew it at once.

"By the way, why aren't you writing?"

"You think writing's worth it?"

"The know-it-alls say it isn't. But if they say it isn't, that means it is. I even have an idea. You should write for one particular reader, that's always best. Me, for example. Reject censorship, *raison d'état*, all your fears, and write like a free man for other free men. You were always proud but never vain. The size of the printing isn't the important thing for you. Better one intelligent reader with a literary head than tens of thousands of coelenterates with toilet paper between their ears. Your book won't die in my hands. Only in my hands will it have a chance of lasting, of living forever."

He offered me his hand carefully, in fear of causing me pain. "I'll be seeing you."

Then, wonder of wonders, he walked past me and out of the room. Zenek came over, tipped me delicately over onto the floor, and began kicking me in the ribs with astonishing subtlety. He did this skillfully, as if his only wish was to straighten out a fold in my crumpled jacket with the tip of his boot. Halfway between a caress and torture, it was easy to endure, and I was able to observe one of the chief's assistants taking pictures of me quite professionally, clicking flash after dazzling flash. Then Zenek lifted me from the floor, brushed off my clothes, removed the handcuffs, and shoved me toward the exit. Some sort of confused play was over, and it had been just as much of a surprise to me as to its silent directors.

I walked out into the corridor by the restroom and was about to head back to the restaurant when I was halted in my tracks by the severe voice of the restroom attendant, who was not a bad-looking woman. "You owe six hundred zlotys."

"I didn't use the men's room."

"You sat there half an hour and you didn't use it?"

"But why six hundred?"

"That's the price. Everybody's got to hustle to make it. You can't be bashful."

So I gave her a thousand, pushed the half-open door, and entered the restaurant—but it was not the restaurant. The door slammed behind me and some mechanism clanked harshly. I found myself in a waiting room which contained armchairs and some half-dead plants. The high official who lived across the street from me, Comrade Kobialka, was sprawled in one of the chairs. It was clear that he had been forcibly dressed, because his shirt was inside out, his shoes weren't laced, and his tie was hanging off the back of the chair.

He looked lucidly at me.

"Hello, neighbor," I said wearily.

"Hello. You recognized me?"

"I always did, every day, but as you yourself know, back then I really couldn't pay you my respects."

"Where did you take off *your* clothes?"

"I didn't, I came to the Paradyz for dinner."

"A bad choice. Who let you in?"

"It must have been Zenek."

He looked intently at me and then with a wave of his hand invited me to sit down.

"So, they interrogated you. It must have been in connection with my case, right?"

"No, my own."

"But you didn't take your clothes off."

"No, I guess it was because I was taking a different line."

"Did they give you an injection?"

"They did."

"Me, too. But now there's practically no pain." He pinched the palm of his hand. "Would you like a piece of candy from the congress?"

"I'd prefer going to dinner."

"Give it a try," he said, shaking his head.

I walked over to the door and tried the handle. It didn't budge. I tried shouldering the door, but it was like a rock.

"You see their little tricks. They still want something. I know why I'm sitting here. I'm waiting for an ambulance, but I'm only third in line. What a rotten day. Somebody's taking off his clothes every hour. You know, this whole thing doesn't have a leg to stand on. One day it will all come massing together, like before a storm. People can't stand it. The enormous tension."

There was a sanguine flash in his eyes, but no fanaticism. Something more like wildness, hysterical determination.

"You know, neighbor, I'm relieved. For the first time in many years I feel relaxed. I'm tired, weak, but I feel good. I haven't slept for a week. This morning, when you saw me, it cost me great effort to keep my teeth from chattering. I have been waiting for this day since the last congress. I wrote my speech in strict secrecy, not in my house, but when I was out hunting. I kept it in the hollow of a tree, and every Saturday I would drive around, memorizing it. I kept learning it and then forgetting it. Then, suddenly, during a conference, a briefing session, or on the plenum, I realized to my horror that those words would never pass my lips. So I forgot them and I wrote a new text, and then, in a fit of courage, or despair, I wiped the new one from my memory and brought back the old one. Yes, my good neighbor, I've been struggling for a good many years already. At night I would deliver that speech to myself mentally. With mockery and with anger, and with a little pathos here and there. I would pause and wait for the applause, I would lift my head to outshout the tumult and the roars of disapproval. I saw it all before me every night. At the last congress, I weighed ninety-five kilos. And now they've weighed me here, and what do you think I weigh?"

"It's hard to say. Eighty?"

"Sixty-seven," said Kobialka hoarsely but triumphantly. "The same as a Soviet color TV set."

"Aren't they about three kilos more?"

"Listen, neighbor, I'm an old-fashioned politician. I was able to stand all of it before, but I can't stand these times now. It's all gone, over, period. They'll put me in an insane asylum, but one for government people of course. They'll keep me there six months and then release me on a pension. They might even issue me a passport to go to another province."

He was talking a blue streak, and it was obvious that he was not about to stop. The flood of words and chaotic thoughts he had held back for years was now crashing down on my poor, hung-over head. But where had that hangover come from?

Kobialka tore a dry leaf off a plant and began chewing it nervously. "Are you retired, too? I can see you from my window. You either spend the day at home or you go for walks."

"I retired myself. But now I'm going back to active duty."

"Have you gone mad? They're at the end, it's all over for them," he said slowly and without much conviction. "That's what I think, that's what I've thought for years. When I was with the First Secretary or at the Presidium of the Council of Ministers. Do you think that they're coming to their end?"

"Everything's coming to an end. Water, coal, the whole world."

"That's not much consolation. You see, neighbor, I crammed it all in, I learned it all, and then, goddamnit, I just blanked out up there. I shouted the words 'Comrade villains, comrade swine'—you probably heard that. Maybe shouting like that is in bad taste. It certainly isn't a good thing, not the least bit dignified either, but I had grown used to the idea. I hesitated,

I went back and forth on it, but in the end I grew used to the idea. I simply could not give up. So I shouted out those epithets and then, goddamnit, I blanked out. I couldn't even remember the next word. What am I saying, the next word, I couldn't remember the next fucking syllable, I couldn't remember what I was talking about. My head was like a ball of hot cotton. But I started yelling out of that cotton, if only to be a pain in their necks. Maybe that wasn't too smart, but they tell me the sound was turned off, anyway. No problem, people could see that I was protesting, isn't that so?"

"Take it easy. Breathe slowly, rhythmically."

"I'll take it easy when I'm with the other madmen. But they won't be madmen. Just others like me. Who knows how it'll be in there—but it can't be any worse than in the ministry."

He stopped talking for a moment to spit out the remains of the leaf. He scraped the pieces from his tongue with trembling hands and then attempted to shake them off onto the floor.

"You don't happen to know what the real date is today?" I asked, taking advantage of the moment.

He motioned with his thumb at the wall. "Only they know. The security forces. They probably don't know, either. Only the minister himself, or just the ruling council. They have an imported calendar hanging in a safe as big as a room. Every day, like a ritual, the minister goes in that safe and tears off one sheet, which is then incinerated. No one knows the date, because for years they've been moving it, sometimes ahead, sometimes back. At one moment they're chasing the West, then they pass it, then they're chasing it again, and then they're behind again. Every branch of industry, every institution, every state farm had its own calendar and had to struggle with it. Five months ahead, then twelve back. 1974 turns into 1972, then 1977 becomes 1979. Everything got all screwed up. We're still going around the sun, but it's a horrible mess."

"Maybe we could find out the right date from the West? I haven't listened to Radio Free Europe for quite a while."

"That's a possibility," Kobialka said, laughing, and then

began to choke horribly. "The West took up the challenge. They started running away when we started chasing them, and then they slowed down when we eased up. They're exhausted, too. They're straddling the fence, too."

"How did the calendar get into the Ministry of Security?"

Kobialka spread his hands apart to indicate his ignorance. "Even I don't know that," he said.

I walked over to the door and listened. Somewhere on the other side of that red door water was gurgling monotonously like a country stream.

"It's all being held together," said poor Kobialka, trying to make sense of his inner chaos, "it's all being held together by a string, by the thread of domestic production, by a spiderweb of hope. We have demoralized capitalism. Utterly and absolutely. By our own horrible example. We have them so tied up in agreements, economic agreements, scientific, cultural, athletic, what have you, we've got them tied up as if with barbed wire, and so we can fail to meet deadlines, cheat on quantity in deliveries, not pay what we owe on time, lie, drown them in vodka, so that after a while the total socialist chaos we have invented and sustained will bare its teeth even there, among them.

"And you should be aware, neighbor, that for a while now they have been letting people leave Poland and go abroad. And what have they been doing there? They've been breaking the pay phones, riding the subways without paying, slipping in ahead of the line everywhere, stealing silverware from restaurants, sneaking out on their hotel bills, getting people drunk, messing up public restrooms, and abusing the local women whenever they have the chance to. If we put all this together and draw our own conclusions, then, my dear neighbor, who will be surprised that the so-called free world is looking more and more like the Soviet world all the time. And here is the one last doctrine, it may be Lenin's, that hasn't been played out yet—if we don't overtake capitalism, then capitalism will wait for us."

He finished his monologue and sank into his unhappy thoughts. Music came through the wall. Smooth, efficient tavern music, timeless and universal in a way. That meant we were close to the restaurant. But how to get in there? I checked the door. A door like any other, a little soiled, cracked in a few places, with an ordinary handle, but all told, it might as well have been an armored gate. A little dog was barking in the depths of that Hades. It had to be my Pikush.

"You should find a more comfortable position," I said to Kobialka. "What you've been through could kill you. You have to take care of yourself."

"I'm a simple, honest man. I have no head for philosophizing. If I see something's black, I call it black. And I call it white if it's white. Have you noticed how they are constantly philosophizing? The worse things are, the more they play philosopher. The more obvious the nonsense, the profounder their thoughts. The more lawlessness there is, the more laws. The more widespread the chaos, the more insistent their love of symmetry. They have produced piles of philosophical rot. What am I talking about—mountains, Himalayas. If we started burning all those hypotheses, theses, axioms, truisms, theories, and dogmas in the stove, there'd be energy enough to last us until the end of the world."

"You're philosophizing too, you know."

"Me philosophizing?" said Kobialka in surprise. "I'm only telling you things are. O God Almighty, it won't be long till I'll be resting. I'll be wearing a warm, quilted straitjacket, I'll lie on the floor of my restful padded cell. I'll think about all the young women I never got the chance to screw, I'll wake up now and then, I'll blaspheme to my heart's content, I'll shout a few horrible curses in Polish and Russian, which I've been itching to do for a long long time. They've started to respect madmen here now, as they do in Russia. It used to be that any jerk who was against the government was taken in for a psychiatric examination. As if being against the People's Republic made you a madman. Nowadays that is out of the question.

Just think of how many of our premiers, secretaries, and professors of Marxism-Leninism are presently guests at various lunatic asylums. In our times insane asylums are a sort of branch of the national academies."

Kobialka was clearly enjoying his vision of his new career. But still, there was a certain anxiety quivering about in that confidence of his. I said nothing, thinking about my own problems, which in the end caused him to grow suspicious of me.

"But maybe I did the wrong thing?" he groaned suddenly. "What good will it do? You can't break a wall with your head. Am I supposed to save the world? Why me, and not, say, Bochenek? Life's not impossible. I could even help other people."

"Bochenek will be taking off his clothes, too," I said peremptorily.

"You think so?" mumbled Kobialka.

"You should look into his eyes sometime."

"What do his eyes have to do with anything?"

"The eyes are the most important thing. If they're fearful and full of pain and tears, that means a person will take off his clothes."

"I'd give a lot for that son-of-a-bitch to do it," sighed Kobialka. "Do you think it's worth it to repent?"

"Nothing's worth repenting. You've just accelerated the course of History."

"Shit," said Kobialka in amazement.

Just then the lock made a grating sound. The door opened easily, like a silk curtain, and in came Zenek.

"Jesus, Mary, and Joseph, what are you doing here," he said, surprised to see me. "Your dinner will get cold."

"I thought I was on my way to the restaurant, but I was mistaken."

"Then you should have gone back out. You really shouldn't be in here."

"I couldn't open the door."

"What are you, a child?" He slammed the door shut and opened it from the inside three times in a row like some performer. "It's very simple."

"What's your chief's name?" I asked without knowing why.

"That's no secret. It's George. Used to be Georgie when he was young."

Kobialka fell back into the chair, which was losing its stuffing. His eyes took on a fixed stare, and he began to kick his feet and make hoarse sounds with his throat. Zenek looked at him with disgust.

"There's no reason to act like a fool. You've already been classified as a madman. There's been a phone call from the Central Committee."

"Really?" said Kobialka, perking up. "Thanks for telling me."

"Don't mention it."

I walked to the door and turned the handle, still warm from Zenek's hand.

"Can I go now?" I asked.

"One moment," said Zenek, and approached while rummaging inside his shirt. "You know, I've decided to read some of your stuff. The chief said it was worth it, and I've taken a liking to you. Of course, I don't have any of your books yet, but I wonder if I could get your autograph in my notebook."

He handed me a datebook with a blank sheet on which *Genia 63-24-71* was the only thing written. I signed my name under hers, and then he shook my hand.

"I see the pain's gone," he said, smiling benevolently. "We're friends now, right? It was just an injection."

"I'll be seeing you, Mr. Kobialka."

My neighbor smiled sadly. "I won't be seeing you again."

"You'll be seeing each other, you'll see." Zenek laughed good-heartedly. "People are always running into each other here."

"Take care," I said.

"Good luck," replied Kobialka.

I was in the doorway when Zenek beckoned me again with a crooked finger. "Please, I have something for you."

He handed me the little box of Swedish matches, one of which his chief, Georgie, had used.

"Nothing ever gets lost here."

The lower ranks can still be charming, I thought, at last leaving that waiting room. They still remember the old days and the old practices of their order. Once they were artists, now they're philosophers.

"Hey, you didn't pay again!" cried the young restroom attendant.

I went to her table, where there was a little plate for tips.

"My dear child," I said. "I am not coming from the stalls you administer but from that door over there. And I'd like to remind you that I've already left a thousand once."

"I'm sorry, really I am."

"Your zeal surprises me. You're such a nice, pretty child and yet so aggressive."

"That's because I'm doing my practical here."

"What sort of practical?"

"My student practical."

"And what department are you in?"

"Archaeology. And they monitor me here. They do. One time the head of our work team, a docent, a horrible person, he snuck in here. I didn't notice and there was trouble afterward. And if I get a lot of credits for my practical, then I can be excused from the exam in the propaedeutics of philosophy."

"All right, Zosia, that's another matter entirely."

"How do you know my name?"

"I know everything. I might visit you again. But in private. Could I?"

"Oh, I don't know, I really don't. And what if they came to check on me?"

"I'd hide in a stall."

At last a smile gleamed in her eyes. The young restroom

attendant liked the intrigue of it. "All right, come; but be careful."

I stroked her hair, rough as the crown of a sheaf of corn. There were still some good-looking girls here, but they were becoming rarer all the time. Soon the boys won't find them pleasing anymore because they're not the right type, biologically alien somehow. It's a shame I won't be around.

The cloakroom attendant's eyes were bleary, and he was gripping the edge of the counter tightly. He had started to get high. Apparently he liked getting started around that time of day.

"You're leaving already?" he asked.

"No, I'm just coming in."

"But I thought you'd already been here and left something. I even remember what it was."

"You're right. I popped out for a while and now I'm back."

He was friendly and severe at the same time. He had to be reserved with the clientele because there were so many people waiting, in a line that went up the stairs and ended outside.

I went into the dining room. I hadn't been there for years, even though that's where the story of my life began. The place must have been rebuilt several times, but it had retained its original shape, that of a deep well bordered at the top by a gallery where the second-class customers waited to be waited on. The small fry in on official delegations. The latest version of the Paradyz was ruined-modern. That means that its architecture and interior decoration were up to world standards, but at the same time it made you think of some old shanty about to collapse. Besides, that's the style of our entire society. As if all the people were expecting to be whisked away to a new country any minute.

All the tables were taken. It was hard for the waiters to squeeze through the narrow spaces on their way toward the gloom of the kitchen. There were a few couples floating on the dance floor. A presentable band of disabled veterans from the Warsaw Musicians' Union was playing. This I learned from a sign on a column made of artificial sandstone. Another sign proclaimed that the waiters were mounting a socialist guard.

But there were no tables. I stood there, my eyes piercing the blue and red semidark. I finally caught sight of Kolka Nachalow, who was sitting at a large table with a blonde, her hair combed back dramatically in a style that hadn't been around for years. She had a large red face with deep wrinkles and large lips enlarged by abundant blood-red lipstick, and she wasn't lacking in the breast department, either. There was no other choice, I had to seek Kolka's assistance.

I walked over to his table and bowed ceremoniously.

"Looking for a table?" asked Nachalow. "Sit down, brother, feel right at home here." Turning to her, he said, "This is my friend, the well-known writer."

It was clear that he was flattered by this connection, which elevated him in the blonde's eyes.

"Thank you very much. It'll just be for a short while. I'll eat something, then I'll run."

"You could stay till morning, isn't that so, Gosia?"

She nodded her golden beehive chicly, and I kissed her hand, patterned with liver spots.

"Gosia's a good person to know, brother," said Kolka. "She runs the cinema."

"Oho," I said with polite surprise.

"Her specialty used to be taking over bankrupt enterprises for the state. Factories, warehouses, merchant ships. But now she's switched to culture."

Gosia smiled pleasantly. "As always, Kolka's exaggerating. You know, I buy up films that were abandoned from the Ministry of Culture. You know what I mean, the ones that never got finished. Because it's getting harder all the time to produce films. For a while the director and the cameraman struggle with the situation, which, on the whole, is just impossible. People are late, they don't deliver the props, they forget about deadlines, they lose tapes, and what they mostly do is hit the bottle. And so after a couple of weeks the production just peters out. Everyone disappears, the office is empty, and the director is close to suicide. Then I come into the picture. I buy the film for half price and I finish it with my own crew."

"It was Gosia who finished *Transfusion*," boasted Kolka.

"Because I pay. They don't have to steal in my crew."

"This is a wonderful discovery."

"You should only know. Professors from the School of Central Planning and Statistics are running tests on my crew. I'm a guinea pig." She broke out laughing, revealing lipstick-streaked teeth.

Kolka called the waiter. Gloomy, dark-haired, in a spotted white jacket, he stood there angrily, his pencil on his order pad.

"I'll take the ragout," I said uncertainly. "But what's it made from?"

"I don't know. That's not my business. There's ragout on the menu, that's all I know. What am I supposed to do, go in the kitchen and look in every pot?" said the waiter, growing excited.

"You're on edge." I wanted to calm him down.

"That surprises you? Everyone's eating and I'm working."

"I'll take the ragout, please."

"That's it? I won't be coming over here every two minutes."

"That's it, thank you."

The waiter walked off into the darkness. Kolka smiled knowingly. "He's always like that at the beginning. By morning he'll be your best friend. By the way, would you like a drink?"

"I'll give it a try," I said.

He filled a crystal glass to the brim with pure vodka made from imported potatoes. But then little silver drops began running down the side of the glass.

"Let's not waste time," said Kolka. "The glass cutter put his whole heart into it and so he ruined the glass. Let's drink to the glass cutter."

We clinked glasses carefully. My sleeve was already wet inside. The drink was repulsive, but I mastered myself and swallowed the stinging liquid.

"But maybe it'll be all right," I said softly.

"Of course it will. Why shouldn't it?" said Kolka.

Now the band was playing some sort of ambitious contemporary work by a Polish composer. Our country lacked hard currency to pay royalties. Nobody protested, everybody was used to it. The couples left the dance floor for their tables. I closed my eyes and it felt the way it used to back then. That evening someone had also been playing his own composition on the piano, and I was sitting with the girl who later became my wife.

"I think I know you from somewhere," said Gosia.

"I remind everyone of someone. To be more precise, I remind each person of someone different. It's as if I never existed. Me, singular, individual, with my own unique genetic code. I, my good woman, am Everyman, I am an ordinary pedestrian. There's a bit of Kolka in me, a bit of the waiter, and I even flatter myself to think a little bit of you, the venerable producer of *Transfusion*."

It was only then that I noticed that the demonstrators who had taken shelter in the Paradyz had left their banners in a few places along the wall.

"Is that a new sect or a whole new religion?" asked Gosia.

"I'm sorry, I wasn't listening."

"What you were just saying."

Cracked walls, the gilding turning to rust, the lighting on the blink. Modernity dying of a heart attack. A blue and red half darkness full of vicious faces. Every face was a mortal sin in itself. Every kisser a sacrilege. There was a rumbling sound in the walls, a racket in my head, a howl in the attic. The voice of divine wrath.

"Yes. That's it. I remember."

"What do you remember?"

"Where I got the hangover."

The band stopped playing and immediately dozed off. They simply rested their heads on their instruments and went right to sleep.

"Let's drink," said Kolka. "I'll go see why the kitchen's so slow."

My head began to clear. Now the buttermilk, the Siberian elixir, the glass of Caucasian wine, and our own Polish vodka were all working together. I was still alive, but I'd soon be catching up to my fate. Kolka rose unsteadily from the table and set off toward the mysterious gloom of the kitchen, which was haunted by the invisible ghosts of our cuisine.

"You're an oppositionist," said Gosia in an undertone. "I always imagined the oppositionists as wild young men with long hair."

"What do you want, the regime's gotten old and so have we. It's all been going on much too long. The whole spectacle has its tedious passages. The playwriting is not up to snuff."

"Are you founding a new sect or have you done that already?"

"I'm my own sect. Me as I am in each of you. Because the real biological me, with an address and a life story, does not exist. I live in you like a virus, a moral virus, or like the bacteria of conscience. Or perhaps like some criminal enzyme. The point is, my good woman, that I am not here or rather that I do not exist. What you're hearing now is just a loudspeaker, stray waves in the air, not purposely transmitted by anyone, just some sort of echo, your own waves ricocheting back on you, a monotonous murmur in God's throat."

"When did you think all that up?"

"I didn't think it up. It was revealed to me."

"Today? When the salutes were being fired?"

"No. Last night. That's why I have a hangover."

I could see part of the cloakroom counter through an oval niche. Pikush had just hopped up onto the counter and, looking fondly at me, signaled me with a wave of his tail that he was still there and waiting for me. I signaled him that it wasn't time yet.

Kolka Nachalow came back to the table, his face flushed a shade brighter. "Gosia, the chef would like to see you."

"Excuse me for a moment." She rose from her chair, and it was then that I saw she was wearing pants. Stout women like pants.

There was a roar going on around us as in the Valley of Josaphat on the night before the Last Judgment. All the voices fused into one piercing, plaintive moan. The faces of evil angels observed us from on high as if they were in Purgatory. But they were only the second-class customers in from the provinces who had managed to wangle themselves a passport to travel to the capital for the greatest holiday of the century.

"Who are you sitting with?" said a sneering voice.

It was Rysio Szmidt, but he looked completely different. As if he had lost weight and gone gray.

"With the people with the money. Sit down, they'll treat you, too."

"I don't need that," he said haughtily, and sat down. "May I?" he said, pointing at the bottle of vodka made from imported potatoes.

He poured some into a glass of soda water, drank it down, then looked me in the eye.

"He's not with us anymore," he said.

"When did it happen?"

"Even before they started with the life-support systems I knew he wouldn't make it. He could see God already. His eyes were staring off, he couldn't get over his surprise. He's on the other side now."

The musicians awoke all of a sudden and began playing their own rendition of the waltz "On the Hills of Manchuria." So no royalties would have to be paid. It made me feel even more wistful.

"I would have liked to see him. I know he hadn't told me everything. He was always stingy about coming right to the point."

"You'll see each other soon."

The waiter approached, carrying a plate. "You ordered the ragout, sir?"

"Yes, thank you."

"Your coupon for meat dishes, please."

I pulled out a handful, a month's worth.

"You can take them all. I won't be needing them anymore." The waiter's raven-black eyebrows rose.

"What do I look like, a beggar?" he asked. "You could donate them to the Fund for the Struggle against Colonialism."

He carefully selected one coupon and threw the rest back on the table in front of me. They lay there shamelessly, like money which had been disdained.

"I'm sorry," I said.

But he was already on his way back to the kitchen, angrily elbowing a customer from the provinces.

"He's just being like that now," I said. "Kolka promises that by morning he'll be nice as can be."

"You really don't need those coupons?" asked Rysio.

"I haven't been eating meat for a long time. A philosophical decision. An old man's whim."

"Meat gives you strength."

"I don't need strength anymore."

"But what about the girls? You were always fond of them, even though I've heard in the city that's about as far as it went."

"I can see you'd like the coupons, so take them. They'll give you strength."

"Well, if you want me to. Why should they go to waste."

Ashamed of himself, glancing to both sides, he stuffed the red coupons into his inside pocket. A few couples were bobbing on the minuscule dance floor.

"What time is it?" I asked, suddenly aware of time.

"Two-thirty."

"Plenty of time. A whole lifetime."

"So where's the gasoline?" whispered Rysio Szmidt.

"Don't worry, it's here. In the cool of the cloakroom. Gathering strength."

"Jesus God, Hubert, poor Hubert."

The band was scraping out the waltz, which my mind some-how connected to Nadezhda. It made me feel sad and strangely good at the same time. Would I see her again? I probably would, I had a premonition. And where women were con-cerned, my premonitions were never wrong. The good premoni-tions, and the bad ones.

Rysio Szmidt wrote elegant, intelligent prose. He behaved with dignity and created a certain old-fashioned artistic aura about himself. That morning he had played the good, simple soul, but that was only tactics, and I hadn't been impressed by his phony heartiness. Rysio was a bit contemptuous toward my work. He liked me but he didn't respect my prose. He was a professional, I an amateur. Professionals don't like amateurs. He also knew that I knew he took special pains in writing his books so that they would be easy to translate. Rysio had re-nounced everything and devoted his entire life to his worldly career. He wanted it so badly that he would achieve it in the end.

And now he was watching me pick without much appetite at the dish which had capriciously been named ragout.

"He burned himself out," I said.

Rysio froze, the bottle in his hand. "Who?"

"Hubert burned himself out from the inside. He lived through terrible things. You know I can't collect my thoughts, or my feelings, either. It's as if I'd broken my chain. A wind is tearing at me from all sides. I should be falling to the ground howling. But here I am, chewing my ragout."

Rysio looked up, toward Purgatory, where the ash-colored daylight became silver in reflection.

"Listen, listen," he said slowly, "Caban's sitting up there. He wants to talk to you."

"Where? I don't see."

"Up in the gallery. Near the window. Halina will show you."

"Halina who?"

"The one you already know. Look, she's waiting on the stairs."

And, indeed, Halina was standing on the stairs behind the band. The musicians were still playing "On the Hills of Manchuria," and it felt as if they'd been playing it since this morning. I rose and squeezed my way behind the invalids.

"Yes, I wanted to introduce you," she whispered.

I followed her, and on the way I noticed a burly man in a wrinkled flannel suit who was sitting alone at a small round table by a window covered with a piece of transparent tulle. I stepped into the daylight, the fluffy light of an autumn afternoon.

"Here he is," said Halina, indicating me when we had stopped by his table. I was about to tell her to stay, but she had already walked off toward the door, whose plate glass was missing.

"Please sit down," he said in a soft voice which had a metallic sound.

I sat down obediently, even though I had a good ten years on him. The tabletop was empty. There was only a large ashtray filled with butts left by the last customers.

He was not the least bit interested in me. He looked out the window at the blackened, dingy Party building, on top of which an enormous red silk flag was flapping in the wind.

"I don't like intellectuals," he said after a while.

I looked at him in shock. But he continued to sit with his profile to me. Another group of tipsy demonstrators was walking down the middle of the street toward Aleje. They were carrying a banner with some illegible date on it.

"Hysterical people," he continued. "Hypersensitive women."

"You wanted to talk with me."

"That's just what I'm doing."

His sense of mission had made him insolent and he had grown used to being obeyed. He played the role of dictator with gusto. And that threadbare flannel suit seemed like royal robes on him.

"I'm listening."

"You've been out of it for many years now. Was it your own

self-censorship that didn't allow you to take part in things?"

"Why self-censorship? I have other considerations."

"For example, what?"

"I'm supposed to make confession to you?" I asked a bit sharply.

"What are you afraid of?"

"What do you mean?"

"Well, are you afraid of—prison, interrogation, harassment?"

"I'm not afraid for myself."

"So, so," he prompted me, "for who, then? For us? For the country as a whole? Are you afraid they'll wipe us off the face of the earth because of one of your books?"

I looked over at him and could not believe my eyes. He reminded me of them. A coarse, anonymous face, transparent eyes.

"You see, I'm used to a different form of conspiracy," I said.

"What sort?"

"The sort that was formed by the uprising, and by fighting units of the Polish Socialist Party and the Home Army. You came out of a different batch."

"What does that mean?"

"You were created by this regime. You were excreted by the system, you're part of this tyranny's flesh and blood. You're like a character from Dostoevsky's *The Possessed*, not from a Zeromski story or one by Strug."

He finally turned toward me. Now I could see that his face was neither so coarse nor so anonymous. Something like a smile gleamed in his eyes, which really were quite pale.

"So what do you advise me, then?" he asked.

"I don't know what to advise you. That's not my problem. I'm alone, outside all the systems. And I want to keep it like that, right up to my last moment. But if you want advice, there's one thing I can tell you. Be like the old conspirators. Society remembers those archetypes in its unconscious. They're part of our collective memory. Only they can be effective."

"Could you please be a little more precise about the archetype you're referring to?"

"First of all, things should be voluntary. You have a fondness for blackmail, nasty, oppressive, moral blackmail. Secondly, disinterestedness. You like immediate rewards, you're all business. Thirdly, a willingness to lose. You don't like to lose. You want to win at any price. You're the product of your times. You are indecent, like the era which brought you into the world," I said.

"There's something to what you say. We probably are like our times. How could it be otherwise? How could we transcend the conditioning influence of our times, the social mentality, the political systems, the peculiarities of this phase of the historical process, the tightening or loosening of morality in this time, this epoch? How can we be nineteenth-century types when we're finishing off the twentieth century? How can we be anticapitalist if we're anti-Communist? Are you a romantic or a fool?"

"You use the prudent language of a Marxist. You don't perceive the moral and ideological imponderables which have decided our nation's fate. You are just a shadow cabinet of the crew in power," I said.

"Don't wear yourself out. I heard that you were touchy and quarrelsome. We don't need people like that now. Maybe at some point, when things are better, we'll be able to converse at length. But there's no time now. Many people and many nations are going to their graves now. The final bell is tolling. The Angelus bell. You don't have to keep your word. We don't need you. You can go home."

I rose from the table, but I did not walk away. "And who gave you my life to use? I'll be slow about going to the stake and it'll be a hard thing, because that's human. And in what way are my moral instincts any weaker than yours? And who told you that my death had to win your approval?"

Again he looked out through the dusty tulle at that building illuminated by a few rectangular windows. He clenched his teeth, knit his brows, and looked as if he was restraining an outburst of anger or just a sob. I thought he would reply, but he didn't say anything. I was irritated and was about to speak up again, but I didn't.

I returned to my table. The band was still playing that waltz, somehow unable to finish it.

"How did it go?" asked Rysio.

"It was not a good conversation."

I fell silent and so did Rysio. Someone at the bar had turned in our direction. It was Rysio's brother, the philosopher of allusions. He looked at us mockingly, without saying hello. Apparently Rysio sensed his brother's eyes on him, for he raised his head and glanced over at the bar.

"That's all I needed," he moaned. "What is that jerk doing here?"

"We ran into each other today in a dairy bar. He's running a seminar on political allusions for the censors. He stopped by for a glass like a good neighbor."

"That lousy faggot. To hell with him."

"Are you twins?"

"We are, but from different eggs. And he had a different father."

"You're nuts, that's impossible."

"I don't feel like explaining it all. Ask a doctor. The possibility exists—if a woman has relations with two men a few hours apart and if two eggs are descending. But I don't feel like talking about all that nasty stuff. Mama, God rest her soul, was a hot ticket. And that is why Edek is only a distant relative of mine."

"You're making it all up, Rysio. You dreamt it all one sleepless night while reading some medical encyclopedia. Is it really possible to hate one's own brother like that?"

"He's not my brother. I'll say it again. He's only my fucking cousin."

Edek the philosopher had already polished off his glass, and it was not enough that he was looking mockingly at us, he had to smile contemptuously, too.

"Don't pay any attention to him," whispered Rysio. "Let's pretend we're busy talking."

"You know what, Rysio, I'm going home. You get the gas can from the cloakroom. Maybe you can find another volunteer."

"Have you gone out of your mind?"

"There's something ambivalent about the whole thing. I'm ambivalent, you're ambivalent, the whole world's ambivalent. I'm not feeling well and that's that."

"Sissies put shit under their noses and say the world stinks," lamented Rysio, whose brother was looking daggers at him. "Maybe I should give him a smack in the face?"

"Listen, I'm going home." I rose from my chair.

But just then Kolka Nachalow appeared, leading Gosia carefully back to the table. They were giggling affectionately, and he was carrying her pocketbook, large as a bank safe. They hadn't been wasting time in the kitchen, some unfamiliar alcoholic smell came wafting off them. They were approaching us through the overwhelming wail of a gigantic flute, but it was just the band's Hammond organ, which had gotten stopped up. The musicians set their instruments aside and watched their colleagues struggle with the mysterious organ.

"This is my friend," I said, introducing Rysio, but they paid no attention to him.

"Attention, everybody. Attention, everybody," trumpeted Kolka through cupped hands. "This is the greatest chance of all before the actual end of the world. Gosia invites you all. It's Gosia's treat. Gosia's paying. Follow me. Forward. To victory."

He began pushing his way toward the kitchen, with Gosia actively lending a hand. We tipped over two tables on the way. Someone tried to stop us, but he received a smack in the face from the dark-haired waiter, who had been lying in wait for a chance like that all day.

We were met by a choral ring in the kitchen. The cooks, the

scullions, and the kitchen help sang together, not in unison, but together at least, reaching for the upper registers. They were singing the well-known song of the Volga boatmen, "Dubinushka." The chef, a huge, jolly fellow with a tomato smashed on the front of his tall white cap, was dancing all alone by a cauldron that was steaming dangerously from under its lid. That squashed tomato looked like a ruby stud on a Cossack hetman's pointed fur cap. On seeing us, the chef rose from his squatting position and banged his fist on the cauldron's lid.

"Silence! Shut up! I'm talking!"

But he had nothing to say; all he did was make a deep bow, knocking over a pail of potatoes in the process.

"Hey da uchnyem!" he sang in Russian.

Then he stood with his legs wide apart and began to beckon us with his huge thumb. "Come here, come here, my little kidney pie. Let me see you, my little smoked ham."

Suddenly he grabbed Gosia by the arm and carried her off violently through a dark door into some room. Enjoying the pleasant horror of it all, we started off after him. The room was a large pantry whose shelves were nearly bare. A dusty light bulb swayed from the low ceiling.

The chef had set Gosia down on the cement floor. "Quiet! I'm giving an order!"

With a knowing smile he began fumbling in his pockets under his white apron. Finally, he withdrew a bunch of small keys of different colors. He put his enormous forefinger to his lips, and his thick, black brows rose.

"Shhh. Do you know what this is?" He jangled his keys.

"Hurray!" cried Nachalow obsequiously. "Colonel, we're at your command."

The chef grabbed hold of the edge of a shelf piled with cans of tomato paste. He pulled at it with the strength of a Lithuanian bear; the shelf's concealed hinges groaned, and a tidy metal door opened. It looked like the ones I had already seen that day. Humming "Dubinushka," the colonel/chef pressed an illuminated keyboard, something screeched, there was a flash of light, and then we were descending into the depths of a low mine tunnel of a corridor.

A reckoning with my conscience. My act of contrition. Regret for my sins. My life story in the colors of mediocrity. At first I hated that mediocrity, disdained it, but in the end I made my home in it. Greatness in mediocrity. Mediocrity as the highest form of aristocracy. Mediocrity as asceticism, as proud isolation amid vulgarity, the gray habit of a proud monk. Mediocrity as the final stage of exaltation.

Is mediocrity sinless and innocent? I was pure until my instincts awoke, and I became pure again when my instincts began to slowly die out in me. My sinful period—a dozen-odd years when I was driven by swaggering biology. Some scientist implanted instincts, drives, reflexes in me and then observed the results. I was a guinea pig. And is the guinea pig responsible for the experiment?

I took care not to exceed the temperature of mediocrity. In the cool microclimate where I was tested I did not go to any extreme, and so I spoiled the experiment begun on my person by the Highest Intelligence. Was my sin that I did not sin enough?

My mediocrity was freely chosen. But the mental and physical conditions for being satisfied with mediocrity, for accepting it voluntarily, that I inherited from a genetic chain passed down for centuries and millennia by all sorts of types, oddballs, characters of whom I know nothing and don't wish to either, and they were never able to imagine a certain literary man who would briefly take that genetic code over and perhaps even do it harm, render it defective, or alter it. So my mediocrity, that proud and haughty mediocrity, was, to some small degree, imposed on me. But is a mediocrity I received against my will and which claims to be an act of my will, is that mediocrity without sin?

I never stole a lot of money, I never committed acts of erotic madness, I never transgressed the laws of nature, I committed no crimes. I kept to the herd and obeyed the herd. I listened attentively to the inaudible voice of the human herd which we call society. I committed a few petty transgressions, which did not disturb the general picture, and I immediately hushed them up, feeling myself corrected by society's invisible eye. But still I have a sense of sinfulness and I am a sinful man.

Perhaps that ribonucleic acid I inherited from persons unknown is itself Original Sin. That mysterious code launched from distant, gigantic galaxies of sinfulness. Perhaps sin is that rabid curiosity, that terrible desire to know the unknowable, that perverse temptation to tear aside the dark curtain which conceals the Most Perfect Existence (or does it conceal a lifeless nothingness?). Perhaps the sin is the universe with its billions of galaxies, its trillions of suns, and its quintillions of stars which are born in pain and which expire in pain?

I am flying off into interplanetary space, into the winds of time, flashing with the instants of my fate: the moment when I was drowning in a warm river bright with sunlight, the taste of bitter herbs in my mouth. The second when I saw the wild, terrifying act of two people copulating. The instant when I was shooting at a friend on a frosty, starry night with its choruses of howling wolves. The minute when I betrayed myself and my friends. The shortest eternity when I was waiting to see the hemorrhage of orgasm in the eyes of another man's wife. Moments of despair, suicidal nights. Those moments flash and fly like glowworms carried by the winds of time through eternal darkness. They resemble each other, they resemble hundreds, millions of others. The same, indistinguishable, identical. The Milky Way, the crumbs of our existence. The great roar of human existence.

Perhaps indifference, the child of mediocrity, is a volatile material like the mist which petrifies, forms crags, and rises to the sky in a mountainous mass while crushing our pitiable life? Perhaps transparent, colorless, odorless, formless, sluggish, ubiquitous, nice, cozy, innocent indifference is the only sin which can gum up the sieve of Providence? And could it be that only for that sin, which is not a sin, we will be judged on Judgment Day?

Holding on to the walls, stumbling, giggling as on a school field trip, we floundered our way through the carefully timbered tunnel with its pedantic lighting, its little arrows in two colors, white and red. We were following the white arrows; the red ones indicated the way back out.

"Listen, this could turn into a little orgy," whispered Rysio to the back of my sweaty neck. "Somebody's already said something to me about it."

"We're probably under the street. I can hear the demonstrators walking around up there."

"But under what street? Could we be under Nowy Swiat? What's your guess?"

I could hear the echo of footsteps behind me. I turned around automatically and saw that it was not an echo but actual people creeping along behind me. The kitchen help following their leader.

"Are you there?" asked Kolka, who was up ahead.

"I'm here."

"You won't regret your courage. You know how much this foreign expedition is costing? All the proceeds from *Transfusion*. That's the sort of person Gosia is. You don't know her, but you can see what she's like."

"But where are we going, Kolka? I have a deadline to meet today."

"I know about your deadline. You'll make it. Everyone makes his deadline."

Up ahead Gosia squealed, "Colonel! I see a rat!"

"Come to me, my little smoked ham. Upsy-daisy. Come here, my darling."

"Oh, you're so strong."

"And now you can repay me."

"Jesus, not my breasts, old man."

"I have to hold on to something, my little smoked ham."

We were driven on by the stamping feet of the kitchen help and the persistent voice of that flute-sound made by the stuck organ.

"An excursion to hell," I said softly.

"No, to paradise," said Kolka hoarsely from up ahead. "It's worth seeing. There may never be another chance like this. Even after we're dead."

Something was blocking our progress. Gosia was still squealing. "No hands please, Colonel. I have grown children."

"Ha," grumbled the colonel-chef. "I won't say what I could."

"I have sensitive breasts. I'm sorry, but I'm going to get angry."

"Quiet, shhh, mum's the word now," commanded the colonel in a deep voice. "Come closer, dear customers, I want to tell you something."

He waited until we were all standing in front of the door which we had spotted in the beginning.

"Who the hell is that?" he said, glancing angrily past us into the depths of the corridor. "Those scum, they left the kitchen for God to look after. Do you have something in your bag, my little chuck roast?"

He began gurgling like an oak cask, wiped his lips with the sleeve of his white apron, and then put the bottle into his own pocket.

"I'll be watching, so don't move anything or touch anything," said the colonel-chef. "You can look, but I forbid you to try anything. Understand?"

"Who do you think you're talking to, Colonel? After all, your guests are artists, witnesses to the age."

"I worked with artists once. I almost kicked the shit out of one. But that's beside the point. So, it's hands off and keep it down. Everybody understand?"

"We understand, we understand," said Kolka.

"And that bird?" The chef pointed at my modest person

panting by the door frame. "Why are your eyes so puffy?"

"It's a hangover, a total hangover."

"Did you have any ragout, you poor guy?"

"I did."

"Then drink three sips of this." He handed me the bottle he had tricked Gosia out of. "The truth is, friends, that I don't know how to cook. I don't know how to and I don't like doing it."

"It's stuffy down here, Colonel," groaned Gosia.

"I'll open the door right now."

His keys made a grinding sound, he pressed the colored keyboard and opened the iron gate. Once again we found ourselves in a pantry but a well-stocked one this time. There were large boxes of canned hams with shimmering colored labels on the tall shelves. To the right were cartons of bottles the likes of which we hadn't seen for years.

"Don't look around, don't look around," the chef reminded us. "Up these stairs now."

There were steep stone steps in front of us, rising toward a black ceiling.

The colonel stopped at the top and said to himself, "They could have my ass for this. And I'm up for retirement in just three years."

"Colonel," said Kolka Nachalow impatiently. "We'll just take a look and tiptoe back out. Good God, what are we wasting our time for?"

"Your father taught me everything I know," said the colonel-chef, calming himself down. "A holiday is a holiday, after all. There're no subversives or enemies down here with you, are there? All right then. On a day like today it's probably all right."

He sighed ceremoniously, examined the most important-looking key by the light from a bulb enclosed in wire, and then kissed the key as if it were a holy relic. He began fitting the key into a slot in the lock on the ordinary, white, unpainted door. A look of indecent delight appeared on his preternaturally huge face, which seemed enlarged by some mysterious biological calamity, a face which was attractive and repulsive at the same time. He fumbled at the lock, flushing darker all the time. The deformed sounds of the Hammond organ penetrated the depths of the corridor, reaching the royal pantry. Finally, the lock clanked merrily open, and then that door, too, was pushed open.

"I haven't opened it for six months," said the colonel, with a sigh of relief. "I check it every six months. Only me, nobody else. There's been no need to use this escape route yet and may God keep it that way."

We crowded into a cramped area full of old brooms, empty floor-polish bottles, and damaged parts from vacuum cleaners.

"Ready?" asked the chef, straightening his back in front of the final door.

"Ready," whispered Gosia solemnly.

He placed his hand on the gilded knob of the final door. He turned it slowly to the left and we could already hear the sort of exalted music played in churches or crematoriums. The slowly opening door revealed a magnificent interior the size of a chapel. The walls and columns were inlaid with marble; though they were, if the truth be told, cracked in a few places, a careful hand had filled them with a putty that matched the color well. From the high ceiling ornamented with classical stucco-work hung heavily gilded chandeliers, their lavish crystals shimmering indecently. But all that was as nothing in comparison with the tables. Tables reminiscent of the days of the Radziwills or when the Saxon kings sat on the Polish throne. Covered with antique tablecloths, decked out with greenery, weighed down with marvelous tableware—museum pieces, the tables were bent beneath the weight of the elaborate dishes and bottles.

"Did you cook all this yourself?" asked Kolka Nachalow, shaken by the sight.

"I don't know how to cook," replied the chef/colonel sincerely. "The whole world has cooked and fried and stewed and baked these wonders. For two years our Party has been scraping together every last cent of foreign currency to put on this secret banquet for its highest leaders. Did you know that for three months now the Polish Minister of Foreign Affairs has not been able to travel to the UN because there's no money for travel? The first dollars just came in today, somebody bought some Swedish matches in a hard-currency store, some Arab purchased three dozen condoms, and so, finally there was enough to put down as an advance for the minister's ticket. Please enter very carefully, because the floor is slippery. Just look, don't touch. God forbid. I'm warning you. I have the eye of a hawk."

We entered the banquet room on tiptoe. Even though the room was lit by the chandeliers, which were in the style of the Joseph Vissarionovich Stalin era, the room was still sunk in a golden half darkness which, in the aisles between the columns, became the mysterious darkness of coral caves.

"Can you guess where we are?" whispered Kolka Nachalow.

"I'm certain I know. A sanctuary. The Ark of the Covenant. The covenant between the Party as king and the Party as servant."

"Come on, let's take a look."

Figures kept darting out from the entrance to the storage room. The kitchen help, drunken customers, and even one of the musicians who still had the use of his legs. Wonderful music, whose composer I didn't recognize, filtered in through hidden speakers. Perhaps the music had been composed by all card-carrying members of all music schools working together.

We stopped in front of the main table, where an enormous sturgeon, a tsar of a sturgeon, lay in a meadow of parsley. The sturgeon was covered by a shimmering pale-green aspic, which reminded me of the depths of Lake Baikal. The sturgeon regarded us with a wise and august eye, which had been hard-boiled, of course. Nearby there were grooved blocks of light-blue ice containing red and black caviar. Crouching more modestly at either end of the table were Old Polish hams, their golden bones bared like the hilt of a prince's sword. Sirloins, roasts, and Lithuanian kielbasa, all cooked old-fashioned style, had been timidly placed between those giants of the culinary art. There were dishes on that table we had never seen before in our entire lives.

"The last time anyone saw a banquet like this was in the Kremlin, under Stalin. He ordered a feast like this before he went mad. He didn't invite anyone. He ate and drank alone, and he conversed with the ghosts of the Russian Caesars. And then he locked himself up in a one-man prison he had built for himself, and it was there, all alone, that he kicked the bucket," said Kolka Nachalow, his voice trembling slightly.

It was only then that I noticed there was a podium by the main wall and on that podium reposed the coronation insignia of the Polish kings with the famous sword of Boleslaw the Brave. A Party art curator had hung paintings, the nation's relics, on the wall.

Kolka Nachalow noticed that I was staring at the sacrilegious altar. "The Rooskies should find out who they're buying. Her Ladyship the Polish Republic. A Roman whore."

His own voice frightened him when he said those words. But the dignified music continued to play, the music which the propaganda department of the Central Committee had been approving and rejecting for several months. But already one of the half-drunk ghosts from the dungeon had come across the volume control and was fiddling with the enormous tape recorder.

"Oh, I can't resist the sturgeon," moaned Kolka Nachalow. "The colonel won't notice; come on, let's pick a little pinch off the back."

"Kolka, that's crazy. The guards'll be in here in a second and shoot us up against those columns."

"No one will be coming in, because all the doors are sealed from the outside. The commandant will only break the commission's seals at five minutes to eight."

We bent over the table where, at quarter past eight, both

Secretaries—ours, the Royal Prince, and theirs, the Tsar—would be standing. Kolka peeled the fine, silky skin off the back of the sturgeon, gouged out a hunk of the pinkish-gold meat, and handed it to me with the utmost care. I waited until he had taken a similar portion for himself. We closed our eyes so as not to sully our senses with extraneous impressions. With ceremonial slowness we placed the exotic treats on our tongues as if they were communion wafers.

But Kolka Nachalow began gagging at once, struck on the back by the heavy hand of the colonel-chef.

"That's not allowed! How many times do I have to say it! Get out of here!" he grumbled.

Kolka's tasty morsel fell to the floor, but I succeeded in swallowing mine. We were behind a marble column which had been patched with imported putty and where someone else was slugging French cognac straight from the bottle.

Grumbling, the colonel began furiously tamping down the cavity in the sturgeon's back with his enormous thumb. He did it, however, so maladroitly that he hacked the back of the fish open as far as the first fin. Finally, he looked around to see if anyone was watching him and then gobbled a large piece of fish which had rolled down onto the aspic. And having eaten a little something, he automatically reached for the bottle of Armagnac. The mysterious kitchen sprite who had been fiddling with the tape recorder had now found some dance music on one track. Suddenly a passionate tango filled that *fin de siècle* temple. Half-drunk, Rysio was busy at work at the less grandiose tables. He was gobbling smoked pork, leaving my meat coupons on the dishes. And someone was already, alas, vomiting by the column next to ours.

Gosia came floating out of the golden darkness. She was struggling with her bag, which was crammed full and would not close. I found her lack of tact irritating. To taste the delicacies was one thing, but to walk out with a ham in your handbag was something else entirely.

"I've got to run, though the fun's just starting here. But

there's a banquet for the film. We're selling *Transfusion* to some Australian buyers. We have the right to sell the film abroad, but not in Europe. Isn't that scandalous?"

Responding to the piercing notes of the tango, she danced a few steps, her pocketbook her partner.

"A unique feeling," she whispered. "Tell me what it's like, young man? Is it true that you play at being an oppositionist?"

"I don't play, my dear woman. I'm too old for games."

She took me by the arm and pulled me behind her into the mysterious semidarkness of the colonnade. I walked with dignity, like a member of the Politburo out with his wife. The rhythm of the tango lent a certain majestic quality to our movements.

"I have to tell you something. It's my obligation as an old woman." She hesitated for a moment. "Well, maybe not that old, but experienced. Listen carefully. I don't believe in any of this opposition stuff. And you should steer clear of that one." She hitched her thumb at Rysio Szmidt. "They all get government salaries. It's all one big provocation. Don't you find it surprising that the years go by and they keep playing at protest, revolution, publication, demonstration, as calmly as peasants in springtime? They've gone gray and fat, but what of it. Ravens don't peck each other's eyes out, if you see what I mean. I feel sorry for you. You've got a good eye. I need a production director. There's money to be made with me. God, what wonderful music! I have to run now. But we've seen what we've seen. No one can take that away from us. You know, I think the end of the world's coming. Why is everything falling apart? East and West. The beginning of the end of the world. But it could last a long time, the end. Centuries."

"Get going, you old cow," I said sleepily. "I see your face every day, everywhere I look. The face of an aging bourgeoise who likes to stuff her face at our funeral repasts."

"You boor!"

"Who's a boor?" The chef appeared from behind a column.

"Me, a boor? I am in charge of evacuating the Central Committee."

"I'm being insulted here. Please show me out, Colonel."

"Oh, my little roast chicken, we don't let people be insulted here, but we don't let them out, either. You have what you might even call Soviet tits."

"Colonel, I beg you, come to your senses."

"Let's dance, my little kitten. After us, the deluge. You see, I used to read books once. Tararala-bum-bam-bom."

"Pardon, excuse me." Someone was pulling at the hem of my jacket. "I am Dr. Hans Jürgen Gonsiorek. Do you happen to know if there is a men's room here?"

"I don't. Wait a little bit. We'll go look for it in a while."

"I'm lost. And my colleagues are lost, too," he said in correct Polish but with a slight German accent. "I can't even remember the name of my hotel."

"Are you from the building or outside?"

"I was in the kitchen when it all started."

Rysio Szmidt walked over with a herring in one hand and a glass of gin in the other. "What's going on?"

"He's looking for the men's room. Maybe I should introduce you first. This is Mr. Szmidt, a writer, and this is Mr. Gonsiorek, a doctor."

"Very nice to meet you," said the German, his face contorted. "I am the leader of a delegation which is negotiating with the Polish government to buy the province of Zielona Gora, formerly Grünberg."

Now there were more and more couples speeding past in the golden darkness, executing the difficult steps of the classical tango. Outside the windows covered with curtains made of gold cloth, the last storm of the year was thundering past.

"Is that you?" Edek Szmidt rose from one of the nearby tables. "What a stroke of fate. I am the Polish commission's expert on the sale of Zielona Gora province."

"I am Dr. Hans Jürgen Gonsiorek."

"I am Docent Edward Szmidt."

"I've already met you."

"That was my twin brother."

Rysio tossed the herring away into the darkness of the aisle. "I'm leaving. That's it. Period. I've had enough for today."

The philosopher moved a bit closer to the table. "Wait a little, brother. We'll go together. I've been thinking about you all day."

"Excuse me," interrupted Dr. Gonsiorek, stopping Edek. "Are you the leader of the opposition? I've read about you in the newspapers."

"Not me, it's that sad sack over there, my twin brother. I'm in the government's camp, Herr Doctor. Tomorrow, after we've sobered up, we'll be meeting at the negotiating table."

"I'd rather not talk about business today."

"Why not, Doctor. I have German blood in me."

"And I have Polish blood."

Rysio pitched an empty wine bottle into the depths of the hall. We waited for it to smash to pieces against the marble, but it just sank as if into water.

"Goddamnit, you have too much of our blood and not enough of our conscience. I'm leaving."

But he didn't leave. He slumped against a marble column and wiped his forehead, which was moist with sweat.

"We Germans have experienced a great historical shock," said Dr. Gonsiorek in a pained voice. "But I represent other Germans, the new Germans. We will never resort to violence again."

Szmidt the philosopher was about to start dancing, but was forced to abandon that intention.

"Nonsense," he said, kneeling on one knee. "Our border runs through the suburbs of your capital. Joseph Vissariono-vich hung a pretty good millstone around our necks. Rysio, what am I talking about? Brother, take care of me. I'm the only one representing the state here. I have lectures tomorrow, no, a meeting of the commission, and meanwhile, reaction is running rampant right here. A grubby deal disguised in fancy trapping, money grubbers knocking at the wrong doors. You've made me drunk, you lowlife. On your knees, scum! And you, the German with the big money! That's our national basilica, the fane of the Piasts, the plinth of Swantawit! Guards, over here! Comrades!"

"Rysio, he's starting to take off his clothes," I said in horror.

"I'd help him to, but he won't do it, you'll see. He's got a dick the size of a fingernail. Mama even had a mass said for it, but nothing helped."

The colonel/chef, the man in charge of evacuation, emerged from among the dancing couples. He walked gloomily toward us, his pants unbuttoned, his apron undone.

"What's going on here?" he asked menacingly. "Where's Gosia? Who took that girl away from me? And who's this fancy guy with the monocle?"

"A German comrade. But stand at attention. I am a member of the review board."

"I'm kicking you all out of here. You've run amok in here, you've gone completely wild, all you do is guzzle free vodka and steal the headcheese. Dance for me now, right now. Take the German by the arm, round and round you go, or else I'll put a hole in his head," he said, suddenly drawing out a large pistol, no doubt a precious souvenir from the old days. "Come on, start dancing! Yohoheaveho!"

"Who, me?"

"Yes, you dildo."

He shoved Edek brutally, and Edek obediently put his arm halfway around Dr. Gonsiorek. They did begin to wiggle around in place, because the tango's tune was hard to resist.

"Colonel, sir," I said confidentially, "I think Gosia's over there in the corner. Some guy is feeling her up."

"The bastard!" The colonel charged frantically off into the darkness.

There was a blood-red flash, a shot rang out, and someone began to flee across the hall with the tail of the sturgeon over his shoulder.

"They're tearing off the seals and breaking in the doors," I said to Rysio. "There's going to be a bloodbath in here."

"Come on, let's go back. I'll take responsibility for you."

"Maybe we should stay. The last Petroniuses in the final minutes as the millennium comes to an end."

He dragged me over to the packing room. On the way we had to step over Kolka Nachalow, who was sleeping on the floor. He was mumbling to himself in the language of his childhood, even though he was asleep.

"Go on, go on, I'll catch up. I'll just get a bottle."

Why didn't I like Warsaw? No, that's not true. I just didn't like it the same way those asses who made a bundle by loving Warsaw did. They start taking drugs in the morning and then of course by evening time they love Warsaw. They love it and they make people pay for that love. I've lived more than half my life in this cripple of a city. A city crippled at dawn, raped by its occupiers, quartered by its conquerors, and strangled by the lariats of Asiatic hordes.

Once I crawled back into this city's corpse. The city was having a tough time reviving itself and I was slowly coming back to life for the first time in my life. We were the same age. Bound together by chance. And, it turned out, bound together for death and for life.

This last day of my life would be my last literary work. The day of a modest "happening." But something had broken inside me. Weariness and powerlessness were overcoming me. My life was repeating itself and I was repeating myself. Instead of uniqueness, a series. My art, like my life, could be sliced like a sausage. That's how things turned out in the end.

Above me my city, its brand-new monuments and old modern buildings. I don't have anything besides that. A common language, a common suffering, a common misunderstanding. What are they guilty of? What am I guilty of?

I started down the corridor which led out, following the red arrows now. A couple were embracing in the alcove which held the fire extinguisher. Someone had dozed off, leaning against the wall like a mummy in an ancient catacomb. It looked like I was climbing back up to the surface of the earth, but in fact I was going into the dungeon of the Paradyz.

My city is reminiscent of the famous city of Irkutsk. It was once a crippled European city, today it is a healthy Asiatic village, a *kishlak*. I am enslaved to this city. Or rather, I chose my own house of bondage here.

I entered the kitchen, which was deserted, as if the Tartars had been through it. Pots gutted, dishes smashed, water running from the faucets. A rat was dog-paddling across the ocean of the kitchen floor.

I know the cause of my hangover. My total hangover. It happens to me every so often. Every once in a bad while. And then I play dice with fate for my life. Not with dice, but with a glass of water and three, four, five sleeping pills. The white man's Russian roulette. Played by presidents and whores, clergymen and poets, proletarians and capitalists.

The disabled veterans' cooperative band was playing a medley of American tunes but, to disguise them, was playing them backward so they wouldn't have to pay any royalties in hard currency. Someone gave my foot a friendly nudge.

"Pikush, have you been looking for me? Here I am. We'll be leaving soon."

He was jumping up into the air, trying to lick my hand. He had licked his coat clean out of boredom and now he looked all new and shiny. A little red dog with fringe-like feet.

"March, Pikush! Back to the cloakroom! Guard that can your master was carrying as if it were blood plasma."

Pikush made sad eyes, tucked his stubby tail between his legs, and went back to the cloakroom attendant, who was having a nice little nap, not the least disturbed by the music, the shouts, or the end of the world, which would take a few million years, not bothered by anything at all.

I sat down at our table. Other tribes had been camping there. Strangers' cigarette butts, traces of strangers' lipstick, someone's spilled lemonade. People were moving dreamily around me. They were heading through the kitchen toward the already-desecrated Party sanctuary, others were floundering back, soaked to their knees, sated with debauchery. Blue faces, red faces. Oblong, oval, pimply, gleaming with sweat. Melancholy, wanton.

It cost me some effort to rise from the table. I raised my hand to quiet the band, then I opened my mouth as wide as I could.

"People!" I bellowed. "The Antichrist has descended to earth. He hopped down here from the next galaxy. Maybe he had someplace else in mind, but he ended up here."

A man was signaling me. "The toilet's over there, buddy. Out past the cloakroom."

I raised both my arms. "People, look at each other. He has divided himself into all of you and into me as well. Don't be waiting for the Antichrist to come, he's already here on earth. An Antichrist diluted, broken into bits and granules. The Antichrist is in every one of us, in me."

The band was playing a sixth song, someone was dancing, someone was dozing. The lights blinked red and blue. Up above, the pale faces of Lucifer's helpers awaiting their hour.

"No one's listening to me," I said in resignation. "The Antichrist has engrained himself in all of us and that is why he doesn't exist. No one's listening to me."

"I'm listening," said Edek Szmidt, looking disheveled, his tie crooked. "But it's too stupid. What unscientific, old-fashioned nonsense. Aren't you ashamed of yourself?"

George, formerly Georgie, was sitting at the bar. He was sitting rather casually, one leg dangling from the high stool, and sipping some drink from his glass through a bent straw.

"Docent, yesterday I took five sleeping pills with a glass of vodka. And it still took me a couple of hours to fall asleep. It's a lottery. Either it knocks you off your feet right away or it has a nasty opposite effect. And so there I was falling off to sleep for a couple of hours, but I couldn't quite make it there. I'd cross the line and then step back. And each time I would enter a different sector of that strange dimension. I would enter the gentle world of childhood memories, the shadow of the uneasy conscience, the red night of malicious demons. Once I even entered the clarity of understanding, a glowing clarity marked with meaningful symbols. I understood everything, everything became obvious, comprehensible in the simplest possible way. But then someone punished me, and at the very last moment, the instant before the cry of triumph and relief, I was pushed away into the dark abyss of dreamless sleep.

"And do you know what my twin brother, Rysio, is living off?"

"No, I don't. I've left literature, I lost my ambition. I'm waiting for my deadline."

"This is worth hearing. Rysio is living off a little book he wrote in the far-distant past when he was still a zealous son of the Party and served in various important agencies where I also held positions. Do you remember the title? That book, which had its own style, a certain flair, praised force, justified the absence of freedom, and reconciled the reader to the evils of the world. That book is reprinted twice a year and forced on every schoolchild, to poison him, to corrupt his moral instincts as they make their first appearance, to instruct him in ambiguity and the first delights of cynicism. It is thanks to that little book that Rysio walks the city safe and sound. He lives off that book, it pays for his milk in the morning and his vodka at night. And it's thanks to that book that Rysio can wage his uncompromising battle against the regime and rouse our consciences, which have gone flabby. And so here, once again, my dear friend, we bump up against the dialectic of our times."

"And where's Dr. Gonsiorek?"

"He got lost. Probably lost in the men's room."

"God, everything's gone black. All that's left is a hangover that won't go away."

"We are only bits of protein in a cruel universe of silica and fire."

"But you believe in God."

"If I do it's in a different one from the one you fools believe in."

George was sweeping the room with his eyes, searching for a new victim. I was about to hide behind the philosopher's crumpled front, but it was too late. He had spotted me. He smiled knowingly and hopped down off his bar stool.

"You're still here?" he asked, shoving the docent unceremoniously aside. "This isn't a good place. A bar with a bad reputation."

"I was just about to pay up. But the waiters have all disappeared."

"Speaking of the bill, you know, this is foolish, maybe I shouldn't even ask you, but I'm a little short for my own tab."

"Short how much?"

"Not that much. Twenty thousand."

I felt around in my pocket to see what I had. I knew his type. As soon as he saw a wad of bills, he'd ask for more.

He lowered his hand discreetly, and feeling his bony hand in the dark, I slipped two bills into it. He appreciated my tact and touched my hand in return.

"I'll return it tomorrow morning, special delivery," he said softly.

"But, then again, you know that your creditor won't be around tomorrow."

He broke into laughter and gave me a whack on the back. "If I wasn't sure of that, I wouldn't have hit you up."

He walked off toward the bar and tossed my money onto the counter as if it were his own. The bartender served him another round but left the same bent straw in the glass.

Hans Jürgen Gonsiorek came staggering out from the cloakroom, bumping against the walls.

"Herr Gott, I don't want any more. I just want to go to the hotel," he moaned, his hands clutching his sides.

"What's going on in the sanctuary?"

"It's the end of the world down there. And it's the end of the world here, too. I want to go home."

"The end of the world is coming to your home, too."

"But at least I'll be in my own bed when it happens."

Then I noticed that Rysio was standing at the bar and drinking out of George's glass while George chatted with the bartender.

"Rysio!" I shouted, a bit too loudly, because the band had suddenly stopped playing.

Szmidt looked staidly over at me, put out his cigarette in George's glass, then staggered over to us.

"That faggot Edek is back again," he said. "No doubt he's been slandering me behind my back. You know, every day he prostrates himself at Holy Cross. He runs to church between a conference at the Central Committee and his lectures to the censors. He falls flat and then gathers strength for his next batch of dirty tricks. He's even gotten God used to it."

"Gentlemen, I have diplomatic immunity," complained Dr. Gonsiorek.

"We spit on immunity," said Edek Szmidt.

"In this country you could end up in Siberia just like that," added Rysio Szmidt.

But then the doctor grew suddenly sober and smiled astutely. "I can go to the Canary Islands or Caracas, but not to Siberia. You can't go to Siberia now. It's become a strategic area."

His pink fingers toyed with the gold-rimmed glasses on his substantial nose. At that moment a sort of tinny racket came from the band. A musician, no doubt a percussionist, had fallen off his chair and, staggering back, had crashed his head against the cymbals. No one rushed to his aid, only the man at the broken Hammond organ rose lazily and started toward him.

"Is there a doctor in the house?" he inquired in no particular hurry of the customers at the tables closest to the band.

A man rose and stipulated that he was only a biologist. He climbed up onto the stage and began turning over the percussionist, who had blacked out.

"He's drunk. Percussionists are great boozers," opined Edek Szmidt.

"Philosophers are great boozers, too," hissed Rysio with hatred. "To poison the worm. That guy just got sick. Everyone's sick when a country's not free."

"Oh, Jesus," I sighed. "That reminds me of Hubert. We're sitting here drinking and he's choking to death in some hospital. One of my last friends. People, I'm an orphan. An orphan on an alien planet."

Kolka Nachalow was crawling between the tables, leaving large stains on the floor. He had swum across the flood in the kitchen. Kolka collapsed exhausted on someone's chair. "You guys, give me a match. You've got some Swedish ones. I want to burn down this bordello."

"But why do you want to burn it down?" asked Rysio cunningly.

"Let it all burn, right down to the ground. All the filth, all the sin, all this devil's brood."

Rysio slapped him across the forehead with the palm of his hand. Kolka and his chair fell over backward, and then he scrambled silently back up to his feet.

"You hit Kolka Nachalow," said Kolka in a strangled voice.

"Yes, I hit Kolka Nachalow."

"My father spilled blood for you Poles."

"And he also gave us a nice present—socialism."

"Russians are still eating potatoes so you Poles can live well."

"So get the hell out of here. Go eat oysters in hell."

"That's gratitude for you. Doctor, you're a witness. You'll hear from me yet."

Edek Szmidt intervened. "Comrade Nachalow . . ."

"I'm no comrade of yours."

I tried to help him back onto his chair, but he pushed my hands away angrily.

"Kolka," I said, "he meant well."

"What do you mean?"

"We're supposed to tease you a little. The White Poles keep you going. Russia needs the sneaky little Poles and all their complexes for stimulation. That holy vocation of Russifying Poland bequeathed to you from Ivan Kalita leads you through history like the morning star. You want us to yield right away. Do you want to spoil the whole thing?"

Kolka Nachalow looked at me long and hard. Finally, he broke out laughing and tried to lift his heavy belly from the chair. "I like you. You're the biggest phony there is, but I like you. Give me your face, brother."

But we didn't get to kiss because Zosia, the men's room attendant, appeared at that moment.

"Someone's here to see you," she said.

"Me?" I asked in surprise. "I'm not expecting anyone."

"You never know."

I started walking straight ahead, clearing a path among the ravaged tables and the dozing customers.

"There's no reason to feel bad," she said consolingly. "The first sitting's just about over. In a minute they'll start throwing everyone out. They have to get the place cleaned up for the Arabs. They start coming in after six."

"Zosia, my dear, I kept meaning to come see you, but somehow it didn't work out that way."

"What are you talking about? I know all about it now. Here's your six hundred zlotys back. You didn't use the stall and I jumped on you because I was irritated."

"No, no, forget about it."

But still she thrust the money on me. In the cloakroom the major had woken up and was listlessly watching a small television which was showing the visiting Secretary, the Chief Secretary, the Super Secretary just finishing his speech and receiving his ovation. A few men wearing black clothes were placing a traditional miner's cap with a magnificent plume on his head.

But there was no sound with the picture. Observing the Polish custom, the major had turned off the sound.

"Major, I would like my package and my dog. I'm setting sail for a distant land."

He lifted up the can and sloshed it to show that all the gasoline was still there.

"Everything shipshape?" he asked.

I pressed the money Zosia had returned to me into his sweaty palm.

"Let's go, Pikush."

The dog jumped briskly out from under the counter, ready to hit the road. Behind us the percussionist was being carried away somewhere.

"Don't forget!" cried Rysio from the abyss of the restaurant.

I started off, led by my eager Pikush. I turned to Zosia, who was leaning against the door frame. "Goodbye. Maybe I'll drop by to see you some evening."

"No chance of that," she said, examining her nails.

I started up the stairs covered with a red carpet which had been stained with every variety of unsuccessfully digested food. At the top of the stairs, by the glass door with the missing panes, stood Nadezhda.

"They're kicking us out," I said. "In the evening this place is for Arabs with petrodollars."

She shook her red hair with pity. "A fine thing. You had to go get yourself thrown out of a bar. You should just see how you look."

Ashamed of myself, I patted down a few hairs on the top of my head. Pikush was already sniffing her legs, full but not too stout, just the kind I like and which he liked right away too.

"Is this your dog?"

"No, it belongs to some friends. At one point he got lost, we cried over him for years, we had poignant dreams about him, dreams of bad conscience, and now he's turned up again out of nowhere. Pikush, give the lady your paw."

"Have you been drinking?"

"Just a little. But the food I ate! A Kremlin lunch. Even if I told you about it you wouldn't believe me."

We went outside, where there were Arabs already waiting to get in. They were standing around in little groups, all dressed almost identically, talking to each other in guttural voices. For some reason they never associated with the local populace. They lived a life of their own in Warsaw, never asking for directions or friendship. The only exception they made was for the girls of the Vistula, whom they screwed with a vengeance, and besides their money, that was the sole tangible trace of their presence here.

"Nadezhda, wait, it's such a beautiful day."

And indeed, the clouds had dispersed toward the far horizon, the sun was good-naturedly warming this poor, cowering, but festive city. Some final notes drifted through the hot air and a mangled butterfly even flew across the street toward Party headquarters.

"Party headquarters," I said to myself, and my heart sank.

Agents dressed as traffic policemen were tapping their feet in boredom by the corners of that building located right in the middle, the heart of Sodom and Gomorrah. I wondered if anyone had managed to paste that sturgeon back together, add water to the bottles, and clean away the muck on the floor. That poor chef who held the rank of colonel, the last man with any dash in the capital!

"Nadezhda, I'm going to take you by the arm."

"Would you like a tranquilizer? I have everything with me."

"What do I need to be tranquil for?"

"You should try to sober up."

"I am sober."

"You're going to give us trouble."

"But Caban said that I didn't have to keep my word."

"Is that something Caban can do? Do you need to be excused? Was anyone ever able to force you to do anything?"

"Nadezhda, you flatter me."

"Anyway, he regrets the conversation. Sometimes men argue for no reason at all."

We went past a grocery store. A hastily assembled team of saleswomen was putting together a modern version of Poland's state seal—a small eagle enfolded in large sheaves of grain—in the rickety display window.

We came out to Three Crosses Square. A small group of half-drunk demonstrators was lying on the concrete square by a pissoir of historical significance. They had placed the banners with their illegible slogans and incorrect dates under their heads.

One ruin could be seen among the other buildings, which still looked healthy enough. It was the building that had housed the editorial offices of the satirical weekly *Szpilki* for many years. It had collapsed one spring, and no one had had the strength to rebuild it.

"Come here, Nadezhda, let's sit down and have a look at God's world."

I pulled her toward the stairs of the ruins. We sat down on a warm step. Pikush curled himself into a ball at my feet. The demonstrations seemed to be dying down, though it was early yet. Bands were still playing somewhere near the Vistula or perhaps over by Parade Square; a shout exploded in the shallow canyon of the streets, maybe a pro-government shout, maybe just a drunken shout. Still, apathy was again covering my city with its fustian shroud.

"It's a good sign that we're together again," I said.

She said nothing, staring straight ahead into the misty distance of Aleje Ujazdowskie.

"You know, I had a revelation last night. I'll tell you about it because I don't feel embarrassed with you anymore. So, I had a revelation, like an old woman but not quite, because it had some meaning. That's why my head's killing me today. And I'd been waiting for that revelation my whole life. I wanted to pass it on to society, but not for selfish reasons. The way you bequeath priceless paintings or statues to a museum."

"You dreamed of the Antichrist."

My hand froze in Pikush's fur. "How do you know?"

"I don't know. I dreamed of the Antichrist, too. It wasn't the first time, either. It's one of my recurrent dreams. Always in color, too. Though once, a few days before I left for Poland, I had the dream in black-and-white."

"But today I can't remember any of the dream. As if somebody had hacked it away with an ax. But still it's making me afraid of people. Not the way a person usually is, no, people terrify me."

All of a sudden she rested her head against my arm. Her light, red, fluffy hair. "Oh, my dear man."

"What is it, Nadezhda, what?"

"Oh, it's hard to live."

"And hard to die."

She pressed herself against me. A solitary balloon which had lost its owner was wandering high through the freshly washed sky.

A drunken demonstrator suddenly woke up, raised his heavy hand, and called out in a hoarse voice to the sky, "Poland, Polska, Polsha, damn your eyes!"

My colleagues A.M. and J.H. were returning from their stroll, emerging from the east end of the square. They were carrying paper flowers that had been dropped by demonstrators. And thus they had a certain festive look about them, even though the flower in his hand kept J.H. from gesturing and pushing A.M., which impeded their literary conversation. I watched them closely, tenderly, helplessly, from a distance, as if looking down on them from the sky.

The sun was low, its rays almost horizontal. A sudden summery hot spell before nightfall, even though the grass my friends were walking on had long since turned the color of rust and died. Only a set of flower beds ingeniously arranged into the Roman numeral LX was still alive, letting us know that the Municipal Parks Department was way ahead of everyone and was already observing the sixtieth anniversary of the Polish

People's Republic. Someone was supposed to have constructed something of importance on that grassy area after the war ruins were demolished. But then somehow everyone forgot who was supposed to have built what.

Little black ants were running in panic over my gas can, as if it were some strange planet. No doubt, the Pharaoh's ants, or those of King Piast the Wheelwright. For them the gas can was an evil, unfriendly planet, or just a gigantic atomic reactor.

"Are you sleeping, Nadezhda?"

"I was, just a tiny bit. I left you alone for just a couple of seconds."

"Evil is like darkness. It goes on forever. And good is a flash, a victory over darkness that doesn't last. The good is mortal."

"Are you thinking about our dreams?"

"I'm thinking about what to do. This day will be my last literary work. Should I polish each sentence and situation like the old masters, or should I rely on spontaneity, the chaotic spontaneity of the incorrigible writer? No, Nadezhda, I'm only kidding. I was really thinking about you. This morning I met a haunted, poetic, slightly daft Russian girl, and now . . ."

"And now?"

"And now I'm sitting with my woman. Are you my woman?"

"I am."

"Even though that doesn't sound too nice."

"Even though it sounds rather trivial."

"How depressing and outrageous that everything can be reduced to a few of the questions in Hamlet's monologue. Centuries have passed, civilizations have fallen, generation after generation has vanished into oblivion, but nothing has changed, so little has changed, and goddamn Providence has even taken away the illusory satisfaction of being first, has deprived us of the rights of the author and made us all plagiarists forever."

"What is it that's tormenting you, my darling?"

"Sin has assumed the form of virtue. The moral imponderables have faded away, and the imponderables of amorality have bled through the design, as when you redye a piece of cloth. Amorality rules us using morality's laws, it uses moral nomenclature, it constructs its own positive systems, it rewards saintliness and hurls the damned into hell. Evil has tapped into our ethical code and turned itself into good. A fatal, cancerous good."

"Do you regret joining up with us? That you didn't get a government license to engage in judicious dissidence, the nonviolent defense of human dignity and the bloodless struggle against force and tyranny?"

"I had to join up with you people. It was written that I would."

"So then don't have any regrets for your greedy pride. Let it suffer, let it envy, let it hurt."

"It doesn't matter."

"Some things matter."

"Do you think redemption is possible, that God's conscience can be moved?"

"We have to try. Until the end of time."

"You love sin."

"Who does?"

"You Russians wallowed dissolutely in sin so you could gain the blessing of absolution. Because there can be no absolution without sin, right?"

"You're confusing literature with life."

"What did you say?"

"You're confusing people's blasphemous dreams and the way they act in everyday life."

"Yes, I am confusing literature with life. I'm declaring my own ordinary life to be a work of literature."

Pikush was compassionately licking my exposed calf. Swallows shot past above the rooftops. That used to portend good weather, but now it portends nothing. A sudden hot spell. Maybe it was the end of the summer, or the beginning of next spring.

"Let me see you, Nadezhda."

She raised her head, her reddish hair which she no doubt got from Lenin spilling around her face and falling onto her shoulders. One eye truly was green and the other truly violet. All in all, my Nadezhda was good-looking, good-looking in a disturbing, dangerous sort of way. But that was my cup of tea.

I put my arms around her and squeezed her hard. She closed her eyes, then I closed mine. Our mouths felt their way to each other. Her lips had such a tender and aggressive life of their own that chills went up my spine.

Somewhere a clock was striking the hour. It rang such a long time that finally we opened our eyes. But it hadn't been a clock. The Angelus bell had been rung in St. Aleksander's Church earlier than it should have been.

Saying nothing, without a single word, we rose from the cement step which was already absorbing the late-afternoon chill and we entered the silent nave of the editorial offices' ruins. All that empty space contained was a staircase which looked like a rumpled rug. The remains of the walls, partitions, and ceilings were lying in the middle of the building, piles of picturesque rubble which seemed arranged by some romantic architect. Astonishingly luxuriant vegetation had entwined itself around those hunks of cement and brick, those dunes of weathered lime. The sun's oblique light made the large, blackish burdocks glow; it gilded the handsome ferns and lit the deadly nightshade bushes on fire. Even fall asters had stolen into that enchanted garden, which had overgrown the junk pile of what once had been editorial offices.

The stairs invited our eyes to the sky, which had grown distinctly opalescent now. I scraped some dead leaves and tobacco shreds off the first step with my foot. I gave her my hand and Hope joined me on the first step; I cleared the way for her and she followed obediently until we found ourselves on a landing which had once had a wooden floor. An incredibly large flock of sparrows had come to rest on a small, solitary tree. Hidden among the yellowing leaves, they chatted away, holding some council. That chattering became a sonorous and uncanny music, a monotonous, metallic moan of piercing anxiety.

Nadezhda leaned back against the jagged wall. She closed her eyes and waited. Again I kissed her lips, which had grown cool in the meantime. My hand found her large breasts, my graceful friends. Nadezhda cringed as if in fear of me, or perhaps from a sudden cold draft of uncertainty. Her huge nipples roughened and went erect in a series of little spasms. She smelled like water that had been warmed by the sun, and she also had the sharp, enticing aroma of birch leaves. Hope whispered something I couldn't hear. Her body grew limp and heavy, and I had to support her so that she wouldn't fall to the moldering floor.

We could hear the desperate pounding of each other's hearts and the polyphonic cry of the birds, like some rising reminder. I parted her legs with my knees and then entered her, deeply.

She said something, but soundlessly, as if reciting a litany. She had closed her eyes so tightly the lids had turned white. Sharp, predatory teeth gleamed in the heathery pinkness of her mouth.

"Hope," I whispered. "Hope, I'm here."

"I know. Only you. Forever you." She drove her back against the wall as if she wanted to push the wall to the horizon, where the sun had now started to set. She seized my hand in both of hers, made a short, muffled cry, and then became so enormously heavy that I could not hold her up. She slid to the floor, the red yarn of her hair covering her face. Water was dripping somewhere from what remained of the ceiling. A stray wasp flew in from the garden and began circling around Nadezhda's head. I tried to drive it away. I bent down for a piece of rust-colored nettle to shoo it away, but just then I heard the cry of broken glass being stepped on.

A man was standing in the doorway. A middle-aged man wearing a small red cap with a long visor with a leather bag on his stomach, the sort parking-lot attendants carry. He saluted

—two fingers at the visor of his cap adorned with an emblem I didn't recognize. It was only then that I noticed that he had a red card that looked like a receipt in his other hand.

"Good day," he said briskly. "Ten thousand zlotys."

"Ten thousand zlotys? For what?" I asked.

"For making love in a public building."

"You mean you can't do that?"

"You can, but you have to pay."

"Is it a fine?"

"No, a tax. It went into effect on the first. You should have come to see me beforehand, I could have loaned you an inflatable mattress."

I was standing astounded over Nadezhda, who was still curled up. Now the wasp was flying around my head.

"There's too many people and not enough apartments, so the state's stepped in," said the official. "There'll be more conveniences fairly soon. There's supposed to be tarpaulins for privacy, and pillows, too. Pay now or I'll call a policeman."

"I'll pay, I'll pay," I said, grumbling, while walking back down the stairs. "But how do you know what we were doing here?"

"We're all professionals. You're not going to say you weren't, are you? Don't I know you from somewhere, were you ever on television?"

"I might have been. I don't remember," I said, fishing out a ten-thousand-zloty bill. He took it politely but decisively from my hand.

"Before I retired I worked as a television director."

He handed me a red card marked ambiguously *Municipal receipt*.

"You can stay here as long as you like. I'll keep an eye out for you."

He saluted courteously, placed the money in his bag, and left.

Bands had struck up again somewhere in the heart of the city. Individual piercing cries rose from nearby gateways. Cries that sounded like wolves howling in winter. But there were no more wolves on earth. Only people. As usual the city was stepping on the gas as night fell.

"Wake up, Nadezhda." I shook her by the arm.

She made no response, and remained kneeling on a molehill of old ashes, her head hidden in her arms as if she were trying to suppress a pain that could not be overcome.

I started to lift her up. She was terribly heavy, inert. Some weather-beaten plaster came crumbling down not far from us. The wasp was pestering me with its buzzing, bumping against my ear.

"Nadya," I whispered into the red bush of her hair.

Suddenly she reeled against the wall. For a moment I caught a fleeting glimpse of her eyes going wild and blank. She shoved me aside and began running down the shattered steps. Then she dashed off to the side, into the thick of the enchanted garden; she must have knocked against an old sheet of tin because a shadow which covered the sun suddenly burst from the tree. But it was only the swallows flashing past toward the heart of the city with a deafening whir.

The sky had cleared again, innocent and pure, as it once had been when it truly had been innocent and pure. Now that sky had been befouled by rockets, trampled by eager philosophers in search of a truth which might not even exist. But now, for this singular dusk, the sky had gotten dressed up, put on makeup and rouge, and looked young again.

"Nadezhda!" I called out, but not very loudly.

A raggedy butterfly, perhaps the very same one which had been flying toward the Central Committee, was now rising unhurriedly over a lovely thistle bush that stood straight as a hussar. Silvery spiderwebs sparkled in the bushes' shadowy, dun-colored recesses.

She appeared suddenly, as was her custom. She walked unsteadily out from behind the tree the sparrows had abandoned. She was walking in her own graceful but ponderous way, like a small boat sailing across a choppy lake.

She smiled to me from a ways off, then wiped the corners of her eyes with the back of her hand. I waited for her, standing up to my waist in ferns which were strewn with white, mysterious seeds left to them from the good old days when they had been trees on this earth.

She walked up to me, put her arms around my neck, and buried her head against my arm.

"I'm tired," she whispered. "Did somebody come?"

"An old man who used to work in the building. He wished us happiness and gave us his blessing."

"That's just what I wanted, someone to give us his blessing. There are good, wise old people in Poland, too."

"We used to have noble, intelligent, dignified old people."

She wiggled her head, which seemed enlarged by her hair. A ladybug hurried down a broad lock of her hair illuminated by the sunlight.

"Listen," she whispered.

"I'm listening, Hope."

"I'll go with you."

"Where, my love?"

"To the Palace of Culture. I'll do the same thing you're going to do, my love."

"No, Nadezhda, I'm directing my final story. From the point of view of mood and composition it's better that you stay and pine away for me for the rest of your days."

She raised her head, amused by my idea. She looked at me with her large, sparkling eyes, one of which could have been greener and the other more violet. The swallows were returning in small flocks to the tree, which was their house of parliament. I gave her a light kiss, first on the left eye, then on the right.

"You really don't want me to?"

I shook my head no. Again she hid her face against my arm.

"Wait, I have to think," she whispered.

I took her in my arms and immediately found those astonishing breasts, so responsive to my touch. They were tired too, warm with a melancholy sleepiness.

"No, no, don't." She pushed me away with her elbows. "No more. That's enough. For my whole life."

"I'll be waiting for you up there in that gloomy, bearded, Russian Orthodox heaven."

She pressed her face harder against my jacket, which was snarled with transparent cobwebs.

"What should I do?" she asked. "Everything has gone to pieces in just a couple of hours. But I knew it was coming. I somehow knew that I would meet you."

"There are plenty more like me. There's some of me in every one of them. I don't exist as an individual. You're hugging a mannequin dressed in pants and jacket from a department store."

"There's only one you. I know. I had a dream about a Poland of ruined palaces and you wearing a knapsack on a long, winding road."

"We have to part, Hope."

"Until we meet again."

"In the next life."

"Or maybe here again. Do you want a tranquilizer?"

"No, not anymore. I feel calm, even though I don't know what I'm going to do."

"You'll do what the God you believe in wants you to do."

"Still, the best thing that could happen would be the end of the world. We could set off, arm in arm, for Purgatory. Along with our enemies and our friends. With a suitcase full of good deeds and a freight car full of sins."

"Yes, that would be a fine end for the world, the one people have been waiting for, for half a million years."

"Nadezhda, I still have a few last things to take care of."

She pulled me to her. Again I could smell the faint aroma of dried birch branches. Then she pushed me away, but not very far, I could still feel her breath on me. "So, go then, my love, I'll pray for you."

She made the sign of the cross over me, in the Russian Orthodox manner, and I kissed the tips of her fingers. The sparrows had started their chattering again, their Chinese chorales. Clouds of mosquitoes were flying over the bushes in that garden now full of gold and the darkness of wells.

"Wait here till I'm gone," she said, looking off to one side. "You promise?"

"I promise."

She brought her eyes to mine. Her pupils widened in a barely perceptible smile and a sudden dampness gleamed in the corner of her eyes.

"Hug me. Very hard. Even harder."

"I can't hug you any harder."

"Harder, love, so I can always remember."

We kissed, our lips wet and salty. Then she turned away with desperate resolve and ran off with her ponderous but strangely fluid gait into the depths of the sunlit street. Automatically I began looking around for my gas can. But the vessel of my agony was nowhere to be found. I felt a sudden heaviness in my head, oppressed by a hangover and by black thoughts. The wasp which had caught my attention earlier now flew out of the garden. It bumped up against my cheeks and ears again. And it was with me as I went back out to the street.

And there, by the collapsed walls of the pissoir, stood Tadzio from Stargard, a smile on his face and the blue gas can in his hand.

"Perhaps at some point in the next circle of infinity I will love you again. You wrote that one, too," he said, shaking the gas can. "I've been guarding the can. You left it outside."

The drunken demonstrators were waking up from their after-dinner nap on the cement square. One of them tore a paper letter L from a banner to wrap his bleeding finger.

I crossed the street, which stank of liquefying asphalt, and walked over to smiling Tadzio from the provinces. He lifted the gas can and was about to hand it to me. But then, without any warning, I grabbed him by the collar of his flannel shirt and squeezed it around his scrawny neck, so that his stupid, kindly eyes began to bulge out of their sockets.

"You scum, you brought me to George. How long have you been working for them?"

Pushing me fearfully away with both hands, he stammered, "Three years."

I smacked him right across his beardless face. He fell to his knees, but nimbly, so that the gas can would not be damaged. He grabbed my hand and began kissing it with his disgustingly slobbery lips. It was only then that I noticed he was not all that young. There was some old cunning in that hairless, infantile face.

"How old are you, you swine?"

"Thirty," he groaned, still covering my hand with ardent kisses.

I struck him again. He rubbed his nose to see if it was bleeding and then he moaned, "Forty. I swear to God I'm telling you the truth."

"How did they recruit you?"

"I write poetry for them. I think up jokes for them. For the Department of Propaganda and for testing the public's mood."

"Get up, you scum. Don't start hamming it up here or I'll tell people who you really are."

Sniffling, he began to rise from his knees. He cleaned the edge of the gas can carefully with his sleeve. He was so devoted to me.

"What sort of poetry?" I asked, and again I grabbed the collar of his disgusting, sweat-soaked shirt.

"Satirical poetry. On the oppositionists, the dissidents. The enemy."

"And the jokes?"

"The jokes are about the people in the government. There are two kinds. One is a probe to sound out the crowd's reaction and the other is against politicians whose time has passed."

"You're a monster. I should call a bunch of people over here and have them lynch you."

He fell to his knees again and seized my hands in his lizard-like hands.

"I beg of you, forgive me, please. I admitted it, didn't I? What was I supposed to do? What could a person from Stargard do, and me a cripple to boot? I wrote poetry for twenty years and not a single soul ever had a good word for me. All the letters from the editors and publishers began with the words: We regret to inform you . . . Finally, I got to the point where I hated the mail. You understand, you'll forgive me. They do other nasty things, worse things. I ask you to forgive me in the name of my parents because I'm an orphan."

"You're as old as the Polish People's Republic and just as treacherous. Perhaps you'd like to quote something else I wrote?"

"Gladly," said the venal Tadzio, cheering up. "I have just the right quotation."

I raised my fist to strike him. He cowered and broke into tears. "I really do admire your prose. One thing has nothing to do with the other. I'm fascinated by your work. You've influenced my poetry. The head of my department even rebuked me for being influenced by your work. I love you. I can't live without you."

The drunks were giving us hostile looks. To an outsider it might have appeared that I was abusing a minor.

"Get up, you provincial dink. Get out of my sight."

He rose from the sidewalk, rubbing his nose and eyes.

"Today has been a shock for me," he said weepily. "You should forgive me. I'm beginning a new life. After lunch I quit my job in the department. Now I'm just the same sort of person you are."

I made a fist and took a step toward him, but he covered himself with his dirty hands.

"Hey, you jerk, leave the kid alone!" shouted a demonstrator, picking up a stick from one of the banners.

"All right," I said, "give me the can and get going."

"I'm going to carry it for you," sobbed Tadzio.

I squinted over at the drunks, who had woken up and were rising shakily to their feet.

"It's so good that I met you. You were a breakthrough for me. In my life and my work. You have saved a human being. Could there be anything more important in the whole world?"

"Shut your mouth and let's get out of here, or else there might be trouble with them," I snarled.

I set off toward Nowy Swiat, the forty-year-old Tadzio with me. Sobering up with great difficulty, the demonstrators followed us with suspicious, hostile eyes.

"So many years wasted," lamented Tadzio from behind me. "Yes, I was a sinner. I won't deny it. But don't the greats sin too, these days? Please have a look at this." He caught my hand and pulled me over to a haberdashery store's display window.

There was an out-of-focus TV inside among the slogans. But the set wasn't so bad that we couldn't view the latest developments at the congress. Now, the presidents of the various art unions were paying their respects to both the Secretaries. The president of the visual artists' union, dressed in a nineteenth-century smock and enormous velvet beret, was holding a palette and brush in one hand. A second president, wearing a white blouse, was holding an enormous goose quill and a roll of paper. A third, in a Roman toga, was holding a Greek mask in front of his face. A fourth, with a wreath on his brow, was plucking a lyre. But one of them was in civilian clothes and carried no symbolic props, though he still knelt on one knee before the two Secretaries. This civilian president intrigued me and I had a sudden desire to learn, at any cost, whom he represented. Tadzio would know, of course, but it would be disgusting to ask him.

"You see. How can they do it? They have everything. Money, beautiful women, fame at home and abroad, but they are kneeling down before those blockheads. So what do you expect from me?"

"Tadzio, you're loathsome," I sighed.

"But is that my fault? I'd prefer to look like you. But what can I do if God had a different idea."

Not knowing what to answer, I just cleared my throat.

"Give me the gas can back," I said finally.

"I'll kill myself."

"You can go right after me if you like, but give me the gas can back."

"Do you despise me?"

I rushed at him, but he jumped nimbly out of the way.

"Give me the can, you son-of-a-bitch!"

Suddenly he took offense and handed me the can, the handle damp with his repulsive sweat.

"You think I don't know anything," he said in an ambiguous tone.

There was no one out in front of the Paradyz. The Arabs were already inside pawing our girls to the tune of Eastern melodies. I stopped in front of the plate-glass door, whose panes had all been knocked out. A piece of cardboard marked ALL TABLES TAKEN was jiggling in the late-afternoon breeze.

"You know," the forty-year-old Tadzio said conciliatorily, "all an Arab has to do is touch a white woman's leg and he comes off."

"Now what kind of filth are you going to start telling me," I yelled.

"It's the truth, the real truth. You should ask the ladies."

I started off toward the traffic circle. The Party building reposed sleepily on a large stone platform. An old tired beast going blind. A slight chill ran down my back because I had again remembered the Secret Banquet For The Highest-Ruling Officials, known by the cryptonym SBFTHRO. Would my bottle buddies have had time to wipe out all traces of us? And my bill. I had forgotten to settle up for the ragout. Tough. It would probably just get lost in the general chaos.

An empty tram car was napping at the traffic circle. The passengers had all surrounded the driver, who was standing beside his vehicle and defending himself against his impor-tuning passengers. "I told you I'm not going and that means I'm not going."

"But what's the problem, you wonderful person, you?"

"I just don't feel like it and that's that. I'm going home."

"But, sir, your route is even shorter now. Just as far as the Poniatowski Bridge, which collapsed."

"Short or long, I don't give a shit."

"Jesus, man, be human about it."

"I don't want to, and I'm not going to make any exceptions. Out of my way, please."

"My good man, I'm bringing dinner to my sick mother."

"What does that have to do with me?"

"I have a quarter of a headcheese. Would you like it?"

"Out of the way. You're bothering me. Everybody's bother-ing me. I'm being straight with you. Let me through."

"We beseech you, act like a Pole."

"Sure, like a Pole, you mean, and join the Soviet Union?" asked the driver.

Suddenly they all fell silent. Someone began coughing, someone else cleared his throat. A child started crying.

"Oh, land's sakes, all right," sighed the driver. "I'm a soft-hearted guy. I'll take you, but only to Narutowicz Square, and that's final. All Poles aboard."

We hopped briskly into the dilapidated interior of the tram car. I could hear Tadzio panting behind me. The tram's bell rang furiously and the car pulled clattering away beneath the setting sun.

"And what's more, you must be confusing me with another writer, you cabbagehead," I snapped, looking out the dust-caked window.

"Come now, I know perfectly well who you are. You're Ryszard Szmidt, right?"

I wanted to kick his ass, kick him out of my sight. "You were quoting me, you idiot."

"Those were your lines. But I thought they were Ryszard's."

I turned around. That face, mustacheless, youngish, wrinkled, was smiling at me with a certain familiar patronizing expression.

"Don't worry. Those are your golden thoughts and I know who you are."

"You can quote whoever you want to, I couldn't care less."

"Some of that stuff is good, even though your luck didn't last you the whole way. I'll avenge you when I get the Nobel Prize."

I groaned softly and went back to the window. Tadzio was squatting on a heating pipe and took the gas can tenderly from my hands. He held it between his knees, and, staring straight ahead with a merry look, winked knowingly to me.

Then I felt someone touch my right leg delicately. Pikush, of course. He looked up devotedly at me and wagged his pathetic stump of a tail.

"Pikush, where did you disappear to this time?"

He was digging his fringe-like paws into my pants and squealing with great love, happy that his unexpected appearance had pleased me.

"Dog, we'll take you to your friends by the Square of the Saviour. They still remember you after all these years. They love animals. And people, too."

Pikush was happy and turned crazy cartwheels around his tail, which did not in fact really exist. We were passing the traffic circle at the intersection of Marszalkowska Street and Aleje. Now the stone mountain of the Palace of Culture was reflected in display windows and apartment windows. Army searchlights were flashing in the sky. Between them a sign made of plastic washtubs for bathing babies, illuminated from below, read: WE HAVE BUILT SOCIALISM! But the washtubs, rejected as unfit for export, were cracked here and there, revealing the light bulbs, most of which had already burned out.

I felt some compulsion to turn around and glance back at what was soon to be my gigantic grave marker decorated with what used to be the seal of Poland and with the seal of the

Soviet state. I even wondered if our eagle would be enclosed in heraldic sheaves of grain tied with a band which read PROLE-TARIANS OF ALL COUNTRIES, UNITE. But I didn't turn around, I was paralyzed by some superstitiousness or some magical counterforce. I'll look back at that building when I have a need to. I'll look at it tonight at eight o'clock, if I look at it at all.

Behind me, above the clanking of the tram, I could hear the loudspeakers roaring, the bands fading. The cadaverous pale-purple reflections of arc lights played over my arms. Pikush slept by my foot.

We went past Central Station, which was surrounded by a lake of broken glass, the last of the panes knocked out by the artillery salute. The setting sun was reflected in the broken glass. We had just passed the blood-red flood around the dark, looming bunker of the train station when our tram car began to jerk as if it were trying to tear itself loose; its iron joints began to vibrate, and then it grew still and coasted for about a hundred yards like a boat coming in to shore. Finally, it came to a stop, lurched forward, lurched backward, and died.

The passengers ran to the front car, where the driver was emerging shakily from his seat.

"But you promised to take us to Narutowicz Square."

"I promised and I'm a man of my word. But the electricity's out. This is driving me crazy," he said, fanning himself with a brass crank that he had taken from the control panel.

"He's lying! He just doesn't feel like driving again. And I'm bringing my sick mother dinner," a woman shouted.

"Then here, please," said the driver, with a bow, suppressing a burp, "take the crank and drive the tram yourself."

A few people were now ferreting around his cabin. "He's telling the truth. There's no juice," they shouted.

Curses rang out, but were not particularly energetic. The little crowd began to disperse into the adjoining streets. The driver sat down on the front bumper, raised his bluish face to the sun, and closed his eyes in relief.

"Let's go on foot, you two," I said decisively.

Pikush went out ahead, I was in the middle, and Tadzio and the gas can were bringing up the rear. We came out onto Oczki Street, which had turned red in the sunset. I knew that the city morgue and autopsy rooms were concealed behind that prison-like wall. Just then we heard sirens howling hysterically behind us. An ambulance with a broken signal light was racing down the middle of the road. Because his light was dead, the driver was leaning full force on the horn. The ambulance passed us, tearing bits of dead leaves from the asphalt, and then suddenly, violently, it slammed on its brakes. It skidded a little toward the curb, but the driver was in control and a second later he had it in reverse. The rear doors opened and Kobialka looked out, happy as a lark.

"See my uniform," he said, indicating his impeccably clean straitjacket. But he was able to move his hands a little because he had used his political connections to have them bound loosely behind his back. "I had to wait for the ambulance. It had been in an accident. But now, thank God, everything's all set. We're on our way to Tworki. Can I give you a lift?"

"Thanks anyhow, neighbor," I said cordially. "We don't have far to go. We're almost there."

"What's happening in the city?"

"Same as before. We're still celebrating."

"We'll be catching up with the West any day now. I mean, they'll be catching up with us. That'll be better. Things will be better then."

"And why do you think that might be better?"

"Because we'll all be starting again from scratch. I mean, we'll be bouncing up off the bottom, as a matter of fact, the world will be bouncing off the absolute bottom, off a sort of cosmic floor. You must forgive me, neighbor, but I am still an optimist. I have a free and independent house of my own," he said, and struck the ambulance roof euphorically with the palm of his hand. The driver was about to pull away, but Kobialka commanded him in a thundering voice: "Stop! Stop! One more minute. I would shake your hand, dear neighbor, but as you can see I'm not suitably dressed for it."

"I wish you good health."

"I am healthy. We should all be wished luck for the next round, for the coming epoch, the next world. Remember that I always loved all of you!" He noticed Pikush, who was peering curiously at the ambulance. "And I loved your animals, too! Love was my undoing! What am I saying, it was love that made me free! Long live the free and independent Polish Soviet Republic!"

And he began tapping out some sort of African drumbeat on the corroded roof of the ambulance from the state psychiatric hospital. He had probably decided to make that last statement because Zenek was looking out the side window and listening closely to what he was saying.

The ambulance pulled rakishly away, its wheels screeching on the street strewn with maple leaves, and headed toward Grojecka Street.

"You've just seen a happy man, you boob," I said to Tadzio Skorko. "Give me the gas can."

"What for?"

"I'll be needing it. I'm going into this hospital. Wait out here for me."

"Take care of yourself, please, I beg you. I love you, too, like a father."

I was about to kick him, but he jumped alertly to one side.

"I'll avenge you. The world will hear of us yet."

He fumbled in his pocket, trying to pull out a packet of some sort.

"I've started writing prose. I've got three chapters here. The world has never seen prose like this."

I started resignedly toward the entrance to the hospital. A few patients were lying drunk on the grass-covered stairs. I was about to warn them about pneumonia, but they looked up hostilely at me, the way sick people look at those who still have their health.

"The Antichrist," I said. "The Antichrist, in the form of a virus. It's an epidemic. Like flu. Or cholera. An epidemic from the depths of the universe."

I went down a corridor lit by small bulbs which kept flashing on and off. The hospital was generating its own electricity. Half-drunk patients were wandering about in dark recesses near the corridor. Those who were less seriously ill were taking care of the seriously ill, but without much enthusiasm. There hadn't been any attendants or nurses in our hospitals for a long time now. They'd gone out of style.

Finally, I caught sight of the glass wall of the intensive-care unit. There were three chairs or beds, or more precisely, there were three rickety catafalques on which three inert bodies were lying in their death throes. The door had not been closed tight and so it was no problem to enter the greenish room, which was full of clock ticks, hisses, and clanks. Small lights were blinking different colors, water was dripping from a faucet, and the air was thick with the smell of carbolic acid or perhaps valerian.

I examined the three bloodless faces. The one in the middle with the graying hair and the slightly Negroid features could have been Hubert. He was in a tangle of tubes and wires, and there was a thick, corrugated tube down his throat. Jerking wildly, shaken by the pulsations of the machines, he looked up at me with his one blind eye. He kept baring his teeth in an odd sort of way, but he must have been doing that for some time already because a yellow foam had already collected at the corners of his gray lips. He looked at me with his blind eye and did not say a word, for he could no longer speak. It suddenly occurred to me that there was a stink of death in there, in that glass room that hadn't been cleaned for a week, that greenish purgatory reeking of corpses.

I could not bear his gaze, I mean I couldn't stand that blank eye which pierced me with its pale-green, phosphorescent light. So I knelt down at the end of the bed with Hubert's waxy feet in front of me. His feet, covered by dead skin, were bony and veiny, as if they'd been boiled in formaldehyde.

"And so, Hubert," I said softly. "You drove yourself through this world for quite a long time. You drove yourself through this city of ours, this dying microcosm in the middle of Europe. But what drove you, what force, what faith?"

Someone sighed moaningly. I raised my head, but it was only one of the machines, an artificial lung, an artificial kidney, or an artificial heart; one of the artificial human organs had changed its rhythm as if one hand had grown tired.

"Well, and so, what do you say, you monk in this epoch of decline, you Savonarola at the end of the world. You didn't have much of a life, you had a tough life, fate wasn't kind to you. You were always in the opposition, and they say you were always changing your views. You stifled your own human impulses, or perhaps it was your philistine habits, and you condemned the bourgeois and the philistine in those you loved. Few people loved you, many hated you. You were loved carelessly but hated with full intensity. What sort of moral logic guided your actions, my pale, stiff, inhuman pang of conscience?"

Then Pikush, who had found his way to me there by paths known only to him, emerged from the darkness. His ears pricked up, he began sniffing the tall, misshapen ends of the beds, the pails, the bits of old bandages. The machines wheezed, their weak lights blinking at regular intervals.

"When you started publishing in the émigré press and in the underground at home, the government's artistic salons chuckled and sneered that you were sucking up to the free West and trying to build a literary career on politics. When the students started copying your work on duplicating machines at night, when the old cranks began knocking out copies on their typewriters, when your works, your desperate thoughts, and your hopeless hopes began to circulate through the country in editions of a few dozen copies, your colleagues, your faithful friends, keepers of Poland's flame, vestal virgins of Poland's watchfires, they stepped up their ambiguous but profitable flirtation with our brainless regime. They rose to the top here in money and recognition, they took off abroad, availing themselves of the regime's support, diplomacy, money, the great machinery of the state. They winked significantly at people in the free world to say that they represented the moral strength of their oppressed country, that they both created and directed that moral force. But neither the one nor the other spared you any kicks, you poor beggar with your medieval upbringing. Now you're pulling the lever which brings down the curtain of your fate. Did anyone else but me grow more beautiful in our dungeons? Did anyone else fail to sleep through the night tormented by his conscience besides me? Did anyone leap into the fire in order to sin and offend the Lord God besides me?"

Pikush was sitting in the middle of the room. He wasn't looking at me, he was looking at the people dying. He raised his head and stared with bead-like eyes up at the greenish tile ceiling, the greenish color of hopeless hopes.

"You're doing the right thing in dying, you old blackmailer. You'll slip away like a plumber who failed to fix the faucet. The world's evened out. There are no good or evil people. There is only a great, unfathomable mob trampling itself underfoot. The life-giving sources of the old morality have dried up and vanished in the sands of oblivion. There's no other source to draw from, no place to refresh oneself. There is no example, no inspiration. It is night. A night of indifference, apathy, chaos."

There was a desk calendar on the table beside a broken lamp. The pages were yellow, dog-eared, and had been written on in someone's hand. It showed the date to be July 22, 1979, another date among all the many dates besieging us.

"You're dying too soon, Hubert. All of them, the lackeys of time or history, they're all waiting for your head. They demand that you abase yourself before them and acknowledge them to be right. They want to hang your scalp on their chest like yet another medal. But perhaps you already have abased yourself? Could you be paying for your capitulation with your life?"

Hubert's plaster-white legs trembled slightly. The edges of

the sheet slipped away, revealing his hairy, dead calves. A door slammed somewhere, but Pikush did not change position in the middle of the room. His head twisted, he was looking up at the ceiling or at something above the ceiling.

"Hubert, we were so distant and so close. It'll be bad for me without you here on earth. And it'll be bad for you in the next world without me. It's time to say farewell for a short while, the twinkling of an eye, God's dead eye."

I stood up and walked to the head of the bed. The machines were not shaking that gray, grizzled head whose face was lined with pain or expectation. I leaned over and touched his cold, wet forehead with my lips. I didn't feel like doing it, but I knew I was supposed to.

Then Pikush began to howl. He was howling at those green tiles of hope as if they were the moon. And for some reason I was afraid to command him to stop howling. And so it was with a heavy heart that I listened to Pikush's dirge, Pikush who had vanished and then unexpectedly turned up again.

Someone was staggering down the corridor. It was a young doctor in a none-too-fresh smock. We had obviously torn him away from sleep, because he was yawning so heartily that his jawbones were cracking. "Who let you in here? And with a dog no less?" He reeked of pharmaceutical alcohol. "This is an intensive-care unit."

"Do you see that calendar?" I asked.

"I see it," he replied in surprise.

"Is that today's date?"

"How should I know? You have to leave this area."

"I came here to say farewell to my colleague. He was a prophet. He wanted to lead us out of the house of bondage."

"Which one is he?"

"The one in the middle."

"Aha. To be frank with you, those machines only create a semblance of life. He's already far away. You understand."

"No, he wasn't a prophet. He may have been an honest man, he may have been a maniac. He was a modest pang of conscience, or maybe the phantom of conscience which is sometimes to be seen in our eyes. Just a tattered piece of modern life. Oh, what a headache I've got."

"Me, too," said the doctor in consolation. "But that's fair, because what would happen if we didn't get hangovers from drinking? There has to be some justice, doesn't there?"

"Yes, in the end, somewhere at the end we can't see, there has to be some justice."

"I won't make him suffer, even though he can't feel any more pain." The young doctor indicated Hubert's ruined body. "I'll unplug him at seven o'clock."

Pikush had quieted down a bit. He was whining heartbreakingly now, looking over at us.

"Could you unplug him at eight o'clock?"

The doctor stroked Hubert's stiff legs and looked me soberly in the eye. "You're still hoping?"

"No. But it's very important to me that it happen at eight o'clock."

"It's a waste of the machinery."

"Please, I'm asking you. It's not a big favor. Maybe fate will even reward you for it."

"You said eight o'clock?"

"Yes. On the dot."

"All right then, I'll set my alarm. But please go now. The dog will be leaving fleas here, I'm sure of that."

He hustled us out into the corridor, slammed the door, and then disappeared into his little hole. I took another look through the glass smudged with fingerprints as at a police station, one last look at those catafalque-chairs lit by the faint glow of the machine's little signal lights.

"I had so much to say to you. I thought it would be about life, but it was only about me. About me as I am in you. Or rather about you as you are in me. But how to disentangle my own so to speak hormone-based despairs and frustrations from those which are general and universal ones and which my time, my little bit of history, has engrained in me? I beg for justice, but how many times was I myself just? I cry out for moral order, but for how many years have I been trampling it myself?"

I waved. Someone screamed in the depths of the hospital. The red light of sunset filled the crevices of the corridor.

"I'm repeating myself. You know all that. And it bores me now, too. I'm sorry."

I took a few steps down the corridor and then stopped, stricken by a dark thought. "I will deprive you of a glorious funeral, I, your brother by chance. Forgive me."

Pikush led the way unerringly, already knowing it by heart. We walked through several corridors packed with the beds of people seriously ill and then came out into the dingy hall.

"And the gas?" I asked myself.

"Here," I heard its liquid voice gurgle in the light-blue can.

My testament. My lavish legacy to those I loved. A hopeless historical epoch. No, not an epoch. A moment, a second. Of which there had already been so many. There was life before us, there will be life after us. Sometimes better, sometimes worse. Maybe tomorrow would be a better day. All that's needed is one imperceptible shock, one slight tap on the finely wrought universe of contemporary psychology, the gigantic bank of the collective sensibility. Epidemics of low self-esteem, universal depression, a total lack of faith, such things come suddenly and disappear suddenly as if swept away by some life-giving solar wind. We weren't that lucky, we didn't end up at a point like that in the infinite extension of time or existence.

I have the body of an animal, but my aspirations are divine. Our hormones have outstripped the barriers that biology and the laws of the animal world had erected for them. Our hormones produce enzymes, hungers that cannot be satisfied, dreams that cannot be realized, longings that cannot be suppressed. And I am in the very thick of it, with a great empty head, a bulging, bloodless heart, my soul diluted by antimatter.

I am tired of myself and my times. I am tired of limitations and powerlessness, tired of not understanding, I who am the statistical average in the Great Accounting.

What can I bequeath to the living, apart from my unpaid debts? Long, intellectual testaments go to the archives, nobody reads them through. Celestial moral appeals are turned into lyrics for popular songs. And so my sensitivity will slip away, taken over by all those sad sacks, failures, goofs. I'd like to whisper some good advice in their ears, I'd like to give them an encouraging word and stiffen their resistance to fate.

Listen, my wretched brothers. Come closer and listen closely, because I'm going to speak of shameful things again. Better that those things never existed, but they do. Come here, you screw-ups in nightly anguish over your wives and lovers. I have read your letters in the sexual advice columns. You complain that your wives and mistresses aren't satisfied, that they complain and ridicule you. Flushed with terrible male shame, you want to know how to prolong it, control it, bring things to a happy conclusion.

But my quick, my lightning-quick little rabbits, would you like to be impressively masculine, full of character and success, at least in the still of the night? Then you should ask me, a dirty old man, for advice. Don't look for any help from those sexologists whose wives are fucked left and right by their colleagues and friends.

First of all, I recommend stubbornness and perseverance. In this competition there are no strong men, only the persistent and the hardworking. You have to keep at it any time you can, morning and afternoon, evening and daybreak, and then, one moment, fate will reward your patience lavishly. On this field, this battlefield, nothing succeeds like success. The first victory will create a chain of other victories.

Here, as in every act, the apprentice has to be sincerely humble. A humble person who is not counting on easy success and is prepared for defeats in the short run has more of a chance than the cocky, energetic types greedy for instant glory.

The humble and the hardworking have raised the difficult art of love to great heights.

A fine time for taking the risk is when you have a hangover, one that grows gentler and milder as the evening passes. At such moments, which are laced with sluggish, metaphysical dread, many people who are by nature mediocre have achieved great results. Vodka is capricious and unpredictable. The hangover is benign, good-natured, stimulating.

This act differs from others in that it tolerates no show, no swagger, no common chutzpah. One may not begin it in order to show off, to brag or to make an impression. If you can resist, don't even start. If you can avoid conflict, avoid it. Only the duels which are inevitable and blessed by the heavens are crowned with success.

I would like to quote my friend Zdzislaw M.'s prescription here. His is a scientifically proven method and a nearly fool-proof one. Zdzislaw gave the following advice to a friend, an actor well known for his haste in these matters: "To control the situation you have to occupy your mind with something else, some abstract thoughts. Reciting some text from memory, for example, works quite well. That wouldn't be hard for you as an actor. What relatively long text could you recite quietly to yourself?" "How about Pan Tadeusz?" asked the actor timidly. "Very good," praised Zdzislaw. "Twelve long chapters. A good length." They ran into each other a week later. "Well, and so?" asked Zdzislaw. "It was working perfectly, but I forgot a word after the line 'and the clover burns like a blushing maiden's glow,' and then I couldn't remember the rest," said the actor. "It was a disaster."

So, first of all we must train the memory.

And now the approach. The horizon looked like a blast furnace. Tomorrow would be windy, there might even be a hurricane. Tomorrow was for the living.

"I'm repeating myself," I whispered. "I'm repeating myself

because the situation is repeating itself. The same situation every day."

"Are you talking to yourself?" said a voice.

I turned toward Aleje, where, to the north, dark clouds were engraved on the horizon, and saw Sacher and his inseparable briefcase. The beginning of twilight had extinguished the fanatical gleam in the old man's eye.

"I have fewer and fewer friendly people to talk to all the time."

"That's how it goes. Are you going in or coming out?"

"Coming out."

"Let's go in for a minute. A friend of mine from the old days is in there, an old revolutionary, an old resister. He should be in a government clinic but he slipped in here among the common people and now, here, he is happy at last."

"It seems to me," I said with a sneer, "that his children used their pull to shunt him off on a long, arduous agony."

"You know, he's not in bad shape. Ha-ha, he's like a bull. But maybe we could step into the lobby, it's gotten a little windy. I can see that you took my advice about going for a walk around the city."

He pulled me back into that dismal interior full of glass kiosks, half-collapsed partitions, and a hodgepodge of out-of-date slogans.

He drew me confidentially over to him by a button on my jacket and looked me intently in the eye. "Was it you who threw me out of the Party?"

"No. It was you who threw me and my colleagues out of the Party."

"That could be. I've been getting mixed up lately," he said in a troubled voice. "But I have a sort of instinctive confidence in you. You know," he said, looking around suspiciously, "I'm writing my memoirs. I carry them around with me all the time, in this briefcase, because I'm being followed everywhere, out shopping, on my walks, visiting friends. I'm afraid to leave it at home. They might break in and destroy the manuscript. Have you heard of cases like this?"

"Everybody's writing and nobody's reading."

"What? I didn't hear you." He put his hand to his ear, from which tufts of gray hair protruded.

"Maybe you should thank God that somebody's interested in reading it. That someone's so eager to see an unfinished manuscript. The passion to read, you know, that's all it is."

"You know, I need someone who is devoted to me through thick and thin. To guard this manuscript. That's what I was thinking . . . that's what I was thinking at dinner . . ."

"There are total states, soccer has become the total game, the whole world is already totalized. Why shouldn't there be a total literature, too?"

"How about you, young man? You could safeguard the truth, the one, the only truth about our times. Now I'm writing a chapter about God. The God who is despised by the Party. A study of the rivalry between the two deities. A vivisection of totalitarian envy and hatred."

"A prose which uses all the methods, the admissible and the inadmissible. Reaching out beyond the paper, making its point with a bloody denouement in life. Death in a manuscript is dead but, in life, death is alive, shocking, real. Well, old man, what kind of prose do you write? You've feasted your eyes on the ultimate. There are no sunrises and sunsets there, no couples making eyes at each other, no old women sobbing. Only falling heads. Proud, foolish, cowardly, saintly heads flying from the executioner's block. Show me your prose, old man, let's see what you're carrying around in the bulging briefcase."

"Get out of there!" He grabbed the briefcase, tearing it out of my hands. "You're still sick. Back to the hospital. March!"

"One minute, one minute. I'm a seeker of truth. I saunter around looking for the truth. Open your briefcase, which used to carry death sentences. One whiff and I'll know what sort of truth you have there."

"Why are you always obsessing about death? What do you know about it, you little shit-ass? I was in the Politburo for ten years and I could feel the rope closing around my neck. Death is my sister. It was only in my old age that it got off my back and moved to one side where it's waiting for me."

"I've got a headache. Last night I understood everything for a moment. Everything from start to finish. Take a look at the sky. It's going to be a starry night. It can wait. But can that revelation happen again, that shocking flash when you understand everything in all its complex simplicity, all its simple complexity?"

"I don't know. The end of the world's coming for me."

"Excuse me, but it's my end of the world that's coming."

"I have to go. A friend's waiting for me. I'm going to read him the first chapter. His Genesis and mine. I'll put him to sleep with my reminiscences before they take the truth away from me. You say that it was me who taught them how to do that? No, you're mistaken there."

"The Antichrist. Nothing permeated with nothing makes evil. Damnit, what are those clouds there. God is closing the damper, the lid. He's leaving us all alone with the Antichrist, do you understand?"

"I have no time. I mean, I have very little time now. Good-bye, goodbye." And he walked away with a jerky, crooked gait into the depths of the dark corridor where the drunken patients were singing indecent songs.

A bit startled, Pikush looked up expectantly at me. It was getting dark. Mighty, ink-black clouds, the likes of which hadn't been seen for ages, were massing in the north.

"Let's go, dog." I shook my gas can, my traveling bag.

Pikush barked and set off into the darkness. But we didn't get very far. Several hunched figures walking carefully came out of Starynkiewicz Square.

"Hands up!" ordered one of them, and poked me in the side with his sawed-off rifle. I noticed that the others had boy scout knives strapped to their fashionable woven belts. I raised my hands, including the right one, which was weighed down with the gas can.

The leader searched my pockets and immediately took all my cash.

"And where's your Party card?" he asked menacingly.

"I don't belong to the Party."

"He doesn't belong to the Party," repeated the leader with a jeer in his voice. He was about to hit me with his rifle butt again, but I dodged and it hit one of his own men.

"And who are you, if I may ask?" I asked.

"We're urban guerrillas. You never heard of them?"

"I guess I have. But in Poland?"

"Yes, in Poland. Now you've heard. What's that you got there in the can?"

"Gas."

"We'll check that in a minute. Please go over there, to the pissoir."

"But it hasn't been open since the tenth Party congress."

"No problem."

We walked down the steps, which were buried under trash. Naturally the door had been nailed shut with boards, which someone had conscientiously smashed in. One of the guerrillas switched on a flashlight, another opened the airtight spigot on the gas can.

"It's gas. Thinner," he confirmed glumly.

Then the leader flashed the beam of light in my eyes. "What do you need the gas for?"

"To pour on myself so I can set myself on fire."

Disconcerted, he switched off the flashlight.

"Are you nuts?"

"Come on, brothers we can go up in flames together. I've got some good Swedish matches."

I grabbed the leader by his cloak. He tried to tear free of my hands, but I was holding on too tightly.

"Help!" he shouted. "He's a nut!"

"Be so kind as to give me the gas can, boys. One of you is nice and fat, perfect for burning."

But by then all I could hear was the sound of their feet disappearing in the underbrush. My victim had turned tail, too, and slipped away, the sly dog. But their flashlight, abandoned on the steps, was shining straight into the darkening sky. I found the gas can and picked up the flashlight, which might come in handy later on. I looked through my pockets. They had taken even the scrap of *Trybuna Ludu* which I'd stolen that morning.

"Well, Pikush, you just stood there gaping and didn't defend your master."

Ashamed of himself, he hopped barking into the bushes.

"Forget it. Maybe they meant well. Maybe they're crawling around on all fours the best they know how. The Antichrist or a divine visitation, I don't know what it was. I'd just like to lie down and go to sleep. Forever."

Then Tadzio Skorko emerged from the darkness, but this time, for some reason, without any quotations.

"So what do you say, you drag-ass?" I asked.

"They have a hideout in the city dump." He indicated the black heaps out past Starynkiewicz Square. "Common punks. Give me the gas can. You're tired."

"And do you have a copy of what you wrote to your department, asshole? Do you have some sort of receipt for your resignation?"

"Of course."

"Show it to me."

He turned and began shooing away some invisible mosquito.

"Don't be ashamed. Show me."

"I can't."

"You mean you didn't resign?"

"I didn't," he admitted shamelessly. "But I will tomorrow."

"Do you see what you're like, Tadzio. And I was about to start trusting you."

"But today's a holiday. The staff has the day off. I'll resign tomorrow. I swear to God."

"That means you're still following me as part of your job."

"Not at all. This is entirely private. I'm here as a fan of your prose. Of your final story. Your absolute novella."

A flock of some sort of forest birds flew past in a panic. More and more animals were being attracted to the cities, which were themselves turning into wilderness.

"I'm young," said Tadzio softly. "I have lots of strength and I've got your experience behind me. I won't make the same mistakes you did. I'll buy a ream of paper and leave for Stargard tomorrow. In a year I'll be famous. I'll finish your work."

"You're a horrible freak. Just my luck."

"I am a horrible freak," he admitted matter-of-factly. "That's my number. You were one step away from being a freak yourself, but God's hand faltered out of pity. You took care of the rest. You created your own freakishness by playing the role of aesthete all your life. But I'll avenge you. I'll avenge us both."

"Who the hell knows. Maybe I really was full of fear. I'm afraid now. I'm afraid of being a fool, afraid of contempt. Only my pride has held up."

"I'm proud, too," said Tadzio calmly. "Maybe even prouder than you are. And that's why I allow you all those tasteless insults. Your pride will remain forever unsatisfied, but I feed mine."

I flashed the light on him. He stood holding the gas can straight and with dignity. The light did not make him blink an eye. A moment later I thought, without quite knowing why, that he was probably right. Right in his own inscrutable way. Even Pikush was staring up at him with his green, phosphorescent eyes.

I was completely lost. I had a terrible headache, it felt as if someone were breaking my neck. My head ached, that was the best thing it could do in a situation like this. Up above us a window opened and a young woman poured something splashing down onto the sidewalk. For a moment her long hair turned red, framed by the gray-white wood of the window. But it was not Nadezhda, and that young woman did not have red hair. An oil lamp with a red shade gave off a reddish glow by the window just as in the old days when this lousy world of mine was first being born.

I started toward the Aleje, Pikush and Tadzio behind me. There were garden plots on the other side of the street where there had once been a parking lot. The parking lot had been built toward the end of the seventies on top of a gigantic slab which covered the tunnel to Central Station. The craze for cars had died down, the parking lot was eliminated, and privileged people began to haul in truckloads of garden soil to cover the cement slab. Then they began planting fruit trees, tomatoes, and cabbages. Although vegetables grew excellently on that flat slab and helped compensate for the state's green vegetable shortage, the apple, pear, and plum trees proved resistant to an equal degree and refused to grow in the middle of the city which had surrendered them the space. Of course they grew, but they did so reluctantly, without real feeling, and none of the trees exceeded a meter and a half in height. And so the owners of the garden plots had to work on them in a permanent squat in order to avoid the intrusive eyes of gawkers. And no doubt that was why that little part of town had been christened Squatville.

A police jeep with one headlight out was zigzagging toward us from near the Old Station. It stopped by us. A half-drunk policeman leaned out. "Can we give you a lift? Won't cost you much."

There was someone lying inertly behind him in the darkness of the cab lit by the faint gauges on the dashboard.

"I don't have any money. I was robbed by hooligans."

"You shouldn't be hanging around on side streets. I'll give you a lift, you can owe it to me."

"Thanks anyway, I don't have far to go. I'm just going to the Palace of Culture for a little fun."

The policeman stiffened at once. He looked me over from

head to toe. But then George's half-conscious face appeared from behind the policeman's back.

"Grab him," wheezed George. "He wants to burn down the city. He's the Antichrist."

The policeman put his arm around George and began pushing him back into the interior of the jeep.

"Easy, Colonel. Don't raise your head or you'll be sick again."

"Scum! I'll have you rotting in jail tomorrow! Hands at your sides! Attention!" said George, mixing Polish and Russian.

The driver, who had not said a word so far, turned around and punched the colonel in the head.

"Look, now the son-of-a-bitch is a linguist," he said, and started the motor.

The policeman who had been talking to me broke into laughter and brought two fingers to the brim of his cap in an amicable salute. "He overdid it, that George. But it's a holiday. Everybody's got the right, don't they?"

"Everybody's got the right to hit the bottle here," I agreed. "That's what life's about."

"That's what life can be about until you're dead."

The truck pulled away and turned off toward Mokotow. We walked in silence for a long while. Then Tadzio from Stargard spoke up: "You see how they kick people around. The entire ministry trembles before him."

"Today they're kicking him around, tomorrow it'll be his turn."

"He should have been promoted to general a long time ago, but he likes the bottle and a good brawl now and then. An artistic nature."

"Yes, there are too many artists."

"But it was artists who dreamed up this whole business. Do you know Stalin's little poem about spring?"

We crossed the broad and empty street. Foamy water from some cracked pipe raced down the shallow gutter. Pikush's interest had been caught by a broken fence. He was intently sniffing the rusted posts and lifting his leg every few seconds.

"I used to know that little poem by heart, but now I've forgotten it," said Tadzio, shifting the gas can from one hand to the other.

"You've started studying my prose."

"You don't know the half of it. It's amusing, you and Stalin make similar comparisons when describing nature."

I let the subject drop. The garden plots were sunk in darkness.

There were little bowers, bolted shut, among the Lilliputian trees. But there was a tiny flame flickering somewhere far within the garden. When we drew closer, we could see that a fire had been built in one of the garden plots and there were some hunched figures sitting around it. It was only then that we felt the cold evening wind. It was blowing out of the northwest, bearing the vast rubble of ominous clouds on its back.

One moment, let me think. I did, after all, have a childhood and a youth. A childhood and a yōuth on another planet. Whatever happened to that planet so much like the earth I was now on, and yet so completely different? If I exerted myself, I could still remember that world, as I had done before on so many sleepless nights without even knowing why I was remembering it all. An oil lamp, a fire's lazy smoke creeping across a meadow, the wind driving frightening clouds across a sky like you'd never see today. My nocturnal fear of the life which awaited me somewhere beyond the mountains and the forests, my sluggish little town that would exist forever—until the next war; the prayers of our forefathers, a rosary of fierce and lovely incantations, exalted and incomprehensible, a train whistling at just this time of day, my love for a girl from yet another planet because back then girls came from other, mysterious planets, a piercing animal longing for a woman's body where both a devil and a white-winged angel dwelled, my longing for an uncommon future, the poignant moods that came when wandering the forest, the unforgettable smell of gillyflower and free wild herbs, the storms which augured the end of the world every summer, the sadnesses, the sudden joys and gaieties, and my terror of the magical fair-haired moon, which wore a mask to make it look like a good-natured demon. Where is that planet of mine, locked in its atmosphere of premonitions, small joys, fragile hopes? Perhaps it is flying away like a pigeon among the distant, alien galaxies.

Why did I wear myself out for so many years? It wasn't only on work but on life's joys that I wore myself out. I wore myself out looking at the thrilling beauty of the sunrise and with love for the women I so desperately desired. I wore myself out taking transient successes from the hands of fate and praying to God in gratitude. I even wore myself out in my dreams when I tore myself away from the earth and sailed off to the far islands of the paradise promised us. But everyone else was wearing themselves out along with me, with the exception of those who don't ever wear themselves out. But in all that suffering, the most painful suffering of all was the consciousness that it was banal, had all been discovered a long time ago, and was known to all the generations past, all just a repeated series, stamped out by our genes. That the universe was filled to its edges with groans as alike as two notes, that those particular groans formed one great groan similar to the shrill parliament of the sparrows and that groan became an interstellar roar, the inaudible groan of the aging cosmos.

"Hey there," said someone behind the fence.

"Hey there," I answered.

"Why are you late?"

"I'm late?"

"You see, you forgot. Who's there with you?"

"A young poet and a dog."

"Come on in. We've been waiting."

We crawled through the fence, which had a good number of holes in it. Lucyna, wearing an old coat and a hat with feathers, was standing behind a three-foot-tall plum tree. She was dressed like a girl from twenty years ago.

"We're roasting our own garden potatoes. We're telling fortunes from the coals and we were thinking about Kazio, because today's our wedding anniversary."

"Yours and Kazio's?"

"That's right. You don't remember?"

I remembered that Kazio had died years ago. She took me by the hand and led me to the fire. We walked down a path narrow as a gangplank between garden plots no larger than a bird cage. The army searchlights by the Palace of Culture gave off a violet glow like a flash of light that had just died out forever. We walked past currant and raspberry bushes, and mounded beds of cauliflower, carrots, and garlic. We passed trees so small there wasn't room on them for even a single pigeon, trees which yielded miniature fruit, each one propped up by a small branch or dried stalk. We entered the warm circle of the fire. The wind tore sparks from the fire and bore them away into the gathering darkness.

"I really am in a hurry. What time is it?"

"The evening is young. It's getting close to seven. Look, do you recognize them?"

There were about fifteen women sitting around the fire. I thought I was dreaming, a dream where my conscience was confronting me with my sins. For they were all women I had loved and slept with, though that is better left unsaid. Some I had loved dramatically, passionately, others just because it had turned out that way, and yet others I had loved naïvely, apprehensively, charily, as if I were imbibing some insidious elixir. I slept with them in various ways and various places, all through Poland, and in some of Europe's out-of-the-way spots. Sometimes I succeeded, more often though I flopped, or rather, to this day I still don't know what really to say about them.

I regarded them with a sort of pious horror. They were all widows, divorcees, old ladies with stormy pasts. Thank God, none of them knew the whole truth about any other, that way I had a chance of avoiding being denounced and lynched. But why lynch me after so many years, years which might never have existed at all.

I bowed just enough to be seen but not to attract any attention.

"Sit down," said Ula, who once had nearly nippleless breasts, lovely breasts endowed with a personality of their own.

Exceedingly nervous, I sat down on a cold stone. Pikush was behind me, his tongue hanging out, panting with curiosity. Tadzio from Stargard was already paying Malgosia crude compliments, which she was delighted to receive.

"Here, this is for you," said Rena, with whom I'd had a not very successful something years ago. She handed me a glass filled to the brim. "You took so long it got cold."

"All right, to Kazio," said Lucyna, raising her glass.

"And to you," I said. I shouldn't have been drinking, but I drained my glass. They were already feeling pretty good. A few empty bottles had been tossed into the bushes. God, keep them from returning to the past, make them forgive my wanderings, the fireworks of untimely associations. The Palace of Culture shone like an indecent erection against the low, cloudy sky. The first test rocket burst over the Vistula.

"I saw you recently on the street," said Lidka, whom I had once dragged through all the hotels in the country.

"Yes, I sometimes go out walking."

Kasia's face emerged from the darkness. "Why are you hiding in the corner? Come over here, to us. We'll give you a nice, hot potato."

That Kasia, she had such an appetite she nearly ruined my health. She could never get enough. People, I really did love them, because I am sentimental and yielding by nature. There was nothing perverse about those gleams of shameful memory. It was life, just life.

"Maybe we should sing," proposed Ola, who had golden hair and wore a black fur coat. I shut my eyes so as not to remember any more.

"Don't be stupid. The police would be here in a minute. There's no private singing allowed today."

Fortunately, the wind was now blowing harder in that mini-

garden. It was shaking the trees as if they were real, tearing off
the leaves and carrying them away toward the faintly lit station.

"Do you have a girlfriend now?" asked Rysia. Better not to
remember her.

"Leave me alone," I said. "I have a terrible night ahead of
me."

She bent close to me and kissed me by the ear. "I was very
fond of you."

"I liked you, too."

"You say that pretty casually."

Tadzio saved me from trouble. He was drinking with
Lucyna and quickly becoming close. They were kissing each
other modestly, but I no longer believed in any of that.

"I dreamed of you sometimes," said one of the women.

"Oho, and what did you dream?" asked another.

"I won't tell. You'll have to guess."

"Girls, to your health." I raised my unfinished glass.

"He's trying to trick us. Fill his glass."

"It's true, he's the only man we've got here."

"How about me?" interrupted Tadzio insolently.

"You're too young. Be quiet."

"Me too young? I'll show you."

Hania, who had wanted to commit suicide over me, came
walking out of the darkness as mysterious and hysterical as
ever.

"Hello," she greeted me.

"Hello."

"Looks like you made quite a career. People whisper about
you in their offices when they're on coffee breaks."

"They might be mixing me up with somebody else."

"You always pretended to be modest."

"Leave me alone."

"You're afraid of your own memories. Go on, be brave, and
say it—get out of here, you old bag."

"You look marvelous, honest you do."

"You always were a pig, but I like you."

I felt hot. There didn't seem to be enough air, even though there was a strong wind blowing in tons of stimulating ozone.

"Maybe we should play a game to see who gets him?" suggested Kasia, a bit too loudly.

I peered into the darkness to check if anyone was eavesdropping on us. But the city was dozing, half cocked on a holiday drunk. When the wind died down, the weak, anemic voice of the bands entertaining tramps and sleepwalkers on the bandstands by the Vistula reached us by the fire. Suddenly a slab of sandstone went flying off the Palace of Culture, taking a wreath of light bulbs with it as it fell. That meant the weather was changing.

One of my ex-girlfriends tossed me a potato. I shifted the half-cooked potato covered with malignant-looking growths from one hand to the other. A Polish potato. My girlfriends weren't that well off.

"How about it? Shall we play a game to see who gets the only man here?"

"What game?"

"It's not worth the effort."

"Spin the bottle?"

"I quit."

"I'll take him without spinning the bottle."

"Forget it. Why should it be you?"

"So, let's play, then."

"Tadzio, go look for a bottle."

"Not on your life. I want to be in the game, too. I'm old enough."

"Don't make me laugh."

"Now where is that bottle?"

"Wait, we should ask him. Maybe he's already chosen one of us himself."

"He wouldn't. He's too timid and indecisive."

"And how come you know him so well?"

"A girlfriend of mine told me about him."

"Don't act stupid. Lucyna is crying."

"She's not crying, she's only got a cinder in her eye."

"Well, what about it, are we going to play or not? God, this is getting boring."

"I had a tough day, too."

"Life's getting harder all the time."

"I looked in the mirror this morning."

"Bad idea."

"Oh, where have all our boys gone."

"Those days are gone forever."

"Why? I still feel young."

"Genia has a thirty-year-old now."

"I don't have the strength for it anymore."

"Stop. Enough complaining. Let's drink, girls."

"To our youth."

"But we're still young."

"What are you blubbering about now, you silly thing?"

"And why are you crying?"

"My mascara's running."

"That's what I feel like, runny mascara."

"Are we going to play for him or not?"

"I protest. Are we supposed to play for the first person who comes wandering by? He walked right by us and didn't even stop. Stupid Lucyna ran after him."

"Kazio loved him."

"I loved him, too."

"That's strange, because I loved him, too."

"That's not possible. What are you talking about?"

"You mean you didn't? The whole city was gossiping about it."

"He's a nice boy."

"More of a swine, if you ask me."

"He'd finish with one and then start right up with another one."

"And he carried on with two at a time. To think that I cried over him like a fool."

"You know what, let's give him a beating."

"For the wrongs he did us."

A few of them had already risen shakily from the fire. Rena was breaking off a branch from a withered apple tree.

"What did I do that was so wrong?" I asked, rising from my stone. "After all, girls, I tried my best. I wanted to love like nobody else could. And maybe if it weren't for you, I'd be a Shakespeare by now. Yes, that's true, I squandered half my life on you."

"The nerve of him."

"Blaming us."

"That's the limit."

"The hell with him."

I pulled a torch-like firebrand from the flames. A little bit for show, a little for self-defense. The wind fluttered the meager flame like a scrap of silk.

"My dears, my darlings. We have the whole night ahead of us. Remember those springs, those summers, those autumns, even those winters. The mornings, the afternoons, the evenings. The silk sheets, the mossy forests, the little rooms off the kitchen. Weigh everything fairly, and only then should your kangaroo court pass sentence on me."

"But I hardly know him," said Rena after a moment.

"And I only know him by sight," added Rysia.

"He's more smoke than fire."

"Let's drink to ourselves, girls."

"To spring."

"To the new year."

"To tomorrow."

I laid the slightly charred stick aside. Carefully, step by step, I slipped away behind a low pear tree. And then, close to the ground as if I were in the forest hunting mushrooms, I stole to the other side of the garden. When the bushes and little trees blocked off the fire and my chilly girlfriends, I straightened back up and was free again.

"Hello," said someone softly.

"Hello."

She walked over to me, slender in the darkness, beautiful in the darkness, young in the darkness. She took my face in both her hands as if she wanted to see it better in the light which had suddenly broken through the clouds.

"I still love you," she whispered.

"Who are you?"

"An old girlfriend of yours."

I tried to recognize her voice, but she had been whispering, and a whisper is only the echo of a voice.

"I love you, too."

"You think of me sometimes, but now you don't know who I am."

She kissed me on the mouth with her young lips.

"I'm leaving, you know."

"I knew you would."

"I'm leaving for the other shore."

"What are you talking about? What's happened?"

"I have no other choice now."

"What does that mean?"

"That the time for jokes is over. My jokes."

"I had a bad dream about you. You brought me a little child. But it wasn't yours, or mine."

"I'll remember you forever."

"But you don't know who I am."

"I'll remember you as a young, mysterious Slavic madonna, dark as a summer dusk. Would you like that?"

"All right, remember me like that."

"And you think of me fondly, too."

"I'll always remember you."

"If I've given you anything."

"And had I been able to give you anything."

We kissed each other long and passionately, like two people who had been wronged. The wind was racing through the garden in autumnal fury, tearing the roofs off the bowers. It overturned what was left of the fence, and howled with an unreal voice down the tree-lined paths.

"Bye," she said.

"Bye."

And then she was gone. I stood there for a moment, collecting myself. My heart seemed to have tensed and swelled a little after that glass of ladies' rotgut. I headed northwest, cutting through a little gully in the stunted garden.

I was thinking about Nadezhda constantly. The image of Nadezhda kept looming before my eyes in this rubble heap of what had once been love or love affairs. Nadezhda with her red hair undone, her hand extended to me, her mouth open to cry out. I felt some terrible regret. What was it? What had happened in those final hours before my final night?

Nothing had happened. I had many witnesses, biology included, that nothing had happened. I had met a girl by chance that I might just as well not have met. A girl with red hair supposedly inherited from her grandfather, a plump girl with fair skin, broad lips, one eye light green and the other blue-violet, a girl who sometimes went wall-eyed and weighed around fifty-eight kilograms. Fifty-eight kilograms of water and lime, phosphorus, iron, as well as traces of other chemicals. Fifty-eight kilograms of water and a few pinches of the elements from her fellow countryman Mendeleev's table. Ten buckets of water brought to life by the great force of evolution or by our provincial God.

Nothing had happened. Driven by our animal instincts we had made love by chance in a secluded ruin, on a staircase fouled by drunkards. I had inserted my genital organ into hers. She had hung on her stiffened legs a millimeter above the burned floor, her inert feet brushing rhythmically against the brittle scraps of plaster strewn over the ground. The plaster had fallen behind her, a rapid chemical and electric reaction had taken place in her body, her own individual magnetic field had formed around her and synergized with my biocurrents. That was followed by a conventional spasm in the nervous system. Nothing had happened, nothing.

We had parted and gone our ways in a jungle which was withering and growing deserted before its end had come. Maybe we would never meet again and those non-meetings would be as meaningless as our making love, once or many times. Nothing had happened. Thank God, nothing had happened. That wasn't true. Something had happened. She had come to me out of a million chance events bypassing millions of alternatives, and I had come to her in the same way. Many stars had flared up and gone out while we were moving toward each other in this life. Many little universes had been born and had died out before we met in that house slated for demolition, that house where the paralyzed veteran of the great war or the coming wars which regularly shake our miniature globe was lying in bed. Nothing good had happened to me.

It had been fated. To happen at the last minute. Could I hide in some mouse hole in this cemetery? And make a little nest where nothing would ever be born? Oh, Hope, my Hope.

"Hey there." I heard a voice from up ahead. "Did you lose the gas can?"

Tadzio and Pikush were standing on a muddy, dilapidated street near a fence enclosing buildings which had been started, then abandoned. It was supposed to have been a high-rise district. A few had almost reached completion, the others had died in embryo.

"Well, what happened?"

"She fell in love with me."

"Who?"

"Lucyna. I won't be going to Stargard because I agreed to meet with her again tomorrow."

"Tadzio, you're an awful jerk."

"You should watch what you say. We'll see who the jerk is.

I've had three wives, all Party Secretaries. I've fucked half the Party in Stargard."

"Perhaps it's time for us to part company. You don't have to follow me, do you?"

"I have to. I'm collecting material for a big article on the last steps of your journey. I'll make you immortal."

I walked around him to the left and started down a walkway made of rotten boards. I had never known this part of town very well, but I knew that I would find my way. There hadn't been any streetlights there for years, for many reasons, thrift chief among them.

"If you have any notes on the pieces you've started or any interesting letters, you should leave them with me," remarked Tadzio Skorko. Pikush was up ahead, leading me skillfully through the trackless wastes. Now I had to light my way with the flashlight.

Finally, I caught sight of some people sitting on cement pipes. A few of them were holding holy images and church pennants. Some girls dressed in white were shielding the flames on their ancient wax candles from the wind. Nearby there was a wheelbarrow containing the plaster figure of a saint. They were all murmuring a slow religious song, their voices sleepy.

"Turn off your light! Are you trying to blind me?" It was a strangely familiar voice. Pikush began to wag his tail amicably, and I put the captured flashlight in my pocket.

"Who could this be?" Kolka Nachalow came walking out of the darkness. He had a black eye. "What are you three musketeers doing here?"

"We're on our way back from a little banquet. You're not on your way there by any chance? The ladies are waiting in the garden plots."

"No, I can't. I'm making a pilgrimage to Czestochowa to-night."

"Did you convert, Kolka? When? Who converted you, was it the Szmidts?"

"No, I'm an atheist. I met a friend of mine from one of the

youth organizations. Today he's acting as a priest. He's leading a pilgrimage there and he has a group passport. I joined up because the Bierut steel mill in Czestochowa is going to be demolished. There's a big boom in steel mills right now. Would you like a converter oven?"

Someone slipped out of the darkness, reported to the priest, and then joined the group of the faithful in waiting.

"Ziutek," shouted Kolka. "Come here for a minute."

The young priest with his breviary, his limpid eyes which did not move around much but caught every detail, that priest of the new dispensation walked over unhurriedly to us.

"Introduce yourselves. My friends here have just been at a banquet, but an innocent one. You might even bless them, they're wandering through the night like lost souls."

"Kolka, I'm taking you along provided you behave decently. We're too many as it is and there could be trouble."

We exchanged bows. The priest gave Tadzio a quick but careful once-over.

"Should we have a drink?" suggested Kolka, nudging the bulging front of his coat with one finger. He had probably swiped a bottle from the Central Committee banquet.

"Later. On the way. But I'm warning you, Kolka. The faithful are waiting," said the young priest severely.

"Well then, have a good trip," I said.

"Same to you," said Kolka. The priest bowed earnestly.

We walked past the pilgrims' rallying point and went off toward Swietokrzyska Street. The Palace of Culture was visible off to one side, a great white column.

"I know that priest from somewhere," said Tadzio. "My parents were religious. I'm not very religious myself. Sometimes I can believe, sometimes I can't. And that one, the one who took off his clothes at the congress, he probably wanted to combine Marxism and religion."

A gale wind came up out of nowhere and nearly toppled us over. I was shaken by a sudden chill. Maybe I had a fever. I might. Doesn't matter.

We crossed Swietokrzyska Street. A band struck up a song in the dark hills of the city. The loudspeakers were silent, only the wind whistled through their lifeless, grated innards. Have you noticed what a great circle I'm making around the Palace of Culture, which is bleached white by searchlights and shedding its stone slabs like some gigantic fish? Have you noticed how I don't let it out of my sight and, at the same time, how I keep my distance from it? For years I have had a premonition that the Palace of Culture would be my tomb.

And now here's Jan's house. An antediluvian apartment building, but in better shape than the new ones. The deathly specter of the Palace was reflected in the building's windows. The house was asleep. All the houses were napping at this time of day. The people are napping, too. Except for those who aren't allowed to, who have to be out having fun and celebrating.

"Wait here a minute for me," I said to my little retinue.

"It's freezing. I'll catch a cold," said Tadzio. "And I have a date with Lucyna, too. You know, she turns me on. A stylish lady, even though I do detest widows."

"Take cover by the staircase," I commanded.

But we were stopped on the stairs by a retired old man who worked for the building's security organization.

"I'm going to see Jan," I said.

"The one who lives on the second floor?"

"That's right."

"All of you?"

"No, they'll wait for me here."

"Just keep it down, will you please? There's a racket up there a lot of the time. People come, they look respectable enough, and the next thing you know they're shouting and singing."

"I'll just be a moment."

"Please remember that we lock the gate at nine."

I clambered up to the third floor. There was a reek of urine everywhere, even though the building was protected by a security committee. Then, at Jan's door, I rang the bell I had rung so many times before.

A mailman wearing his mail cap opened the door.

"It's not locked," he said. "Are you family by any chance?"

"No, a friend."

He led me to Jan's study. The wall by the desk was covered with photographs and postcards. Photographs of friends and girls of varying ages who had been in love with Jan or whom Jan had once loved during his long life. The postcards were pictures of special cities and places throughout the world which he or his friends had visited. Strange, old bills, old letters from well-known institutions or famous people. The great archives of a man who had worked his way up into the world's elite but had never really arrived. There was an electric humidifier in the middle of the room. Jan suffered from asthma.

"You know, I've got a problem," said the mailman. "I brought the gentleman his pension money and I brought it specially at this time because the maestro usually naps until dinnertime. And wouldn't you know, today he must be feeling sick. He's locked himself in the bathroom and he won't come out. I knocked and I knocked, I tried to talk him into coming out, but no luck."

"Maybe I can get him out."

The mailman looked me over with a dubious glance. "And who are you?"

"A friend. A close friend. You've never seen me here?"

"I might have. But it's a large check. For meritorious service. More than a million zlotys."

I noticed the television set by the window. A large color television which Jan's friends had sent him from the West when the West still had something to send. The congress's presiding officers were on the screen again, along with children dressed in all the colors of the rainbow. This was the children's late shift. The early shift had been on in the morning. The night-shift children were tying red kerchiefs around the dignitaries' necks, even though the early shift had already done it once before. Each member of the Presidium took a child in his arms and kissed the child on the mouth. And some of those children were well-developed young girls. The visiting Secretary had been given the most exuberant young lady. His eyes were already blurred because he had had a drink during the recess. There was a faggoty expression on his face, a sort of a put-out faggoty expression, but he had to kiss our young Polish lass with the budding tits. There was no sound. Someone had turned off the sound as people always do when programs like that are on.

"Do you want to see my ID?" I asked the unhappy mailman.

"Are you going to sign for him?"

"Naturally. I've done it a few times before."

Squinting at the gas can, he checked my ID. For some reason the can dispelled his doubts.

"All right then, sign," said the mailman with a sigh.

Then, wetting his fingers with copious saliva, he counted out one million two hundred zlotys in new banknotes.

"I feel sorry for the man," he muttered to himself. "This used to be a respectable home. But when his wife, that actress, when she ran off, all sorts of people started coming by here. They say they're artists. I know artists. My brother-in-law works in porcelain. When he's sober you won't find a better artist, but when he's hitting the bottle, it's the end of the world, I tell you. Would you be good enough to count it once more?"

I pretended to quickly count the money. There was a sheet of paper with a few random letters typed on it in the typewriter on the desk. There were also unfinished manuscripts and drawings on the desk, even some music paper. Jan was a practitioner of several arts. Like Leonardo da Vinci. In small countries the great artists are very versatile. The smaller the country, the greater the versatility.

"Exactly right," I said, and thrust a thousand-zloty note into the postal official's hard, rheumatic hand.

"Thank you kindly," he said with a certain relief, because he had taken me for a gentleman and he was not the sort who fawned for small change. "I wish you good night."

I locked the door after he left. How many days and nights had I spent in that home which, at one time, had been affluent, rich, full of cognac, salmon, venison, and, at other times, had been terribly poor, on its last legs, with only crude vodka, bacon, and boiled beans. Now the room was laid shamefully bare before me. I could look at the manuscripts, I could open the desk drawer, I could stick Jan's money in my pocket.

Jan was our Starets Zosima. No one had known him as a young man. Maybe he had never been a young man. Maybe he appeared on earth already a grayish, dry, older man with an enormous forehead which had room enough for both a good-sized novella and a moody rural landscape. You went to Jan for moral support, a glass of vodka, a kind word. Nobody ever brought Jan anything, everyone always took from him.

I walked over to the bathroom door and tapped gently. "Jan, it's me."

Silence. There wasn't even any water groaning in the pipes.

The bathroom was stone silent. Only the gale wind came hurtling in through the back window bearing howls, groans, and the sound of feet.

I turned the handle. The door wasn't locked from the inside, and opened with a soft squeak. A candle, nearly burned out, was flickering on the edge of the bathtub. Long wax icicles hung down to the floor. The light bulb must have burned out in this house, which was itself on the verge of ruin.

I entered, stepping on some rags which were strewn about the floor. Only then did I see Jan lying in the bathtub. He was wearing only a shirt, which had risen up, revealing the pitiful genitals of an old man. His weak hands were touching his legs, which were pulled up toward him and had been sprinkled with some sort of liquid, maybe medicine, maybe sweet vodka.

Jan looked up at me with half-closed eyes. He looked, but he did not react. He was neither glad, nor ashamed, nor troubled.

"How are you, Jan? Having a little rest?" I asked, to make that unnatural situation a little more natural. He didn't say a word, only looked me straight in the eye through the slanted slits of his eyelids.

I bent over him. "Are you feeling ill?"

He shook his head ever so slightly. I sat down on the edge of the bathtub by the candle, which was giving off a black, sooty smoke.

"Do you need any help?"

He looked motionlessly at me. There was a fine white growth of hair on his cheeks and chin. The flame heater was flickering as if mimicking the candle flame, each of them twisting and twitching in its own way.

"Jan, you know I have a terrible decision ahead of me."

His parched lips began to move. Only then did I notice that the side of the tub behind him was caked with vomit, the horrible contents of a stomach fed only on alcohol.

He began to whisper. I listened intently.

"We lost our way in a great forest—the infamy of nations and individuals."

"Jan, why did you kill yourself all those years?"

"What about you?"

"I tempt fate every once in a while. In my worst hours."

"The earth . . . total disintegration. Constant, eternal agony. A drawn-out death. The planet of death."

"Jan, we all got our start from you. You nourished us, you warmed us, you taught us for years. What happened?"

I had been so afraid of Jan for so many years that I would mentally present each of my actions to him for his approval before undertaking them. Whenever I said yes, I thought of Jan, and whenever I said no, I'd see his face before me. But now I no longer had to be afraid. He was lying in front of me naked, befouled, bereft of his humanity. Without even the most pitiful of dignities, the dignity of death.

"Jan, I'm going to take one final flight so that I can fall into the freezing abyss. You see this can? It's gasoline. I'm going to the Palace of Culture because I've made up my mind now—I will end my days in pain there. I have been given a mandate by the foolish and the wise, the cunning and the naïve, by hustlers and saints. Tell me, is it worth it? Am I squandering my miserable life on splendid ideas?"

He tried to swallow. I lifted his head, his silvery hair matted like mouse hair.

"History," he whispered, "up close, History is repulsive, foolish, stupid. Only when seen at a distance is it tragic, beautiful, majestic."

"What should I do, Jan?"

It cost him effort to move his eyelids, but even so, I could see a little of his red, unhealthy eyes, eyes that were intent as if he was struggling to overcome some enormous pain. He had been proud once, too. Prouder than us all. In my country the survivors still waited on his word.

"Someone has to break this lethargy, Jan. To wake the sleepers with a wild cry."

He was trying to nod his head. His neighbors were running the water in their bathroom. A little waterfall raced through the pipes near the old man's head, that old man who had never been an old man even though no one had ever known him as a young man. To my own surprise, I lifted his wet, dirty hand with its terribly long fingers and kissed the flaccid skin on his palm. When I let his hand drop, it fell along the side of the tub until it found a place on his hitched-up shirt by the greenish hair on his groin.

"Goodbye, Jan. Pray for me if you can, if your mind clears, if a good angel comes to you in the morning with bad news."

The candlewick had fallen over into a little puddle of wax. It would go out soon. Let it go out.

I closed the bathroom door, leaving it open enough so Jan could see his room, his cell on death row, and so that anyone who came here would be able to find our Starets Zosima.

I wanted to have one more look at Jan's little world and commit it to my memory forever. His books translated into many languages, books which no one read, publicity photos from his films which had flopped on all five continents, his canvases to this day never exhibited publicly. The walls with empty spaces for the laurels heaven never sent him.

Then the phone rang, which seemed strange because I didn't remember there being a phone in his place. But there it was on the windowsill by the television, clanging urgently.

I picked up the receiver. "Hello?"

"Is this 87-13?" asked someone whose Polish was not the best.

"Yes," I said, glancing down at the cardboard label on the phone. "It is."

"May I speak with the person who lives there?"

"Unfortunately, he's extremely ill."

"And who are you?"

"I'm a friend of his."

"Aha, I see. This is Krulick speaking. I'm a senior journalist with the Associated Press. I wanted to ask what was going on in Warsaw today."

"Nothing too interesting. The usual holiday commotion."

"Aha, I see. The same here. The usual commotion. Thank you. Goodbye."

"Good night."

I hung up the phone. I had to hurry. The chairman of the congress had been handed a great stack of telegrams of welcome and was now reading them. Soon they would be rising for the "Internationale" and leaving for the banquet funded by our Party's thrift.

Then the phone rang again. "Hello?"

"What was the number of the person who just called?" asked an edgy, aggressive male voice.

"God only knows. All I know is that he called from America."

"We already know that. Give me the exact number or else we'll cut off your phone service until further notice."

"Cut it off and hang it up on Mr. Dickowicz."

"On what?"

"On your dick."

There was a terrible grinding sound in the phone and I hung up. Through the curtainless bare window, pocked with raindrops, I could see the city, crouching, quiet. Had I strained my eyes I could have seen Zoliborz and Bielany, the whole expanse of sorry, crookedly constructed buildings and wild vegetation. Over the ages, that city had been built under the knout and had been burned by anyone who cared to. I didn't have much love for that city, my love for it wasn't very strong, not like those packs of flunky artists who love it so much, so madly, for the money they squeeze out of its sentimental citizens, who have to love their city because they have nothing else to love, artists who love Warsaw for the money they squeeze out of the cunning Party, which had identified itself with the city, the state, and the Lord God Himself.

Somewhere out there in the abyss of the night, the Ukraine was dying, Lithuania was perishing, Belorussia was breathing its last, and the Tartars had left on the long journey to Mohammed's paradise. Somewhere out there in the swamps and bogs of this earth, which was small as an atom, people were dying and unfortunate nations were perishing before their time. An interstellar bell had rung its Angelus. The heart of the cosmos beat in alarm.

I went back downstairs, where Tadzio and Pikush were waiting for me by the door.

"Another infinity is coming to an end. Another eternity is passing on its way," quoted the aging boy from Stargard by way of a greeting. "We were frozen stiff down here. Don't you see what's going on?"

I could not believe my eyes. A few scattered snowflakes were falling. A sweltering, muggy afternoon had been followed by a short winter night. Pikush was chasing the slow, gliding snowflakes, which made him think it was some happy Christmas for dogs.

Tadzio drew confidentially close to me and took my sleeve timidly.

"I know," he whispered, with horror in his voice, "I know everything. You want to take your own life because you've had no success."

Something collapsed with a deadly-sounding crash on a nearby street. But fortunately there were no victims, no human cry rang out.

"I'll avenge you."

Without saying a word, I walked into the small brick enclosure for garbage cans, which weren't being picked up anymore. At the foot of a reeking pyramid of trash I found a brick in good condition.

"Tadzio, come here for a minute, would you?"

His interest aroused, the poet from Stargard entered the stinking crematorium confidently. I set the gas can aside and grabbed Tadzio's wet jacket collar.

"What's going on?" he said, trying to free himself from my grasp.

"You know what, you know," I said with deliberation. "You can shout all you want in here. No one will even look out the window. I've got a good brick here, a good Warsaw blackjack. And now we'll cut off your vile little life in a scientific manner."

"You're only joking. You only like to kill people in your novels."

"No, Tadzio, I'm not joking. Enough imagination, enough fiction. We're going to commit a common, banal crime."

"You see, I'm not shouting, I'm not grabbing you by the throat. I know you're just trying to see what it feels like."

"No, look, I'm lifting the brick. In one minute I'll smash in that freckled forehead of yours. We'll see how that looks in real life."

Tadzio gazed without fear at the jagged brick I was holding over his head. "I have a terrible desire to tempt fate. It gives me the willies. We'll meet right afterward, all right? I'll be waiting for you precisely fifty kilometers above the Palace of Culture, at the point where our atmosphere and planet earth's life comes to a definite end. But you won't do it because two thousand years ago a certain young Aramaean told his savage companions: Instead of killing a lamb, your neighbor, or your brother for a sacrifice, make a sacrifice of yourself. There are seven atoms of the Antichrist in me, but there are at least seventy-seven in you."

"Look how easy it is to kill a person, Tadzio. In six months, when there's some volunteer clean-up campaign, you'll be taken out with the rest of the trash to some suburban woods where the last useless mushrooms and poison herbs grow. How easy it is to terminate another person's existence."

"But how about your own?"

He took the brick from me and weighed it in his hand. "I'll take it with me as a souvenir. It'll be my talisman. A piece of the noose. Are you hungry by any chance? I've got two lumps of sugar."

"What are you raving about?"

"I should wipe your face with a handkerchief, but I don't have one."

"Was this our last station of the cross?"

"Yes. The sacrificial altar is ahead of us now." He pointed at the sky-high iconostasis of the Palace, white in the snowstorm.

"Why didn't I kill you when I could have?"

"I don't have any silver pieces in my pocket. Five pages of prose will be my honorarium if someone doesn't steal the idea from me. You know how that is these days. I've been working by the sweat of my brow since this morning, I've been leading you around like a blind man to your destiny, and then, at the last moment, some clever jerk will come out of nowhere and swipe the ending, the premise, the whole metaphor."

"Tadzio, you can have my life story as a present."

"Good, good. But it's time now. You can't be late."

We began taking a shortcut toward the Palace of Culture. I had to search my pockets for the flashlight to light the way, for there were no streets where we were. Pikush had waited discreetly for us to finish our little business and was now running briskly ahead of me, selecting the safest path. The snow was becoming thicker and thicker.

Just then we were accosted by an unhappy-looking woman. "Do you happen to know where the pilgrims for Czestochowa are meeting?"

The voice sounded familiar. I shined the light in her eyes for a quick second. I caught sight of a large head and a face furrowed with wrinkles and smeared with garish makeup.

"Not far from here, Gosia. Keep to the right, it's over by the unfinished high rises."

"Oh, it's you," she said without surprise. "A fine thing, I tell you. That slob took advantage of me. I've been defiled. And it cost me money, too."

"But the priest who's leading the pilgrimage is kind of a suspicious-looking character, too."

"That's no problem. The priest can be a fake as long as the penance is real. Are you giving some sort of performance over by the Palace?"

"Who told you?"

"I can't remember now. My poor head. So much trouble and all at once. Do you know what the road to Czestochowa is like? Half of it is a desert now from all the strip mining. They've lowered the ground water, ruined the ecology. There are sandhills and wild dogs everywhere you look. It used to take a week to get there, but now maybe we'll be on this pilgrimage until New Year's Day. I'm a ruined woman."

"Would you please pray for my soul, too."

"I don't even know if I can redeem my own. What a slob he is, but he is strong, I'll say that. I barely got out of it alive."

She walked away without saying goodbye, cursing the chef-colonel. Pikush was about to start barking but thought better of it. He only bared his none-too-pretty teeth and snarled, looking off into the darkness.

Then the Palace of Culture loomed out of the darkness, shining like the moon in the reflected light of the searchlights. It drew nearer to us, wading through the shifting clouds of the blizzard. I could already see the steel posts, the large palisade which had been mounted above the Congress Hall to protect the delegates from any large sandstone block that might suddenly fall from the building. An enormous rainbow made of colored lights had been strung across that palisade, and the rainbow's arc bore a series of blood-red letters which read: WE HAVE BUILT SOCIALISM.

I could still run away to my little mouse hole. I still had one last little morsel of time. To hide in some hole, like Stargard, change my name, join the Party, start a new family. Save myself a few years for Nadezhda; that is, Hope. But that way I would only lose her. She would die in my arms or in my mind. Nadezhda of the large breasts, an elixir of femininity from the steppe, the consoling bliss I had been longing for all my life. For only now had I suddenly understood the mysterious feminine element borne here by the solar winds from the viscera of the universe. I had slept with creatures half woman, half man. I had caressed puppets made of protein and loved sexless biological mannequins. I wanted to lay my head on Nadezhda's lap and fall asleep forever.

A certain Czech and a Lithuanian had preceded me on this path which led to a Buddhist monk's pyre. And people of various races, languages, and religions had walked that blazing path before them. Why is a solitary suicide a pitiful act? And why is a public suicide performed with all the majesty of ritual an Ascension to heaven? Why is a solitary death at one's own hand a sinful violation of divine law, and a death witnessed by others a victorious challenge hurled at God?

Where are you, penitential souls, who accompany us in our earthly struggles but cannot be of any help to us? I've been talking with you since this morning, I've been spinning a tale, multiplying the repetitions. I am a slave to repetition because slavery is repeated every day. I've even bored you, and so you are waiting in silence for the moment when I join you, you sinful, penitential souls who of course do not frighten people at night, souls whom the living do not fear and who have never kept the living from any crime.

In my life I did not create any prose that was sober, epic, objective, all-embracing, full of meaning, voluminous, like the Bible or the Koran. My times compelled me to monotony, unmodulated groans, stammers, repulsive hysteria, hurried stammerings, one-sided accusations, to an ugliness that was none too appealing. It forced all that on me, an anonymous writer, an unknown man, a perfect mediocrity from a decadent era, a mediocrity with unbridled ambitions.

Hold on, stop. Aren't you even sad about losing the few months or the couple of lousy fall days which fate might still have in store for you? Hours warmed with hope or even by the lack of hope, which is itself one dismal variety of hope. Or maybe the something which the world has been awaiting for millions of years will happen?

We come to Parade Square. The uneven colonnade of the Congress Hall is before us now. The spotlights are trained on a row of exit doors or perhaps on that stone platform which awaits me like my native earth. I see two movie cameras which look like machine guns ready to fire. And standing in the middle of the film crew and the equipment is Wladyslaw Bulat wearing a big sheepskin coat. He put off his trip to America, and he was right to do so. He is going to film the delegates filing out and then film my death as well. Those thirty-some meters of film recording a person's death will make him immortal.

I catch sight of my friends. Nadezhda with a hairy young man. Rysio Szmidt. Caban looking gloomy, Caban with whom I had had words when it was still summer outside. I see the clochard from my part of town, a man of indeterminate age, bald, with a spatulate beard, holding a shepherd's stick in one hand. Mooing with delight, Docent Edek Szmidt is taking a piss in the middle of the crowd, a new but popular custom. They are all standing in a shabby semicircle composed of onlookers, demonstrating activists, delegations of sleepy people, and children quick as sparrows. A few television monitors have been set up in front of that outdoor audience so it can watch the congress live. The Presidium is just rising to its feet, followed by the audience. A hodgepodge of voices begins singing the "Internationale." Our Secretary links hands with the highest Secretary of all, the one who rules the world.

But who really rules the world? After all, I am a slave, our Secretary is a slave, and that imperial lord who looks like a slightly offended Kalmuck is also a slave. We, the whole world, are ruled by a politburo of ghosts, a cell of specters, an emergency committee staffed by the sinful corpses of Stalin, Dzerzhinsky, Zhdanov, Beria, and all the rest of them hidden away in the darkness of cemeteries.

Someone puts his arms around me from in back. It's Caban. Without a word, he kisses me on the shoulder, the way Poles used to kiss each other. He shakes me, stiff with cold, and then steps to the side. Nadezhda runs up to me. She begins sobbing and tugging at my sleeve.

"Don't cry. No crying allowed," I say.

The groan of the "Internationale" reaches us through the walls. It sounds like the wailing of people being walled up alive.

"I'll go with you. Maybe it'll make it easier for you," whispers Nadezhda through her tears.

"No, you stay here. Someone has to stay here. Take Pikush. The wandering dog. He knows everything about me now."

The hairy young man, who looks like John the Baptist, walks over to me.

"Roll up your sleeve, please," he orders.

"But why? Leave me alone now."

"Marek is standing in for Halina. She was arrested this afternoon and he was released," whispers Nadezhda.

Before I have time to protest, he pushes back my sleeve and

jabs a needle into my forearm. I give a little cry, but he is already patting the spot with a damp cotton swab.

"A painkiller," he informs me.

"That's my second shot today."

Nadezhda lifts my arm and kisses the little wound with her cool lips. Hold it. Stop. Don't I regret losing this crummy world? Aren't I sad to lose life's everyday defeats, its failed loves, its eternal fear of the unknown?

"All the penitent souls are in me," whispers Tadzio from behind me. "You're looking for them, you're waiting for a sign from them. It's me, it's me. Like the floor creaking in the night, a lunar phantom, a larynx strangled in a terrible dream."

Now, on the monitors we can see that everybody has linked hands and is singing a song which once, in my youth, had been beautiful but which now, in my old age, sounds like the lamentation of slaves. Even our Secretary is singing, but somehow more anemically than everybody else. He keeps stopping, looking behind him, swallowing hard, until, finally, he lets go of his mainstay, the Soviet Secretary's hand, and then begins to collapse, falling back onto the second row of Presidium members, sinking inertly under the table, his eyes rolled up blankly. But he is caught from behind by the vigilant chief of his own personal guard, a large man with the face of a pig, but whose nose is strangely thin and pointed, as if someone had pulled on it for a good long time. He catches the Secretary by the arms, other agents come dashing over, and after a short tussle they drag him off toward the wings. However, on the way, they give up on it and sit him down on an empty chair; at that very moment the image of the auditorium disappears, replaced by the card with the two red birds, one of which has a white tail.

"In the end he fainted, too. Everyone faints," says Rysio Szmidt. "Listen, old man, so there won't be any misunderstandings. You remember what Edek said about my propaganda book, the one I live off and which pays for the opposition. That was the fine, the penalty I imposed on a rabid state, a levy made by a slave on his oppressor."

One of the spectators begins chanting weakly: "Polska! Polsha! Forward!"

"It's time now," whispers Caban.

"No, no," says Nadezhda, shielding me, weeping desperately. I stroke her wet hair, which by day was red.

The snow is falling as if wishing to soothe and anesthetize us, to put us to sleep. Black, the city regards me with unseeing eyes. But still it is my city. It has added to my suffering, but I have spared it no suffering, either. A city of innocent sinners. Like me.

> After the labors of my life,
> if I've deserved some respect,
> I do not want my coffin borne
> by those whom I could never bear.

Antoni S., the poet, my friend, my protector, my godfather, had written those lines to me before his death. Those he had loved had borne his coffin and I was among them. I'll be smashing my way violently in to join you, a little before my time would have been up. How will you greet me, old friends? I will come among you charred with the terrible mark of mortal sin on my brow. O God, out of love for Your laws, I will break Your most sacred law.

Tears of snow streak the gas can. The matches are in my trembling hand. My ears are ringing. A cataract of scattered thoughts, gleaming bits of memories, a moan-like song, a song-like moan.

All the lights in the semicircular colonnade have been turned on. The security police open the heavy gates of hell, or heaven. The cameras are rolling, their little red control lights blinking.

I kiss Nadezhda hard on her lips, which part in a soundless sob. I want to close her lips with mine so they will keep silent and not remind me of my unfinished life, my unfinished dreams, my unfinished loves.

Out of the corner of my eye I see Tadzio fall heavily to his knees in the melting snow. Pikush is fidgeting about, not sure what to do. He wants to run after me, but some sudden wisdom tells him to stay among the living. Rysio Szmidt bows his head, and some of the unexpected snowflakes drift down his collar. Caban raises his hand as if giving me a signal, or perhaps he is just blessing me.

"Goodbye, Hope. If freedom doesn't come after me as sudden and surprising as the beginning of summer, then it will come after one of the next poets, workers, students."

"I loved you my whole life."

"And I will love you as long as I can."

A revelation, a revelation. Yes, now I see, now I remember what happened last night. A sudden luminosity at the threshold of a fall or summer night. The sudden, all-embracing certainty that it is we, people, that biological river flowing from one nowhere into the next, we who have created God. Not in seven days, but through ages of glaciers and tropics, through ages of continents being born and seas drying up, through centuries when the cerebral hemispheres developed and the gills died out, through evil centuries and good, through eras that have been fathomed and eras still sunk in mystery, throughout our human eternity we have created in toil, pain, and agony our God, the God of mercy and goodness, so that He would protect us against the evil of the universe, the cosmos, or even from that heavenly sky which strikes us with lightning bolts. So that He would protect us from ourselves.

God exists. A God formed of our electromagnetic waves or some other sort of waves, waves vibrating with our suffering, our despair, our anger. A God against the other gods.

Our God is growing mightier, He encompasses the farthest galaxies, and finally, He will rule the entire universe, our universe, for we know of no other universe, and He will make us the chosen race out of the promised land. The God of Mercy. The God of people.

Now I begin walking slowly toward that stone platform

wreathed with a short flight of stairs. My legs are becoming heavy and my head is pulled down toward the earth from which I had arisen and to which I must, of my own free will, return. People, give me strength. People, give strength to everyone in this world who is, at this very moment, going, as I am, to make a burnt offering of himself.

People, give me strength. People . . .